P9-CCP-680

SHARP CURVES
Ahead

A NOVEL

ALLISON HOBBS

SBI

STREBOR BOOKS

NEW YORK LONDON TORONTO SYDNEY

Strebor Books
P.O. Box 55471
Atlanta, GA 30308
www.simonandschuster.com

ISBN 978-1-59309-676-2
ISBN 978-1-50111-938-5 (ebook)
LCCN 2017941828

First Strebor Books trade paperback edition October 2017

Cover design: www.mariondesigns.com
Cover photograph: © Keith Saunders/Keith Saunders Photos

10 9 8 7 6 5 4 3 2 1

Manufactured in the United States of America

For information regarding special discounts for bulk purchases,
please contact Simon & Schuster Special Sales at 1-866-506-1949

The Simon & Schuster Speakers Bureau can bring authors to your live event.
For more information or to book an event, contact the Simon & Schuster Speakers
Bureau at 1-866-248-3049 or visit our website at www.simonspeakers.com

Dear Reader:

Allison Hobbs, in her milestone thirtieth novel with Strebor, focuses on the relationship of two best friends, both of whom are plus-sized. In *Sharp Curves Ahead*, readers will discover that she remains true to her brand of erotica while spinning this tale about the world of curviness.

Jayla Carpenter and Bailee Evans struggle with their weight and its effect on their lifestyles and identities. Jayla is single and copes with her body image by promiscuity, perusing a web site where fit men hook up with curvy women. Jayla, a real estate agent, becomes accustomed to being victimized with fat shaming in her personal life and believes her size determines the properties she's assigned to sell. Bailee is married—not as happily as she pretends—and resorts to food binges to satisfy her needs. Despite their closeness, they both harbor secrets about how they truly define their self-images and the efforts they take to feel better about themselves.

The novel is a roller coaster of surprises, twists and turns. It presents a new spin on women and how they compensate for their weight while challenges threaten to destroy their bond.

As always, thanks for supporting myself and the Strebor Books family. We strive to bring you the most cutting-edge, out-of-the-box material on the market. You can find me on Facebook @AuthorZane.

Blessings,

Zane

Publisher
Strebor Books
www.simonandschuster.com

In Loving Memory of my son,
Carl "Korky" Johnson
March 20, 1979 - August 30, 2017

Chapter 1

Jayla had gone to a great deal of trouble to get the Vance family's home ready for tomorrow's showing. In an effort to appeal to potential buyers, she'd decluttered the place, pulled furniture away from the walls for better traffic flow, replaced family pictures with contemporary art, accessorized tables with trendy pieces from her arsenal of home accessories, and she'd put fresh flowers in every room.

Staging a home to sell wasn't a job for those that lacked creativity. Some realtors hired professional home stagers that charged high fees to make the home look more welcoming. When a home was placed in Jayla's capable hands, she employed her uncanny talent for transforming shabby spaces into what appeared to be stylish, move-in-ready, model homes.

Of course, it was all an illusion. Instead of replacing outdated bathroom tiles, she slapped on a fresh coat of paint. By the time the paint started to crack or peel, it would be the new owner's problem—not hers. Another trick that worked like a charm was to strategically place area rugs, disguising worn flooring.

Jayla possessed a magician's bag of tricks that came in handy whenever a buyer was hesitant to sign on the dotted line. When it came to selling houses, Jayla was passionate, but despite her zealousness, she was not among the higher-paid real estate agents in the area.

She roamed from room to room, admiring her special touches: candlelight, a baby's breath centerpiece on the dining table, and blue pillows on the living room couch that added a pop of color.

Tomorrow would be a long day. She was scheduled to show the home to four prospective buyers. Getting through the day would require lots of energy, a perpetual smile, and an endless stream of conversation that touted the qualities of the neighborhood, the merits of the school system, and most of all, the unique features of the house.

Typically, she'd return home after spending hours decorating. But, having full access to the home while the owners were conveniently out of town for the next two days, Jayla decided it would be wasteful not to put the lovely space to good use.

She climbed the stairs and entered the master bedroom, smiling in approval as she kicked off her shoes. After all her hard work, she'd earned the right to have a romp in the sturdy sleigh bed she had upgraded from frumpy to hot with a white cotton duvet, bold-patterned decorative pillows, and a graphic blanket at the end of the bed.

The ideal candidate to help her christen the renovated bedroom would have been Sadeeq, her on-again, off-again boyfriend, but he'd been fading in and out of her life lately, breaking dates at the last minute and not responding to texts.

Fuck you, Sadeeq! It was time for Jayla to fall back and make Sadeeq realize that she wasn't desperate for his attention. Time would tell where his heart and head were really at.

Feeling empowered, she tapped on her favorite dating app and began scrolling through the photos of guys who were currently in the vicinity.

Eyes narrowed, she scrutinized the pictures and zoomed in on an exceptionally good-looking guy who was posed on an elegant balcony and wearing a smile so confident it bordered on a smirk—a sexy smirk. There were a range of pictures of him: sitting astride a motorcycle, on the beach with a group of guys playing volleyball. In yet another shot, he was aboard a yacht with a bottle of champagne in hand, and in the last picture, he was posed with his fraternity brothers at a formal event.

Although he was obviously physically fit, he hadn't posted any cheesy pictures standing in front of a mirror with his shirt off, which Jayla appreciated. The picture with his fraternity brothers was proof that he was educated, which was another plus. This guy had the potential to be more than a random date; he was husband material.

With a flicker of excitement, she swiped to his profile. His name was Niles Beckworth and according to his bio, he was a tech entrepreneur who traveled often. During the week, he managed his business, but when the weekend rolled around, he was all about playing hard. He lived in Miami, Florida.

Damn, why couldn't he be closer!

Briefly let down that Niles was only passing through the Philadelphia area, she reminded herself that she didn't need a relationship. What she really needed was for someone to slide through and blow her back out to distract her from thinking about Sadeeq all the time.

She sent Niles a message and he responded within ten minutes. Over the phone, his voice was like liquid silk, and his easy laughter made her smile. After putting up with Sadeeq's moodiness for the past month, she was ready for some fun.

Inside her overnight bag were sexy underwear, two negligees, a pair of heels, and condoms. She plopped the bag on the bed and padded to the master bath. After a shower that was longer than she'd intended, she glanced at the clock. Niles would be arriving in fifteen minutes. There was no time for her usual makeup ritual. Luckily, she was pretty enough to get by with only blush, a little mascara, and a few swipes of lip gloss.

The bell rang and Jayla's phone dinged at the same time. Phone in hand, she swiped the screen as she descended the stairs. It was a message from Sadeeq: I miss you.

She sucked her teeth and refused to respond. Wearing heels and a lace chemise that accentuated her curvy figure, she moved smoothly toward the door. She set her phone down on the bamboo plant stand in the foyer before swinging open the door.

"Niles?" she asked in a voice that registered surprise. The man standing in the doorway was on the pudgy side with a visible gut. His once-handsome face was bloated from the weight gain that had occurred at some point after he'd taken the pictures that were posted on the dating site.

Hit with crushing disappointment, Jayla's first impulse was to slam the door in his bloated face.

He had the same smirk he'd worn in the pictures, but it now seemed grotesque rather than sexy. Holding a brown paper bag, he squeezed inside without waiting for an invitation. Jayla noticed that the hand holding the bag looked rough, as if it belonged to a mechanic or someone who did field work. His thumbnail was discolored with something that appeared to be a horrible fungus. The repugnant nail looked as if it were about to sprout mushrooms.

A close look at both of his crusty hands told her that the so-called tech entrepreneur had created a fake profile to make himself more appealing.

Before she could come up with a convenient excuse to rescind her invitation, Niles pulled a chilled bottle of cheap red wine out of the paper bag and handed it to her.

His eyes travelled up and down Jayla's ample body. When his

gaze finally settled on her face, he said, "I should have asked if you preferred red or white. Since most chicks go for sweet red wine, I figured you'd be okay with it."

He'd struck out with the $7.99 bottle of wine. She cast another glance in his direction, searching for any redeeming qualities, but all she saw was a cheap-ass, overweight, sloppy-looking man with an infected thumbnail. The pictures he'd posted had to be old as fuck and time had clearly not been kind.

The dating app she'd selected was a site for physically fit men and plus-sized women to hook up. If Jayla wanted to bump tummies with a fat person, she could have easily found an overweight dude in the grocery store, standing in front of the freezer aisle, and salivating over Turkey Hill ice cream.

Think, Jayla, think! What can I say to get rid of him? She didn't want to come off as rude or shallow, but she didn't want to waste too much time making small talk either. Niles had only himself to blame for luring her in with pictures from back in the day when he was athletic and hot.

"Do you need me to uncork that?" he asked in an impatient tone, nodding toward the bottle of wine.

Oh, the gall of this fool. Only in his dreams will I be drinking wine with him.

She grabbed her phone from the plant stand. Brows creased, she glanced down and pulled up Sadeeq's message. Looking up, she smiled apologetically at Niles. "Something just came up. Uh, why don't you keep the wine? Hopefully, we can link up some other time."

"You gotta be kidding," he said, his eyes wide with disbelief. There was a mixture of anger and hurt glimmering in his eyes that forced Jayla to look away in guilt. She quickly reminded herself that she didn't owe Niles, with his fake profile, one iota of truthfulness or consideration.

"I have a family emergency," she said, keeping her voice purposefully light. She extended the bottle of wine. "Here, you go. I appreciate the gesture, but you can keep it."

Niles grudgingly took the bottle and turned to leave. He suddenly whirled around and stared at her through hostile eyes. Without warning, he threw the bottle against the wall.

The sound of the crash was as loud as a gunshot, causing Jayla to duck and utter a small, shocked scream. Shards of glass rained down into her hair. Wine splashed her face and the front of her negligee. Before she could fully process what had happened, Niles picked up the neck of the broken bottle and pressed the jagged edge against her throat.

"Do you think you're better than me?" he growled, poking her in the neck.

A surge of fear caused her adrenaline to spike like crazy. "No, I don't think I'm better than anyone," she said in a shaky, horrified whisper. She detected a vein pulsing at his temple, informing her that he was on the brink of more violence.

Her gaze flickered downward and she noticed a single droplet of blood trickling from her neck and down her chest. Her terrified eyes darted around the foyer, taking in the appalling scene of broken glass and a wine-soaked area rug.

Oh, God, this cannot be happening. Is this madman going to kill me?

"I'm sick of fat bitches acting like they're too good for me just because I put on a little extra weight." Sneeringly, he ran his eyes over Jayla's plump body. "You have a lot of nerve discriminating against an overweight man when your big ass obviously weighs a ton."

Ordinarily, the insult about her weight would have caused her to flinch, but under the circumstances, she had more important things to be concerned with—like how to escape with her life intact.

As if reading her mind, he twisted her left arm painfully behind her back, and then steered Jayla out of the foyer and into the living room.

"Nice place," he remarked casually. The calmness in his tone was so chilling, she lost her balance and stumbled as her heart drummed furiously in her chest.

"Be careful," he cautioned with a sneer. "I don't want to end up with a hernia or a back sprain, trying to pick your big ass off the floor." Niles laughed scornfully as he led her toward the couch that was adorned with cheerful blue pillows.

He shoved her onto the couch, bent over and whispered menacingly in her ear: "Make love to me like I'm your man. I like lots of foreplay before I go in, so don't rush through it."

He began removing his clothes and Jayla turned her head, unable to watch. He grabbed her by the hair and yanked hard. "Look at me," he spat, the corners of his mouth curled up in cruel triumph. "Look at all this prime beef," he demanded, gripping his dick. "You can get it if your tongue game is tight."

Tears sprang to Jayla's eyes. Feeling humiliated wasn't new to her. Countless popped buttons, split seams, broken zippers, and fat-shaming epithets had familiarized her with embarrassment, but never had she felt the heat of shame as profoundly as in this moment. Never had she felt so vulnerable and pathetic.

She was in the hands of a psychopath, and she only had herself to blame.

Chapter 2

Bailee glanced up from her laptop. "I can't decide if we should add an orange chocolate lava cake to the dessert table or couture cupcakes."

"Either choice is okay with me," Trent replied absently, his eyes fixed on the TV screen.

"Can you show some interest and give me a little support, babe? Our tenth anniversary party is a big deal, you know," Bailee said.

Seeming not to hear her, Trent jumped up in excitement and let out a roar as his favorite football team charged across the field, forcefully knocking into their opponents.

It was a barbaric sport that Trent adored, but Bailee didn't understand it and wasn't interested in learning the rules of the game. Realizing there was no point in trying to have a civilized conversation with her husband until the commercial break, Bailee retuned her attention to the computer and continued scrutinizing a plethora of insanely decadent desserts. On the night of the anniversary party, she planned to go overboard and indulge in all the sugary treats she'd been denying herself in order to fit into her anniversary dress.

When a commercial came on, Trent got up from his recliner to get another bottle of beer. As he moseyed near the couch, where Bailee sat, he cut an eye at the extravagant desserts on the computer screen, evaluated the cost, and let out a whistle of surprise.

"What is it, hon?" Bailee asked.

"How much are we spending on dessert?"

"You don't want to know," Bailee warned.

"Don't you think you're going a little overboard?"

"Listen, we both work hard and we can afford to splurge on our special day. Most of our friends from college didn't make it past five years of marriage. We're one of the rare few who made it to the ten-year mark without separating or having to deal with any other kind of drama." She smiled at him warmly and added, "What we have is worth celebrating and spending a little extra on the dessert station."

"You're right. Get whatever makes you happy."

"It's not only about me—it's about us, and I want you to be a part of the planning."

"Whoa!" Trent held up his hands. "Party planning is your thing—it's not mine. Besides, what happened to your girl? I thought Jayla, with her sense of style and impeccable taste, was going to help you out."

There was an awkward silence as Bailee pondered Trent's remark. "I don't know what's going on with Jayla. She's been acting odd."

Trent raised his brow.

"I feel like she's been blowing me off. She hasn't been answering my calls. Instead she responds with a text, telling me she'll return the call. But she never does. Jayla realizes how important our anniversary party is, and I can't help wondering why she's not being more helpful."

"Maybe she's jealous," Trent suggested.

"Listen, I know Jayla like the back of my hand, and she's not jealous of me."

"Maybe you don't know her as well as you think."

"Why do you dislike Jayla so much? Are you threatened by her?"

Trent scoffed. "Why would I be threatened by someone so fake and pathetic?"

"Wow, I had no idea you were harboring so much animosity toward her."

"Now you know," Trent said unapologetically. "To be honest, I hope she does bail on our party. I'd rather hire a professional than let her turn our event into a Jayla Carpenter freak fest."

Bailee scowled in puzzlement. "What are you talking about?"

"I didn't want to bring it up, but you need to know that your girl was in rare form at our wedding reception and also at your twenty-ninth birthday party."

"What do you mean by 'rare form'?"

"Are you sure you want to know?"

"Of course."

"At the reception, she let two of the groomsmen smash in the bathroom. She gave one dude top while the other was all up in the cooch."

"Who told you that lie?" Bailee asked bitterly.

"I wouldn't lie about something like that. My homeboy, Chance, told me what went down. I didn't believe him, so I asked my boy, Tone, about it. He corroborated Chance's story and added that Jayla told them it was her secret desire to have sex with two men at once."

Bailee's face froze into an expression of complete shock.

"I've been giving your girl the side-eye ever since. I don't get involved in lengthy conversations with Jayla. I'm courteous, but all I say is 'hello' and 'goodbye'—that's it."

"It's clear that you keep her at arm's length, but I figured you were envious of our friendship."

He laughed derisively. "I've never been envious of that trashy ho."

"She's still my friend, so please don't call her that. I'm curious about why you kept this information to yourself for so many years. Didn't you think it was important enough to share?"

"You and Jayla are tight and I didn't want to be the cause of any bad blood between you. I hoped the bathroom stunt was a one-time thing; the result of too much alcohol at the reception. But after her performance at your birthday party, I realized—"

Bailee held up a hand. "Wait, what? What exactly happened at my party?" she asked, dreading the answer.

"I hate being the bearer of more bad news, but you asked," he said with a placating smile. "Jayla was behind the bar serving up brains while the mixologist served drinks. You remember the bartender—the dude with the blond dreads piled on his head in a man bun?"

"No, I don't remember the bartender," she said sharply.

Trent shrugged. "Anyway…the bartender mentioned it to a few of my friends and it got back to me."

"I don't believe it." Bailee folded her arms across her chest.

"Babe, open your eyes. Everybody can't be lying on your girl."

"But I know Jayla. Sure, she can get a little loose at times, but she would never stoop that low." Bailee's voice trembled at the thought of her friend down on her knees, providing oral sex to a perfect stranger in a public venue.

"Face it, Bailee. Jayla's a dusty 'hood chick, and she fronts like she's high-class."

"Trent, please. I can't deal with the way you keep calling her out of her name."

Trent lifted a shoulder indifferently. "It's the truth. She's a cum-bucket, and it's time for you to acknowledge that fact and make the appropriate adjustments in your relationship with her."

"Are you suggesting that I abandon my friend?" Bailee's voice was shrill.

"I'm suggesting that you reassess your relationship with her and determine whether it's prudent to associate with a thot who's fucking out of both sides of her drawers," Trent said in a delivery that was a low and measured mixture of professional attorney and former resident of the 'hood.

"I'm aware that Jayla has body image issues. It's clear that she tries to disguise her insecurities with provocative behavior and inappropriate clothing, but for her to denigrate herself in such a manner..." She paused, searching for the right words. "I didn't realize she was *that* damaged."

"Now you know," Trent said. "I'm trying to get ahead at my law firm. I'm in the running to get the Craver account, which could do wonders for my career, and the last thing I need is for there to be rumors around the office that my wife's best friend was tricking in the bathroom at our anniversary party. You know what they say, 'birds of a feather...'" His voice trailed off and he made his way to the recliner, carrying a chilled bottle of beer.

He flopped into the chair, turned the bottle to his lips and focused intently on the game.

Unable to focus on the dessert samples on the computer screen, Bailee gazed into space. Trent had given her a lot to contemplate. Should she speak to Jayla about her conduct or pretend she didn't know? She decided she couldn't ignore it. Jayla's slutty behavior was obviously a cry for help. She grimaced as she imagined Jayla behind the bar, giving head in the midst of a crowded ballroom. *Who does that?*

Maybe Jayla was a sex addict. Her inexcusable behavior couldn't be chalked up to merely indulging sexual fantasies. There had to be some underlying, deep-seated emotional problem. Bailee would be less than a friend if she didn't suggest that Jayla get therapy or join a support group, at the least.

Another commercial interrupted the football game and Trent

reached for his phone. Usually, Bailee looked forward to the breaks in the game, but she found herself feeling relieved that Trent was using the downtime to tweet about his team instead. She couldn't deal with the way he was berating Jayla and she didn't know how to defend her friend.

At one-hundred-and-eighty pounds of solid muscle, Trent weighed sixty pounds less than Bailee. Their weight was approximately the same when they'd gotten married, but Bailee kept gaining. For the most part, she was comfortable with her body, but she wanted to drop at least thirty pounds before the night of the party.

She cut an eye at her husband, taking in his exquisite bone structure and facial features. Admiringly, her eyes skimmed to his low fade haircut and the spinning waves he was obsessive about. High school friends and college sweethearts, he was the only man she'd ever loved.

Big-boned with skin the color of dark honey, Bailee had inherited her late father's physical characteristics. Unlike her thin and dainty mother, who would never be caught out in public without coiffed hair, a full face of makeup, and clothing that was the height of fashion, Bailee was much more down-to-earth. She dressed conservatively, wore very little makeup and her natural hair was styled in medium-length locs. The most time and effort she put into her appearance were biweekly trips to the salon to get her locs maintained.

The average woman would kill for what Bailee had: a handsome, smart, successful husband. But Bailee also had a successful career. Being the only African American managing director at the bank where she worked, she believed that she and Trent were equally lucky to have each other.

As a couple, Bailee and Trent were practically joined at the hip, except on Tuesdays when he had to entertain clients until late in the night and also when he traveled for weekly, overnight business trips.

Bailee was a lucky woman to have such a devoted husband.

Bearing that in mind, she decided that tonight she'd show her appreciation in bed. Pull out the blindfold, a couple of toys, and do some extra special tricks to prove how much she cared.

Headed for the fridge during another commercial break, Trent walked past Bailee, brushing her neck tenderly as he ambled past her. "I'm getting some ice cream. Do you want some?" he asked, looking over his shoulder.

"No, I'm good," she replied as she inwardly drooled over the goodies that were displayed on her computer screen. More than anything, she would have loved to open a bag of potato chips and dig into a bowl of cherry vanilla ice cream, but she resisted the urge.

You're not hungry. No emotional eating until after the party.

Trent strolled up to her and offered her a spoonful of ice cream from his bowl.

"You're mean," she said, laughing as she leaned away from the spoon. "Why're you trying to tempt me when you know I have to get rid of some of these pounds before the party?"

"You're sexy no matter how much you weigh." Trent punctuated the statement by leaning in and giving her a kiss.

She gazed at him adoringly. "That's why I love you, babe. You overlook my flaws and only see the best in me."

"What flaws? All I see is beauty." He took a few steps toward the recliner and then stopped abruptly. "But, speaking of flaws..."

"Oh, God. What now?" Bailee could tell by the determined set of Trent's jawline that he was going to say something disparaging about Jayla.

He walked slowly toward her, his expression grave. "There's something else I've been meaning to tell you." He expelled a huff of air. "That dude that Jayla's been seeing is married."

"Sadeeq?" Bailee shook her head. "No, you're mistaken. He's single."

"He's married, babe."

"How do you know?"

"My cousin, Javari's baby mom is tight with Sadeeq's wife."

"Your con-artist cousin Javari? How can you believe anything that comes out of the mouth of a man who has three different baby moms and who defrauded us out of fifteen-hundred dollars?"

"He didn't defraud us. It was a loan that he's going to pay back as soon as he gets on his feet," Trent asserted.

"I'm not holding my breath."

"Javari had a rough childhood and a lot of bad breaks—"

Bailee sucked her teeth. "He had the same bad breaks that you had. You were both raised by the same grandmother and you turned out just fine. Javari made a decision to be a lowlife hustler."

"Yo! You're talking about my cousin. As you well know, Javari and I did not have the same opportunities. Through scholarships, I was given a private school education, which was how I met you. Our paths would have never crossed if I hadn't attended your school as a charity case."

"And look how well you turned out. An attorney for one of the top law firms in the state, and eventually you're going to have your own firm," Bailee said proudly.

"Running my own firm is far off in the future. In the meanwhile, I have to play the part of a model employee. As you know, my firm is extremely conservative and I won't stand a prayer for getting that new account if my wife's best friend literally shows her ass at our anniversary party."

Bailee found herself growing defensive. "What are you saying?"

"I'm saying that all the big bosses are going to be at our party and I don't want to have to return to work the following Monday and hear that your girl was topping off all the male guests inside the restroom."

"You're being ridiculous. She's bringing Sadeeq to the party."

"Don't you think it's in poor taste for her to flaunt a married man at a respectable event?"

"If Sadeeq is actually married, I'm fairly certain Jayla isn't aware of it."

"Why don't you ask her about it," he said, jutting out his chin challengingly.

The sudden roar of the crowd emanated from the TV, and Trent, holding a bowl of ice cream, hurried over to the recliner.

Chapter 3

Jayla remembered the vileness of last night in laser-sharp detail, and it was difficult to get through her morning routine without vomiting. She listlessly applied makeup as she tried to prepare for the long day ahead. As she gazed at her reflection in the mirror, the woman looking back at her showed no outward signs of sexual abuse, but she could feel a silent scream pushing at the back of her throat, waiting to explode.

It had been an act of straight-up rape, yet that scumbag, Niles, had not only worn a condom but had also penetrated her tenderly, like it was a consensual act. If he really wanted to be considerate, he should have covered up his disgusting thumbnail before stroking it against her delicate skin and touching her intimate body parts. She hoped she hadn't contracted anything from his nasty hand.

After forcing himself on her, he kissed her goodnight—with tongue—and then had the audacity to ask if she was free next weekend. She wanted to slap the smirk off his face and kick him in the groin, but afraid of prompting him to do something worse than he'd already done, she forced a smile and assured him that she'd give him a call.

The moment he left, she should have called the police. She

should have gone to the hospital and let them do a rape kit. Besides the skin prick on her neck from the broken bottle, her body showed no signs of trauma.

It would be his word against hers.

Besides, she had no business inviting him to the client's home, and a police investigation could cause her to lose her job. Not wanting to make any trouble with the real estate agency that employed her, she thought it best to pretend the devastating night had never happened.

But forgetting was easier said than done.

Never before had she felt so vulnerable and helpless. Never had anyone made her feel so dirty and worthless. After he left, she'd taken a scalding hot shower and scrubbed her skin until it was raw, but it was going to take more than soap and water to make her feel clean again.

It could have been worse. I could have been beaten within an inch of my life. Or murdered.

Last night had been a wakeup call, and Jayla made a promise to herself to stop looking for male companionship online. If she and Sadeeq didn't get back together, she'd become celibate until she was emotionally healed. She vowed that the next man she got involved with would have to be carefully vetted before she risked being alone with him.

Needing to feel better about herself, Jayla paid special attention to her makeup, placing a double layer of lashes to her lids and then further embellishing them with gray eye shadow and perfectly applied winged eyeliner.

She created lip artistry by carefully brushing on a soft plum shade to her lips, adding a dash of hot pink to the center of each lip, and then blending in the bold color. She admired her reflection and concluded that her flawless makeup disguised her pain. It concealed her victimization and gave her the look of a woman who was in charge of her life. It gave her the appearance of someone who was happy and successful.

Jayla's phone trilled and her heart tumbled with panic. No one called that early on a Saturday morning except Sadeeq, and she longed to hear his voice.

Thank God he had come to his senses and realized he couldn't make it without her. His timing couldn't have been more perfect because she needed him in her life, more than ever. She needed to be held in his arms and comforted after the hell she'd endured last night.

Prepared to tell Sadeeq how much she had missed him, she hastily snatched up the phone.

A glance at the screen revealed Bailee's name instead of Sadeeq's. Disappointed, Jayla frowned and hit the ignore button. It was too early in the morning to listen to Bailee's happy ass talking nonstop about her damn anniversary party, acting like it was the most important event of the century.

Jayla regretted getting involved in the planning aspect, and was looking for an out. Until she came up with a believable excuse to not be the party planner, she'd have to continue ducking Bailee's calls. Bailee was her girl and all, but her extreme enthusiasm over her upcoming party was too much to deal with. Her tenth wedding anniversary celebration was all she talked about. Frankly, the way she was acting was reminiscent of the bridezilla she'd been ten years ago.

There was a saying that you never really knew someone until you'd lived with them, but Jayla begged to differ. *You never really know a bitch overly until she's about to get married!*

Usually a nice, polite, and considerate person, Bailee's entire personality changed and she had become a monster during the months preceding her marriage to Trent. And the monster had reared its ugly head again with the planning of the anniversary party.

Nothing was good enough for Bailee. She shot down all of Jayla's great suggestions, causing Jayla to wonder why Bailee needed a party planner at all. Obviously she was quite capable of organizing her own event.

After showing the property to the fourth potential buyer, Bailee received an offer. Going up and down the stairs from the basement to the upper level had worn her out. She was bone weary and couldn't wait to get home and relax. Maybe she'd stop by her favorite Vietnamese restaurant. The nippy temperature warranted a piping-hot bowl of pho soup along with a double serving of smoked beef ribs and also a double serving of mussels smothered in onions.

But the restaurant's meager dessert menu was less than desirable; she'd have to stop at the grocery store and pick up some snacks for after dinner. Her miserable mood justified buying a large container of ice cream, bakery goods, a bag of Doritos, and a large pack of gourmet jelly beans.

During the drive to the restaurant, her thoughts shifted from food to being raped by a lunatic with a slow stroke and a gentle hand. A predator that spoke softly in her ear during the assault that had lasted such an agonizingly long time.

She would have preferred if he'd used brute force. At least the attack would have ended sooner had he exerted himself by thrusting forcefully.

Jayla wondered how many women Niles had raped. Conceivably, too many to count. He was definitely a seasoned rapist. Like her, most of his victims were probably too ashamed and too confused to press charges. Rapists were supposed to rip off your clothes, slap you around, tie you up, and choke you. They weren't supposed to tenderly caress your hair and your body while coercing you to do unspeakable sex acts.

The tears she'd been too numb to shed last night began to fill her eyes, obstructing her view, and forcing her to pull into the parking lot of a strip mall. Slumped over the steering wheel, she cried unabashedly. Tears darkened by eyeliner trailed down her face and dripped from her chin.

Unglued by tears, the double set of lashes slid down her cheeks. She cried for a full five minutes before fumbling inside the glove box and searching for a tissue. Her fingers landed on a napkin and she used it to wipe her eyes and blow her nose. When she checked out her appearance in the mirror, she realized that her makeup was smeared all over her face and she had bloodshot eyes. She looked too bad to be seen in public.

Resigning herself to the idea of having Chinese food delivered, she placed her hand on the gear shift. Suddenly, she was hit with a yearning for Sadeeq that was so profound, it was visceral, and she gasped with need.

She groped inside her purse, searching for her phone. As if reaching for a lifeline, she desperately wrapped her hand around the device and called Sadeeq. She had no words planned and when she heard his voice, her only response was to sniffle and whimper.

"Jayla? You okay?" Sadeeq questioned.

"Uh-huh," she said, sniffling.

"Why're you crying? What's going on?"

"Nothing."

"Something's wrong. Where are you?"

She sobbed. "In the car, on my way home."

"Do you want me to come over?"

"Uh-huh. I really need to see you." Her voice broke and she began to cry openly.

"What's wrong, baby?" The concern and warmth in Sadeeq's voice felt like a soft blanket had been wrapped around her.

"I miss you," she choked out.

"I miss you, too. How long before you get to the crib?"

"About ten minutes."

"Okay, I'll meet you there. I'm on my way."

Heart pounding with excitement, Jayla tore out of the parking lot. She sped through several red lights, trying to get to her big, beautiful man as quickly as possible. The pain of last night was no longer relevant. If she could convince Sadeeq to leave his wife and move in with her, she'd find a way to tuck the memory of being violated somewhere deep inside herself. She'd force herself to forget the tragic night had ever happened.

Tonight, she intended to give it to Sadeeq so good, he'd never want to leave her bed.

Chapter 4

In the midst of a command performance, Jayla was crouched between Sadeeq's hard thighs, working both fists as she took in his massive shaft, alternately licking and sucking. The sounds he made low in his throat motivated her to rotate her fists even faster as she guided his hot meat back and forth over her tongue.

He pounded into her juicy mouth, going a lot deeper than she was prepared for, but she quickly braced herself. His guttural moans sounded so sexy, she was encouraged to withstand the unexpected intrusion of an enormous erection driving into her pharynx.

She gagged a little and tears stung her eyes, but after a few moments, she created a rhythm, tightening her lips around his thickness while delivering tongue flicks to the underside of his dick and then moving upward to the smooth crown, giving it a lavish tongue bath.

Peeking through half-opened eyes, Jayla watched with satisfaction as Sadeeq's head lolled back in defeat. She had that muthafucka moaning like a bitch. In that moment, he was under her control. He was all hers and he wasn't going anywhere.

His dick was like a trapped, helpless creature and her tongue was a boa constrictor, coiled around his length, mercilessly imprisoning it.

Listening to the rasping sounds he emitted was a turn-on, making her want to stop mid-suck and hop on the dick and cream all over it. But needing to finish what she'd started, she was forced to press her thighs together to suppress her own desires.

Grunting, Sadeeq fought to compose himself so that he could take control of the situation. When he entwined both his hands in her hair and held her head in place, Jayla recognized the gesture as her cue to open wide.

It was time to let her hot mouth become a boundless fuck zone, a place where his dick could run roughshod without constraints or restrictions.

Sadeeq had often told her that the way she allowed him to push the full length of his thickness deep into her throat was one of the many things he loved about her. He said he respected the way she sacrificed her comfort for his pleasure, granting him permission to clog up her esophagus until her eyes rolled into the back of her head and she was on the brink of collapsing.

"Damn, you good, baby," Sadeeq growled. "You the only woman who lets me beat up the pussy and clog up your throat."

The sound of his voice seemed distant as she began to slowly lose consciousness. Sensing her body going slack, he pulled out of her mouth before she passed out. He heaved her onto her stomach and immediately shoved his dick into her from behind.

"I love fucking this thing—it's so damn tight. Don't you ever try to leave me again. You belong to me. You hear me, Jayla?"

"Yes," she said in a whimper.

"You're my tight-pussy bitch."

His words and the gruffness of his voice caused liquid heat to pool in her center.

"Say it," he demanded.

"I'm your tight-pussy bitch," she responded breathlessly as he plunged into her slippery depths.

"The way your ass is jiggling and bouncing—I'm not gon' last much longer," he admitted, both captivated and weakened by the sight of the back and forth motion of her ass cheeks. "That shit looks good as fuck and I'm about to bust all up in your guts."

It was too soon for him to cum; she wasn't there yet. But, tonight was all for Sadeeq. It didn't matter that her pussy was throbbing with the need for release.

Selflessly, she helped him along by tightening her inner walls. Clenching his dick, she coaxed him into letting go of the ejaculatory gush he'd been trying to hold back.

"Grip that shit," he encouraged in a shuddering whisper. "Oh, fuck! I can't hold—"

Unable to finish the sentence, Sadeeq grimaced as he flooded her walls, forcing her to loosen her pussy grip.

Afterward, Sadeeq keeled over and lay flat on his back, panting and groaning. While his eyes were closed, Jayla gazed at him worshipfully. His pretty, red ass reminded her of the 'hood version of actor Jason Momoa.

Sadeeq opened his greenish-gray eyes and Jayla smiled down at him. She stroked his curly sideburns and alternately kissed his forehead, his cheek, his lips, and his neck. All she needed was a signal that he was ready for more and she would dutifully wiggle down to the bottom of the bed, prop his legs up, and slather her tongue all over his balls.

"What did you do to me?" he asked as he wiped perspiration from his forehead. "Your box is addictive and your head game is crazy. You got mad skills, baby."

"Thank you," she murmured as she lay beside him, lovingly caressing his chest.

"While you were going down on me, it felt like you were about to suck out my soul. I damn near lost it when you were working your mouth and using the two-hand-twist combo."

"It's called the pepper grinder," Jayla divulged, beaming with pride. Her head game was tight, no doubt about it, and she hoped he was hooked enough to finally walk away from his family.

It was time for him to stop dragging his feet and pack his shit, and then move in with her. He'd admitted that he wasn't happy with his wife and was only there in body. He said that his heart, mind, and soul were always with Jayla.

She wanted so badly to wake up in the morning with him lying next to her. She wanted them to celebrate the major holidays together. No more creeping around. Sadeeq was her man, and it was time for them to become an official couple.

He sat up and lit a blunt. "This here shit is like a mental massage. It blocks out all the bullshit that goes on in my life," Sadeeq said, blowing out a cloud of smoke. He reached over and patted between Jayla's thighs. "That box is the best, baby. But if I had to make a choice between the cooch and weed, it would be a hard decision." He gave her a devilish smile.

Laughing, Jayla tossed a pillow at him.

He held up an arm defensively. "Chill, I'm only fucking with you. I've been miserable without you. These past few weeks have been pure torture. You gotta stop messing with my head like that. Promise me, baby." He cuddled close and kissed her on the cheek.

Jayla felt wanted and secure and she wished the moment could last. It was the perfect time to discuss their situation. Caressing his arm, she cooed, "I missed you, too, Sadeeq. You know I love you to death, but I can't keep ignoring the problem between us."

"It's only a problem if you make it one. I'm not in love with Radiance. I'm in love with you."

That bitch has the nerve to be named Radiance. How ghetto is that? Ain't nothing radiant about that basic bitch.

She nuzzled closer to Sadeeq. "Bae, we're in love, so why can't we be together?" It was a question she'd been asking for over a year. "I'm not saying that we need to get married or anything. At least not right away. I'm simply saying that sharing the man I love is beneath me. After all I've done for you, I deserve something more permanent. I've earned something more respectable than side-chick status."

Jayla hated having to bring up the financial support she'd extended to Sadeeq. It wasn't pleasant throwing it in his face, but he needed to be reminded that she had been ride or die for him. After taking out loans on his behalf and maxing out three credit cards, sadly, she'd be facing bankruptcy soon if they didn't combine their resources and start paying off some of the bills Sadeeq had accumulated.

Her finances had never been great, but they were adequate before Sadeeq entered the picture. Maintaining her own lifestyle while contributing to his was more than she could handle.

"I'm doing the best I can, baby. But I'm not trying to mess up my relationship with my kids, though. I don't want to walk out on them the way my pops did me."

"In other words, nothing's changed," she said solemnly. "I still won't be able to count on you. You'll make plans with me and break them without an explanation. You're still going to have me sitting around waiting and not knowing if you'll show up or not."

"The only time I don't show up is when there's a family situation."

"But your family situations happen all the time. I can't count how many times you've stood me up. You have no idea how awful it feels to be dressed and ready and not even get the courtesy of a phone call."

"Bae," he said gently, eyes lowered. "Bae," he repeated as he stared deeply into her eyes. "I never lied to you about my marital status. You knew there'd be complications from the gate."

"Yeah, but when I met you, you told me you were separated."

"I was at the time."

"Well, what happened?" Aggravated, Jayla threw another pillow at Sadeeq and this time it wasn't a playful toss.

"Chill! You don't have to get aggressive with me. Look, it's not a good time for me to leave right now."

She stared at him, but didn't utter a word.

The awkward silence got to Sadeeq, prompting him to give her an explanation. "Radiance lost her job, okay? She got turned down for unemployment compensation. Now that I'm the only one bringing in a paycheck, it's not a good time to make moves."

Jayla shook her head.

"Radiance has been looking for work and sending out her resume, so it shouldn't take much longer for her to get straight. As soon as she gets back on her feet, I'm out. I swear, baby."

"Do you mean it this time?"

"Yes. Don't you realize how much it hurts me to see you looking so sad? More than anything, I want to put a smile on your beautiful face."

"Everything you're saying sounds good, Sadeeq, but I need a specific timeline. Is that asking too much?"

"No, it's not. I promise you…six months, and then it's go time. My hand to God."

"Okay, six months," Jayla reluctantly agreed. She didn't want to wait that long, but loving Sadeeq the way she did, she didn't have any other choice.

He pulled her into his arms and the feeling of his embrace was heavenly. She truly dreaded having to hear him say it was time for him to go home.

"Are you hungry, baby?" she asked, attempting to prolong their time together.

"Yeah, I could go for some of your kettle-fried chicken."

Jayla frowned. "Aw, I wish I could fix you some, but I've been working so hard, I haven't picked up any groceries in a while. We can order something, though. Wonder Wok makes fried chicken that almost tastes as good as mine."

"Sounds good," Sadeeq agreed, stretching lazily and reaching for the controller. He clicked on the TV and leisurely surfed through the channels, sending her the message that he was in no rush to get home to his wife and his two kids.

With a happy lilt in her voice, Jayla picked up the phone, called the Chinese restaurant and ordered half the menu.

Her purse was on the vanity stool, and when she walked over to get it, she caught a glimpse of her naked body in the mirror. Oddly, she didn't feel the quick impulse to grab a robe and cover her imperfections. She felt beautiful in her skin, which was a brand-new emotion.

With happiness coursing through her, she took out her credit card and began rattling off the numbers to the person on the phone who had taken her order.

She tucked the card back inside her wallet and traipsed back over to the bed.

"The food should be here in forty-five minutes," she informed, snuggling up to Sadeeq. Instead of putting his arm around her, his body stiffened and there was a slight shift in his body that alarmed her.

"Is something wrong?" Jayla asked, searching his face.

"I'm good," he replied curtly, avoiding eye contact.

"No, you're not good. Something is wrong. What is it?" Perplexed, she looked around the bedroom, wondering what had offended Sadeeq.

"I thought you said all your credit cards were maxed. If you didn't want to help me out anymore, you could have just said so. You didn't have to lie about your financial situation."

"My cards are maxed out. I had to use my company expense account to pay for our food," she explained in a faltering voice. She had one credit card left that wasn't maxed out, and there was no way she would let Sadeeq know about it.

Sadeeq narrowed an eye. "So, we're keeping secrets now?"

"I've always had an expense account. There's no secret about that."

"I didn't know. The thing is, I'm in a jam. I really need to use your card for something important."

"I can't use the company card for anything personal," Jayla said firmly. "I've been working over the weekend, showing a listing, and so my food is covered. I can't use the card on something that doesn't fall under the category of work expenses."

"This is important. If you could help me out, I promise I'll pay you back next Friday when I get paid."

"But we already have way too many unpaid bills. You don't understand how bad it is. I've got all kinds of creditors breathing down my neck."

"I told you I'm going to handle those bills as soon as Radiance goes back to work. But right now, it's about my baby girl."

"What about her?"

"Lux's eleventh birthday is Wednesday." Sadeeq blew out a long, frustrated sigh. "With her mom unemployed, I'm really strapped for cash. I can barely afford to pay for her cake and that makes me feel like shit. Like I'm less than a man. I should be able to give her a nice party and whatnot. At the very least, I have to get her a decent gift."

"I could pick up something for her at the mall tomorrow," Jayla offered. "Does she still play with dolls?"

Sadeeq laughed. "Sometimes, but she's got enough Barbies. She wants a phone. She has her heart set on the new iPhone."

Jayla almost choked. The new iPhone was over seven hundred dollars, and she hadn't splurged on an upgrade for herself yet. How in the hell could she justify such an extravagance for a little, young 'hood rat? She hated to think of Sadeeq's daughter in such harsh terms, but she was certain the child was a replica of the mother.

Although Jayla had never personally met Radiance, she secretly followed her on Instagram. Radiance was a bum bitch, always posting ignorant-ass shit. She was a terrible role model for her daughter.

"I wouldn't ask you to do this if I wasn't jammed up," Sadeeq continued. "All of Lux's friends have the new iPhone and my baby girl feels left out. I promised to get her one and I don't know how I'm going to look my daughter in the eye if I don't come through."

"Ordinarily, I could make a purchase like that without blinking an eye, but I've helped you out with so much, I'm experiencing the worst financial crisis of my life," Jayla explained.

"I know, bae. I'm so sorry that I'm the cause of your money problems. Believe me, once we're living together, I plan on working two jobs to get us out this hole. It's just that…" He paused and shook his head woefully. "I hate the fact that when I walk out on Lux and Nafeese and move in with you, my daughter will have a shitty memory of her last birthday with Daddy living in the house. Nafeese is only four years old and he won't remember much, but Lux is a daddy's girl, and it's gonna hurt her to her heart."

"Well, it's not like you're leaving the city. You'll still be able to see your children regularly," Jayla reasoned.

"It won't be the same as living with them. When they came into the world, I had a responsibility to be there for them all through their childhood. But, I fell for you," he said, glumly, shrugging his shoulders.

Feeling responsible for breaking up a family, Jayla blurted, "Listen, I'll get the phone, but I can't put it on my expense account. I'll hold off on making my mortgage payment and put it on my debit card. But you have to promise to pay me back on Friday."

"No doubt. A couple of the fellas at work owe me some money from the football game, so I should have enough to pay you back and take you out to dinner," he said, taking Jayla's hand and bringing it up to his lips.

The gesture was so sweet and so loving, Jayla found herself getting the feels. After what she'd gone through last night, she felt raw and emotionally vulnerable.

"Thank you for hanging in there with me, bae. Luxurious is going to be so happy."

At the mention of Sadeeq's daughter's full name, Jayla's mood shifted from tranquil to aggravated. The nickname, Lux, was much more palatable than Luxurious.

When the day came that she met his kids and became involved in their lives, she'd be damned if she'd ever call that child by her first name. She'd give her a cute pet name, something like Luxy. Or she'd stick to calling her Lux. But never, ever, would she utter such a ridiculous name as Luxurious.

Jayla's thoughts wandered to her financial situation. Instead of playing around with her mortgage payment, she needed to be figuring out a way to make arrangements on all the bills she'd allowed Sadeeq to accumulate.

She cut an eye at him. He looked so fine and sexy, she decided that he was worth every dollar she'd loaned him. She made a mental note to throw in a nice case for the iPhone, a secret gift from her to Sadeeq's daughter.

She wouldn't receive the commission from the Vance home until closing, which would take approximately sixty days. But knowing that something substantial was coming in was like having money in the bank. Everything was going to be okay, she assured herself.

One more purchase on Sadeeq's behalf wouldn't hurt.

Chapter 5

Bailee slammed her phone down harder than she'd planned and immediately checked the screen for a crack. Luckily, it was intact.

But she was still irritated. It was unbelievable that she'd been trying to get in touch with Jayla for over a week and Jayla had been treating her like a pest, ignoring her texts and calls. It was unforgivable, but she couldn't afford to hold a grudge. Not at the moment. She needed Jayla's input for the party.

She wondered why she'd been avoiding her, and figured there was only one way to find out.

Bailee marched out of her big office with a great view and strutted up to her assistant's desk, the latest of a succession of young college grads who only stayed in the position until they found something worthy of their degree.

"I need to borrow your phone, Macy," she said authoritatively.

Being the managing director at First Mutual Bank, Bailee was accustomed to giving orders, but didn't usually speak so sharply to her assistants. But there was something about Macy that bugged her. She seemed cunning and sneaky, though she'd never done anything overt.

Taken off guard by Bailee's presence, Macy scrambled to pull up the quarterly reports she should have been working on.

Too late. She was busted. Bailee had already seen the Jobmagic employment listings but pretended not to notice. She made a mental note to begin interviewing new administrative assistants. She'd be damned if she'd be left in the lurch without adequate help.

She headed back to her office, sat down, and called Jayla from Macy's phone.

Jayla picked up immediately. "Hello, this is Jayla Carpenter."

"And this is Bailee Evans. Why are you ducking me?"

There was a moment of shocked silence and then Jayla emitted a groan of exasperation. "This is stalker behavior. Don't you have any shame? Isn't it obvious I need a break from you?"

"Why? I don't understand. My anniversary party is in a month and this is not the time to act petty."

"You're the petty one. I'm sick of you and your infuriating party. You veto every idea I come up with, and it's clear you don't need my help. Just go ahead and plan your own party the way you want. That's what you've been doing all along."

"Can we discuss this like adults?" Bailee asked.

"No!"

"Jayla, you're being ridiculous. Let's have dinner. My treat. We can go to that seafood place downtown, the one across the street from the theater."

"Marty's?"

"Uh-huh. You love their lobster bisque," Bailee reminded Jayla, certain that free seafood from an expensive restaurant was an offer she couldn't refuse.

"Okay, but my mind is made up about planning your party. Our friendship will be at stake if I continue in that role."

"Why do you feel that way?"

"You're not easy to work with, Jayla. It's okay to be a perfectionist, but it's your attitude. I was donating my services as a friend, but you were treating me like hired help. I can't deal with it. You wonder why you go through so many assistants. Well, let me enlighten you. It's the way you talk to people when you're in a position of authority. It's sickening."

"Really, Jayla? You never mentioned anything about my attitude before."

"I was never in the position of an underling before. You have a problem with looking down on people."

"That's not true. Sounds like you're describing my mother, and I'm nothing like her."

"You may not be pretentious and shallow, but you think you're smarter and more refined than most."

"No, I don't."

"Can I finish?"

"Go ahead."

"You've always had a snobby air, but that's you. I love you anyway. You can also be extremely overbearing when you want something done. You want it your way and on your time. But we're supposed to be friends—equals—and I don't like being in the position where I'm being treated like an underling. I took a lot of shit off you when I was your maid of honor and I don't intend to go through that again. That said, I think it's best for me to attend your anniversary party as a guest. You and Trent can afford to pay a party planner."

"It's not the money. I want *you*. Would it be insulting if I offered to pay you?"

"Yes," Jayla said unwaveringly.

After a few moments of awkward silence, Bailee half-heartedly agreed to hire a party planner.

"Good. Does the offer of a seafood dinner still stand?" Jayla inquired.

Bailee laughed uncomfortably. If she couldn't convince Jayla to help plan her party, there really wasn't any reason to have dinner with her. But she feared that backing out would put an additional strain on their friendship.

"Yes, dinner is still on," she said, injecting false cheer into her voice. "I miss my best friend and want to spend some quality time with you. Is seven o'clock good?"

"It's perfect."

Bailee hung up and paced in her office before returning Macy's phone. Jayla had given her food for thought. It was time to check herself. There had to be a reason why Macy seemed to quietly resent her. Realizing that she tended to be impatient with the young woman, Bailee decided to be friendlier toward her assistant.

Still, it bothered her that Jayla felt the need to point out her flaws. As Trent had suggested, it was possible that Jayla was envious of her. After all, she had a hot husband, a great career that didn't depend upon commission, and a hefty trust fund that she would be entitled to in a few years.

Bailee wasn't the least bit surprised when Jayla showed up wearing a tight pink dress that revealed way too much cleavage. In the past, she'd always viewed Jayla's clothing choices as her way of trying to keep up with the skinny girls, but she now viewed her provocative style as straight-up slutty.

Sticking to her diet, Bailee had controlled her cravings and had ordered only a single crab cake and a small salad, which she ate as slowly as possible. She'd read that masticating food thoroughly, and putting the fork down after every bite, allowed for savoring the food and tricking the tummy into believing it was full.

Jayla, on the other hand, had not exercised any restraint. She started off the meal with lemon-butter shrimp and an oversized margarita. Then, after gorging on steak, lobster, clams, garlic crab legs, corn on the cob, and cheese biscuits, she unapologetically ordered a hefty slice of chocolate-fudge cake and asked for another mammoth margarita.

No shame in her game, Bailee acknowledged as she observed Jayla launching an attack on her cake, stabbing into it as if it might jump off the plate and run away.

Bailee had too much class to publicly flaunt her love of food. She was a closet eater. She tended to eat daintily in public, but behind closed doors, she shoveled the food in with both hands.

Trent never judged her and had never even hinted that she should lose weight. With his many compliments about her body and the passionate way he made love to her, it was clear that he loved and adored her exactly as she was. Ironically, Trent shared Bailee's passion for food, but luckily for him—due to genetics— he could eat whatever he wanted and remained fit by playing a little racquetball with his colleagues a couple times a week.

But Bailee, with her sluggish metabolism, seemed to pack on pounds by merely looking at food.

Sipping lemon water, Bailee waited until Jayla was halfway through her dessert before dropping the bombshell. Though she told herself that she didn't have malicious intentions and that she was only bringing up the subject so that Jayla understood that any nasty sex acts at the anniversary party would not be condoned, a part of her was well aware that the rumors about Jayla's fetishes had angered and embarrassed her. She wanted to lash out at her friend.

"Trent heard a rumor from his cousin, Javari." Bailee took a sip of water before continuing. "I don't believe a word his lying cousin says, but I wanted you to know what he's saying about you."

"Javari's dumb ass can't say a damn thing about me."

Bailee stared at her.

Jayla stared back at her.

"The streets are talking about you," Bailee said calmly.

Jayla put her fork down, and the clink of metal against porcelain was loud and confrontational. "And what exactly are the streets saying?"

"According to Javari, Sadeeq Samuelson is married with two kids. Did you know this?"

Clearly distressed, Jayla dragged her fingers down her face, and then nodded.

"Why would you mess with a married man, Jayla?"

"We're in love."

"Oh, Jayla," Bailee said pityingly.

"I'm serious. We're moving in together as soon as his wife finds a job. She got fired and can't get unemployment. Sadeeq's a good dad, and he can't leave his kids under those circumstances."

"So, you're okay with being a homewrecker?"

Jayla sucked her teeth. "It's not like that. Their marriage is over. It was over long before he met me."

"But he was with his wife when you met him?"

"Yes, but—"

"That's not cool." Bailee's mouth turned down in distaste as she held Jayla in a long, judgmental gaze.

Jayla tried to match the stare, but she gave up, her eyes guiltily shifting downward.

"You can't blame me for Sadeeq's marital problems," Jayla said, trying to keep the frustration out of her tone.

"Didn't it strike you as a bad idea to get involved with a married man?"

"The heart wants what it wants," Jayla replied with a defiant flip of her hair.

"I realize Sadeeq's a fine male specimen, but he's clearly rough around the edges. If he hangs with Javari, it's highly possible that Sadeeq has shady ways. I don't think he's the kind of man that you should be involved with."

"Just because he knows Javari doesn't mean they're friends and it certainly doesn't mean Sadeeq has shady ways. Seems like you're judging him based on the neighborhood he comes from."

Bailee shrugged.

"Well, I'm from the 'hood, too. Does that make me an uncivilized person?"

"No, you rose above your circumstances, but Sadeeq hasn't. Also, do you realize how rare it is for a 'hood dude to be a family man? Sadeeq is as rare as a unicorn. So, why would you want to be responsible for breaking up a family that has managed to stay intact, despite the fact that statistics are not in their favor?"

"Sadeeq is not happy."

"Oh, God, you sound like the stereotypical homewrecker."

"Stop calling me that. He's going to remain in his kids' lives, and I'm going to make sure of it."

"Aren't you the noble one?" Bailee quipped.

"Look, he's moving in with me in six months and there's nothing else to discuss."

"And you're good with leaving two children fatherless? Do you feel that it's okay to take another woman's husband?"

Jayla didn't say anything.

Bailee shook her head. "I had no idea you were so selfish and heartless."

"Yeah, well, if his wife was throwing the pussy back the right way, he wouldn't be leaving her for me."

"Wow, so his wife is to blame—due to her limited bedroom skills? Is that really your defense?"

"Partly."

"I guess I don't really know you, after all. Trent told me some unpleasant things about you that I refused to believe."

"Trent needs to keep my name out of his mouth and mind his

own damn business," Jayla barked. She shoved her partially eaten dessert away and stood. "I'm ready to go. Thanks for dinner."

"Sit down, Jayla. We need to have a discussion."

"About what?"

"About your behavior at my wedding reception."

Jayla scowled. "What behavior? You want me to go back ten years and try to recall everything I did at your reception? What's this about, Bailee?" Jayla pulled her chair back, sat down heavily, and impatiently drummed her fingers on the table.

"You have no memory of getting in a compromising position with two of the groomsmen—Chance and Tone—in the bathroom at the reception venue?"

Jayla gasped. "Are you crazy? Who told you that lie?"

"So, you don't recall? Maybe you can remember your more recent depraved activity," Bailee said stonily.

Jayla lifted her brows in bewilderment. "Recent depraved activity? I don't have a clue what you're talking about."

"You don't have any recollection of going behind the bar and giving the bartender a blow job in the middle of the ballroom during my birthday party?"

The color drained from Jayla's face. "Oh, Jesus! Who told you that bullshit? I'm insulted that you'd think that I'm capable of going that low. I've always known that Trent disliked me, but I had no idea that his hatred was so intense that he'd make up some vile shit in order to break up our friendship."

"Trent got the information from reliable sources."

Jayla folded her arms and glared at Bailee. "His sources are lying on me and I can't believe you're feeding into malicious gossip. How the hell do I look giving top in the middle of a fuckin' ballroom? A bitch ain't never been that pressed to suck a dick." Jayla's voice rose, attracting attention from the other diners and prompting Bailee to look around in embarrassment.

"But his sources weren't lying about Sadeeq's marital status, right?" Bailee spoke in a whisper that urged Jayla to lower her tone.

"That's comparing apples and oranges," Jayla replied wearily. "Falling in love with a married man is totally unrelated to happily fucking two men in a public restroom and openly sucking a random bartender's dick. Damn, Bailee, how could you come at me with this kind of bullshit?"

"I don't know what to believe, but Trent is convinced."

"Fuck Trent. Your rumor-spreading husband can kiss my ass," Jayla said viciously.

"Trent isn't spreading any rumors. His boys have been reporting horrible stories about you for years."

"You waited long enough to tell me about my sordid reputation," Jayla said, sounding hurt and betrayed.

"Trent didn't have the heart to tell me—until recently."

"It's not true," Jayla insisted. "And I shouldn't have to keep repeating myself." She pushed away from the table. "I can't deal with this," she said with tears welling in her eyes. "I just went through a horrific experience that I've been trying to forget."

"What happened?"

"I was raped," Jayla said quietly as tears rolled down her face. "I've been trying to keep my emotions in check, but it's not working. I can't help from blaming myself. I feel like shit for allowing myself to be in such a vulnerable position. And now, after hearing this shit you're talking, it's just too much."

Jayla dropped her head in her hands and began to sob, attracting much more attention than Bailee was comfortable with. Credit card in hand, Bailee beckoned the waiter and hastily paid the check.

Outside the restaurant, Jayla became even more hysterical. Her shoulders heaved, and then she began to wail—a deep, mournful, animal howl that possessed such ferocity, the sheer volume of her lament attracted attention.

Some pedestrians drifted past and had the decency to keep it moving, but most stopped and gawked, the looks on their faces a mix of embarrassment and perplexity. There were a scant few who watched with open delight, as if witnessing a provocatively dressed, curvy woman, in the midst of a public meltdown, was entertaining.

Appearances were everything to Bailee, and being perceived as a participant of a spectacle went against everything she stood for. "Pull yourself together," Bailee said through gritted teeth.

"But it wasn't my fault," Jayla wailed.

"Not out here. Don't say another word until we get in the car." Tugging Jayla by the arm, Bailee led her to the parking garage and guided her toward her shiny Volvo, which was conveniently parked on the lower level.

"Who raped you and when?" Bailee probed, her face contorted in confusion.

"Last Friday night. Some guy I met through a dating app." Jayla sniffled and shuddered. "I invited him to a house I was showing and he raped me."

"You invited a stranger to one of your listings?"

"Don't lecture me, Bailee," Jayla snapped. "I know it was stupid, okay?"

"I don't understand. What about Sadeeq? I thought you and he were—"

"I wasn't speaking to him at the time. I called myself teaching him a lesson by getting with another dude and it backfired."

"Did you call the police? Did you go to the hospital and let them do a rape kit?"

"No. I didn't do anything. If I involve the police, my job will find out and I'll be fired."

"If the guy did it once, he's probably done it before and will strike again. You can't let a possible serial rapist remain at large."

"There's nothing I can do about it," Jayla said tearfully.

"If you don't want to involve the police, then the least you can do is to notify the dating service and let them know that a member is using the app to victimize women."

Jayla shook her head. "I want to forget it ever happened. Being back with Sadeeq is the best therapy for me right now." A fresh batch of tears sprang to Jayla's eyes and streamed down her face.

Bailee put her arm around her friend and murmured, "It's going to be all right, Jayla. You're strong and you'll get through this. I've got your back, girl, and don't ever forget it."

Jayla squeezed Bailee's hand and whispered, "Thank you."

After Jayla calmed down, Bailee drove her to the top level of the garage and waited until she was safely in her car. She tailed her and waited patiently while Jayla fumbled for her credit card and then paid the parking attendant.

Bailee drove behind Jayla until it was time for her to hop on the expressway. She honked her horn and Jayla honked back.

Bailee was convinced that Trent's no-good cousin and his homeboys had lied on Jayla. She'd known Jayla for far too long to start accepting silly locker room talk as fact.

Chapter 6

Jayla was too emotionally drained to be furious with Chance and Tone for running their big mouths. The bartender's accusation didn't really matter. She wouldn't recognize him or his dick if they ever had another encounter.

Nowadays, she didn't get involved with people she knew personally. She limited her hoe-ism to random dudes she met through dating apps. But after the disastrous encounter with disgusting Niles…

Feeling herself getting worked up, she took a deep breath and let it out slowly. There was no point in reliving that night, crying about it, and beating herself up over what happened. She had to learn from the mistake and move on.

In the midst of getting ready for work, her phone buzzed on the nightstand. To her dismay, it was a collection agency calling at seven-thirty in the morning. It was shameful the way the representatives for the company had grown bolder and more demanding with every passing week. Jayla blocked the number, refusing to be bullied so early in the morning. Irritated, she postponed putting on makeup and stomped to the kitchen, where she stuck two fast-food sausage biscuits in the microwave. She'd bought four of them along with other items at the drive-thru late last night after Sadeeq had stood her up, yet again.

While waiting for the food to heat, she sent Sadeeq a text, asking if he was going to be able to keep his promise and come through tonight.

She had to do something about her weight, she thought, as she bit into the first greasy sandwich. Her clothes were getting too tight and she'd soon have to either shop for clothes in a larger size or make an earnest attempt to reduce her caloric intake.

Depressed about her finances and her married-man situation, she removed the wrapping from the second sandwich and ate it so quickly, it was as if she'd inhaled it. After swallowing the last bite of doughy goodness, she closed her eyes blissfully. She yearned for a third sandwich, but she'd eaten the other two last night, along with fries and a double burger.

Trying to fill an intangible void, she swung open the fridge and grabbed a withered-looking egg roll from earlier in the week. After nibbling on it and deriving no satisfaction, she tossed it in the trash.

Starting tomorrow, she'd cut back on eating. She had to if she wanted to look hot at Bailee's anniversary party. She had a month to slim down. If she didn't, she'd end up having to wear a tent, and that would not be cute. Plus, she wanted to look as good as possible while showing off Sadeeq at such an elegant affair.

Hopefully, Chance and Tone wouldn't be there, giving her hungry looks. She'd have to give them both the finger if they had the audacity to try to lure her away from handsome Sadeeq.

Besides, she didn't get down like that anymore.

The one day of the week that Jayla was required to be in the office was long and exhausting. She lost a new and prestigious listing to a skinny, blond real estate agent named Isabelle. Isabelle wasn't the least bit pretty with her long, horse face, but all the men at the agency acted as if her skinniness, pale skin, and hair color made her the second coming of Princess Di.

Ordinarily, when Jayla felt she had been treated unfairly at work, she'd jump in her car and drive to a fast-food joint to get a quick, emotional boost. Unfortunately, the big boss, Griffin, called a last-minute meeting, which was scheduled to commence in fifteen minutes.

Thwarted from dulling her pain with a food run, Jayla did the next best thing. She logged into her fake Instagram account and felt an adrenaline rush when she tapped on Radiance's page, where she hoped to find indisputable signs that the bitch's marriage was falling apart.

Disappointment couldn't begin to describe Jayla's reaction to the most recent photos that she'd posted, photos that depicted marital bliss instead of strife. In one picture, Radiance and Sadeeq posed with Lux, who was grinning while holding up the new iPhone that Jayla had paid for.

In another picture, Lux sat on a new bike that had celebratory white balloons tied to the handlebars. There was a photo of an elaborate birthday cake that was a replica of a pink Chanel bag. The child's awful name, Luxurious, was spelled out in full and in sparkly letters on the edible cake platter.

And if all that ghetto-style braggadocio behavior wasn't enough to make Jayla's blood boil, there was a recent family portrait posted on Radiance's page that nearly pushed Jayla over the edge. In the picture, Sadeeq stood with an arm around Luxurious and the other arm around his wife, while the little boy, Nafeese, stood in front of his mother with a wide grin.

Jayla glared at the family photo, noting that Sadeeq's son had acquired his good looks while Lux was a smaller version of her unattractive mother.

Fuming with anger, Jayla entered the meeting. She was usually the most vocal participant at the company meetings. It was normal for her to rage, snarl, and sulk about unfair company policies and the subpar listings that she was saddled with. Her colleagues had grown accustomed to her behaving like the stereotypical, angry black woman, but today they all exchanged puzzled looks when Jayla sat quietly without a word of complaint.

Uncharacteristically quiet, she kept her head down as she sent Sadeeq a barrage of angry texts. She couldn't tell him that she was upset after spying on his wife's Instagram page, so she blamed her displeasure on his lack of remorse for standing her up last night.

His only response was: *At the barbershop. I'll hit you back later.*

She wondered if another family emergency would prevent him from spending time with her. The idea of not seeing him sent her into a panic. She was weary of her empty existence and was anxious for her and Sadeeq to start building a life together.

She could never reveal to Bailee how much she'd done for him. Bailee would think she was a fool, and who could blame her?

Times like now when Sadeeq was treating her like a total piece of shit, it seemed apparent that he was using her, taking her to the cleaners for all she was worth.

Shame on her for presenting Sadeeq as a single man who was devoted to her. She deserved to get busted for her lies. Maybe now she would gain some self-respect, cut her losses, and tell Sadeeq to do her a favor and lose her number.

On the other hand, the constant worrisome thoughts of the enormous debt she had incurred brought her to the conclusion that she couldn't end the relationship with Sadeeq until he paid her back all the money she was owed.

But who was she kidding? She was hooked on the good dick, mesmerized by his gorgeous eyes, and blinded by his sculpted physique. She couldn't walk away from that pretty muthafucka, even if she tried.

Jayla barely listened to what was being said during the meeting. When Griffin mentioned that a delegation of Japanese engineers was arriving next week and looking for apartments to rent, she immediately began to tune him out. The commission in rental property wasn't anything to get excited about.

While her colleagues paid rapt attention and scribbled notes, Jayla's fingers were busy sending Sadeeq more texts, which he ignored.

She was deeply offended and thought about making up an excuse to get out of the meeting. She wanted so badly to pull up on the bastard while he was sitting in the barbershop. It would be all his fault if she went inside the barbershop and showed her natural ass, and it would teach him to stop playing with her all the damn time.

Imagining herself as the kind of bitch who didn't take any shit off a nigga felt good in her mind. But in reality, if she actually had the heart to roll up on Sadeeq, she'd probably say something weak like, *Sorry to pop up on you, but I got worried when I didn't hear from you.*

The boring meeting dragged on and on. The droning sound of Griffin's voice was causing Jayla's eyes to grow heavy, but she immediately became alert and sat up straighter when he announced that a new client was putting his million-dollar Jersey beach home up for sale.

She was instantly deflated when, in the next breath, he said that the client had specifically asked that Isabelle handle the sale.

If that's the case, why the fuck did you even bring it up? She blinked rapidly and then slumped in her seat and scowled down at her phone. She tapped an icon, deciding that a game of Angry Birds would match her mood. Putting all her energy into pulling back the slingshot on the screen with the pad of her finger, she concentrated on her aim, refusing to listen to anything else Griffin had to say.

Playing the mildly violent action game didn't take her mind off her troubles. If anything, wielding a digital slingshot heightened her annoyance. Made her feel more aggressive. Isabelle, with her upper-middle-class background and her huge network of well-to-do friends, always got the high-end properties. Even when rich clients didn't request the skinny bitch, she was still given much better listings than Jayla.

Griffin automatically assumed that Isabelle was more at ease dealing with wealthy clients than Jayla was.

The token African American in the office, the majority of Jayla's clientele were African American, buying and selling homes for well under two hundred thousand. Occasionally, she sold more expensive real estate, but it was rare. To keep up with her colleagues, she had to sell five or six houses to their one. Life was so fucking unfair!

After the meeting, the male real estate agents concealed their envy and congratulated Isabelle. Their disingenuousness was enough to make Jayla want to puke. Refusing to play their game, she didn't utter a word as she pushed past the group of phonies that huddled around Isabelle.

Jayla's cold silence informed them all that she was pissed off at being overlooked.

Acting chivalrous, a tall, reedy agent named Tom drew Isabelle close, in case Jayla became unruly and elbowed Blondie.

Glaring at her coworkers, Jayla yanked up her briefcase and stormed toward the exit sign.

With the collar of her coat turned up, she cut across the company parking lot. When she reached her car, she pulled out her phone and stared glumly at the screen.

No messages from Sadeeq. Nada! Not a damn word!

Every aspect of her life was shitty: her money, her love life, her career, even her friendship with Bailee seemed tenuous. She deserved better than her crappy life and it was her responsibility to start treating herself like a queen.

On a quest to feel better, she got in her car and steered the vehicle toward a small, grungy-looking takeout place that had excellent seafood. She didn't have to ponder what she wanted; the spot had the best fried catfish she'd ever tasted.

Merely imagining herself pouring hot sauce on top of the golden-brown-crusted fried fish made her feel warm and fuzzy.

While driving, she called ahead and placed an order for three fish platters with sides of potato salad, collards, cornbread, and peach cobbler for dessert. She told herself she'd eat one platter when she got home and save the other two for later, to be shared with Sadeeq when he came over.

If he didn't show up, she'd end up devouring all three platters, and would hate herself in the morning when she awakened with a queasy stomach.

The way she consumed food was a vicious cycle of misery. She ate when she was anxious, she ate when she was bored, she ate when she felt celebratory, she ate, ate, ate whether she was hungry or not. And she was helpless to control herself.

A tiny baby, Jayla had weighed only three pounds at birth, and it became Lorraine, her mother's life mission to fatten her up. Lorraine Carpenter doted on her baby girl, and even when the pediatrician warned her that her toddler daughter's weight was not in a healthy range, she continued to overfeed Jayla.

During her elementary years, she always carried a large, insulated lunch bag to school. The bag was so thoroughly stuffed with Jayla's favorite foods that it bulged on all sides. It seemed perfectly normal for Jayla to unzip her bag and find a turkey and cheese hoagie, cut in halves, a peanut butter and jelly sandwich, two cans of grape soda, a bag of cheese curls, a bag of barbecue chips, a pack of Tastykake Krimpets, two candy bars, and several packs of apple-flavored Now & Laters.

Whenever she came home from school complaining that the kids had taunted her over her weight, fat-shaming her with names like: *Blubber Butt, Crisco Kid, Roly-Poly,* and *Fat Mama Cheeseburger,* Lorraine soothed Jayla, telling her that her classmates were envious of her beauty.

She would cheer Jayla up with an extra helping of mac and cheese at dinnertime, followed by a double-serving of dessert.

With her mother insisting she was beautiful the way she was and promising that one day in the future, so many boys would be chasing after her, she'd have to beat them off with a stick, Jayla tried her best to let the taunts roll off her back.

But as she grew older, she discovered that Lorraine had not been truthful. Teenage boys were not fans of fat girls and Jayla had to give them extra favors if she wanted to get their attention. And to this day, she continued to go the extra mile for the men in her life.

To this day, whenever she felt sorry for herself, she turned her thoughts to food and the anticipation of steaming French fries or a juicy cheesesteak would cause her heart to flutter with joy.

Since birth she'd been taught that food equaled love, she didn't know any other way to deal with life's many disappointments other than to stuff her face.

Although she planned to eventually switch to a healthier diet, until the day came that Sadeeq was secured in her clutches, she realized that her frazzled nerves would only get worse if she had nothing to look forward to except a diet of rabbit food.

Jayla arrived at the seafood spot feeling like Sadeeq's silence was justification to gorge herself. Inside the place, an assortment of enticing aromas enveloped her, and she added a dozen fried shrimp to her fried catfish order.

Feeling somewhat content, she sat on a chair near the window and waited for her food.

Chapter 7

Snuggled together on the couch, Bailee and Trent watched *The Blacklist*. They were both TV addicts, one of many things they had in common. Riveted, they watched with their bodies pressed together, Bailee's head resting on Trent's shoulder. While the star of the show bantered humorously and remained inexplicably calm during an edge-of-your seat moment, Trent anxiously twirled one of Bailee's locs around his finger. As the main character and his sidekick smoothly took out the bad guys in a hail of bullets, Trent released Bailee's hair and his hand slid to the side of her neck, gently massaging until she was practically purring.

A commercial filled the TV screen and when Trent's hand fell away from her neck, Bailee whined, "Don't stop," in a childlike voice that usually persuaded him to indulge her whims.

But this time he stubbornly folded his hands together. "I've been thinking," he began, the three words hanging in the air, hot and heavy.

Uh-oh. Bailee felt herself stiffen. After ten years of marriage and four years of being college sweethearts, Bailee had developed the remarkable ability to translate Trent's tones. Sensing that he was about to bring up an unpleasant subject, she steeled for the discussion he was leading into.

The discussion of their childlessness, a subject he'd recently started bringing up with increasing regularity.

She turned and faced Trent. "What's up?" she asked, chewing her bottom lip.

"We're not getting any younger, honey. It's time to start working on a family," he said in a tone that apologized for bringing up a touchy subject.

As much as she loved Trent, she had to repress the urge to punch him. Why would he ruin their peaceful evening with *this* discussion?

"We've been over this before," she said with evident exasperation.

"I know, but I can't help it if I don't want to end up being a fifty-year-old dad, trying to toss a football to my kid," Trent said tersely.

"It's so unfair for you to put this on me. It not fair for you to make me out as the bad guy when we both agreed before getting married that having kids would cramp our lifestyle."

"We made that decision back in college, when we were still *kids* ourselves. At that age, how could we make a critical decision when we didn't even know what life was all about?"

"I was very much aware of what I did and didn't want. I assumed you were equally certain about your plans for the future."

He clasped her hand. "The future is now, Bailee. It's not normal for two healthy people to choose to remain childless. Don't you realize that society will view us as cold and selfish if we don't have at least one child?"

"Will society help us teach a black son why he might get shot by cops even if he follows their orders?" Bailee asked derisively. "Will society tell our black daughter that her dark skin and kinky hair are positive characteristics? Or will she get the message that she needs to adopt a more European look?"

"We don't have to rely on society to validate our children. As their parents we'll be the ones to ensure they have high self-esteem and—"

"But the images they'll get from the media will destroy all our hard work," Bailee said with a sigh. "Our daughter will want to be stick-thin with a disproportionate butt and wear a long, silky weave. Our son will be singled out by the cops, suffering the indignity of being stopped and frisked for merely walking the streets while black." Bailee shook her head. "It's irresponsible and reckless to bring black children into this messed-up world we live in."

"You're making excuses. It's absurd to refuse to reproduce due to social injustice."

"It makes good sense to me and there was a time when you and I were in agreement." Bailee rose from the couch, indicating the discussion was over. Trent turned toward the TV and flicked the channel to a cable news station.

After she'd exited the living room, Bailee expected Trent to trail behind her, saddened by their discussion but easily mollified with a blowjob. But when she came out of the shower and discovered he hadn't come to bed yet, she worriedly nibbled on her lower lip.

The TV had been turned off in the living room, but she could hear the CNN anchor's voice emanating from the guest room.

Usually, it was Bailee who relocated to the spare bedroom after an argument. She couldn't recall Trent ever willingly separating from her. She ran a hand through her hair, trying to figure out what she could say to persuade him to stop being silly and join her in bed.

But she was keenly aware that the only thing he wanted to hear were the words, "I'll stop taking the pill."

And she couldn't agree to that. In all actuality, she was the one who should have been upset. She'd stuck to their life's plan while Trent had gone off script. A part of her suspected that Trent didn't actually want children, but he believed being a parent would make him seem more well-rounded. Better suited for the position he coveted at his law firm. He wanted to fit in with his male counterparts at the office and have a good little wife at home, dutifully taking care of the kids.

Throwing back the comforter, she slid into the king-size bed, which seemed as wide as the Pacific Ocean without Trent lying beside her. She slept fitfully, waking every hour, reaching out and patting the empty space beside her. A few times, jolted by his absence, she pushed herself up on an elbow and gazed around in bafflement.

It wasn't like Trent to hold on to resentment. It was his motto to never go to bed angry, and whenever she had camped out in the spare bedroom, at some point in the night, Trent would join her, taking full responsibility for whatever had pissed her off.

Did he want her to initiate their make-up? Should she creep into the guest room and tell him that she'd had a change of heart and was willing to have his baby?

But it wasn't true and she couldn't lie to him.

Resolute, she plumped her pillow, burrowed beneath the comforter, and willed herself to go back to sleep.

In the morning, Trent came into their bedroom to get dressed. He moved back and forth from the en suite bathroom to his closet in utter silence, and with his face tightened in a scowl.

Attempting to brighten the dreary atmosphere, Bailee got out of bed and pushed her lips into an apologetic smile. But Trent maneuvered around her, refusing to accept her goodwill gesture.

A morning person, Trent was typically chipper and talkative when he got ready for work. He had never given her the silent treatment before and she wondered how long he could hold out.

When she heard the alarm indicating the front door had opened and closed, a knot formed in the pit of her stomach and hurt throbbed in her chest. Throughout all the years of their marriage, Trent had never left the house without giving her a kiss and telling her to have a good day.

He was really going out of his way to make a point and it wasn't fair.

She decided that two could play his game. She could be as un-yielding as him. Trent had a lot of nerve, acting as if she'd misled and betrayed him when he was the one attempting to alter the course of their shared journey.

If he wanted to sleep in the guest room, then it was fine with her. In fact, she'd help him out by transferring his clothes from their closet into the one in the guest room.

Infused with energy, Bailee began picking up stacks of folded sweaters from the shelf and moving them to the closet in the guest room across the hall. Next, she grabbed suits, shirts, and pants that were held up by hangers. Growing tired, she didn't bother to neatly arrange his sneakers and dress shoes; she dumped them in the middle of the floor. Items from his drawers were moved last, and when she checked the time, she realized she was already an hour late for work.

But, evicting Trent from their bedroom was an hour of well-spent time.

Drenched with perspiration, she felt a sense of accomplishment.

Tonight, instead of wondering if Trent was coming to bed, she'd lock the door to make sure he realized she wasn't pressed to have his warm body next to hers.

Two could definitely play the same game, but she could play it better.

Chapter 8

S adeeq's pay day came and went without any communication from him.

Jayla texted, emailed, and went as far as ringing his phone from early morning until she cried herself to sleep that night.

She loathed herself for being such a dumb bitch. She deserved everything that had happened to her. Signs that Sadeeq was using her had always been there. But she'd been so needy and desperate, she bought into every lie, clinging to the hope that his feelings for her were sincere.

Now, it was Saturday night, snowing outside—practically a blizzard and she was stranded in the house. No one was making deliveries and with her car buried beneath the snow, there was no way to get around. All she could do was warm up leftovers and watch movies on Netflix. Too bad she didn't have any devoted side dudes that were so sprung they'd come out in inclement weather and rescue her from hunger and the devastating loneliness that engulfed her.

There was no one who cared enough to come through with some grub. And she was too spooked from Niles to risk using a dating app to set up another encounter with a stranger.

Her heart had been set on attending Bailee's anniversary party with Sadeeq, but it looked like she was going to end up going alone. There was something sad and tragic about going solo to her best friend's ten-year anniversary celebration. Maybe she'd ask Bailee to fix her up with someone from the bank where she worked. Or maybe Trent could introduce her to one of his colleagues.

Oh, that's right, Trent thinks of me as a ratchet ho, too unscrupulous to introduce to any of his distinguished colleagues.

Beneath her living room window, she heard the familiar sound of a shovel scraping concrete. It had finally stopped snowing and apparently one of her neighbors was eager to clear the sidewalk of snow. It annoyed Jayla when people chose to shovel snow at night. The sound was loud, intrusive, and annoying.

Out of sheer nosiness, she paused the movie and drifted to the window and peered out. As she suspected, Mr. Murphy, who lived in the green house directly across the street from her building, was responsible for the racket. The old buzzard had better watch it before he had a heart attack.

She was about to turn away from the window when she noticed another, much younger man joining Mr. Murphy, helping him clear his steps and porch. It was a nice and neighborly thing to do, but it was too late at night for all that noise.

The two men talked loud, cracked jokes, and laughed heartily while their shovels hitting the pavement added to the commotion.

Mr. Murphy thought of himself as the mayor of Mount Airy and prided himself on being personally responsible for the pleasant appearance of their street. Jayla wouldn't be surprised if he roused all the neighbors and guilt-tripped them into coming outside and shoveling snow at night.

Damned big mouth, self-important, meddling busybody!

Giving up on watching the movie in peace, Jayla decided to discard the funky pajamas she'd had on since yesterday and take a long, hot bath. Maybe when she got out of the tub, the racket from across the street would have stopped and she'd be able to enjoy the movie peaceably.

Luxuriating in the tub wasn't the best idea. Too much time to think, and of course, her thoughts all focused on Sadeeq and the horrible predicament he'd left her in. There was no doubt in her mind that in order to get the creditors off her ass, she'd have to file for bankruptcy.

Live and learn, she told herself as she stared into space. She'd been kind, loving, and generous toward Sadeeq, but he'd ruined her for the next man. If a muthafucka ever had the audacity to ask her for any type of financial assistance, she'd laugh spitefully and swiftly escort his bitch-ass to the door. She wasn't giving up one fuckin' penny to anyone, ever again!

For a few fleeting moments, she'd felt empowered and ready to take on the world, but the reality of her financial troubles slumped her shoulders. She pressed her palms against her forehead and groaned.

Obviously, Sadeeq had considered her as a trick-ass bitch, and had treated her like she was nothing more than a human ATM. Accepting that she'd been used hurt to the core. Lips trembling, she allowed herself another long cry and by the time she heaved herself out of the soapy water, the skin on her palms and the soles of her feet were shriveled up.

A glance in the bathroom mirror revealed red, puffy eyes. Hers was the face of someone who had suffered sorrow and humiliation. She was the picture of despair.

The sudden sound of her doorbell caused her to nearly jump out of her skin. She pulled a robe from a hook and threw it on. As she padded out of the bathroom, she couldn't imagine who was at her door late at night, right after a snowstorm. Probably one of her stupid neighbors who felt the urge to shovel and wanted to borrow some rock salt.

I'm not loaning out shit. I need my damn rock salt for myself. What the hell do I look like, Home Depot or something?

Grumbling in her mind, she trudged to the front door. Closing one eye, she spied through the peephole and nearly toppled over from shock. Trying to get her bearings, she took a deep breath, exhaled and took in another burst of air before opening the door.

"I shoveled your car out of the snow," Sadeeq said, speaking in low decibels as he gazed at her appreciatively.

For the longest moment, Jayla was speechless. A thousand emotions coursed through her. As her heartbeat thudded out of control, she silently pleaded for it to settle down. She wanted to slap him. Shout at him and call him a string of vile names with the word, *pimp*, at the top of the list.

But she remained silent.

She studied him with an intense gaze as he stood there, filling the doorway. Despite the extra layers of winter clothing he wore, discernible musculature bulged beneath the sleeves of his jacket. Sadeeq with his big, rugged, fine-ass self was built like a tank, and no amount of clothing could disguise the fact that he put in lots of work at the gym. His emerald-gray eyes flashed with genuine contrition, and the tip of his tongue flicked against pouty lips that looked more kissable than ever.

He held her in a tender gaze that weakened her resolve. She collapsed into him and he wrapped his arms tightly around her, and his lips brushed the crown of her head.

"I'm so sorry, baby," he murmured, his soft words breezing warmly through her hair. "I never meant to hurt you. Things got out of hand on the home front. But it's all good now."

She untangled herself and pulled away. "Okay," she said with a question mark in her voice and dragging out the word, prompting him to explain further.

"Radiance been trippin', lately, but she's under control. Aye?"

Jayla nodded uncertainly, wondering what he meant exactly by having his wife under control.

"Oh, yeah," he added. "I brought the money you loaned me for the phone." He pulled a wad of bills from his pocket and stuffed them in the deep pocket of Jayla's robe. "I'm gonna need a little more time to pay off those credit cards."

She nodded somberly. The balances on the credit cards were ridiculous and there was no way he could pay them off anytime soon, not on a cable technician's salary. Bankruptcy was unavoidable unless they pooled their incomes immediately, and that wasn't likely.

"Another thing, I want to apologize for ignoring your texts and calls. I hated knowing that I was causing you pain, but there was nothing I could do about it."

"I don't understand why you couldn't communicate. All you had to do to put my mind at ease was send a quick text," she said, feeling hurt and exasperated all over again.

"I know. But shit got real a few days ago."

"What happened?"

"Radiance went through my phone. She found our texts and all hell broke loose." He closed his eyes as he shook his head unhappily.

Jayla did her best impression of looking concerned, but on the inside, she felt a secret little thrill. She had to hold herself back from dancing and cheering in triumph. It was about time that bitch realized that her marriage had been on life support for far too long and it was time to pull the plug.

"Did you tell her that you want a divorce?" Jayla asked hopefully.

He took a seat on the couch. Bent over at the waist, he massaged his forehead. When he looked up, he heaved a sigh. "Yeah, I told her, but it didn't do any good."

Jayla sat next to Sadeeq. "I don't understand."

"She started acting the fool, crying and breaking shit. She even involved my daughter in the bullshit."

"In what way?"

"She told Luxurious that—"

Jayla uttered a soft groan. That name, *Luxurious*, was too much.

"She tried to turn Lux against me," he explained, switching to his daughter's nickname as if he'd read Jayla's mind. "She had my baby girl upset and crying, telling her that Daddy was leaving them for a new family."

"But that's not true. We don't have a family." *At least not yet.*

"Radiance doesn't care about the truth. She don't play fair. She says what she thinks will get the results she wants. And she got what she wanted by getting Lux all worked up and upset, and the next thing I know, my baby girl's wheezing and choking and she's in the midst of an asthma attack."

Jayla reared back in surprise. "Are you serious?"

He heaved a heavy sigh. "We had to rush her to Children's Hospital. It was touch and go the whole ride. She stopped breathing a couple times while I was driving through the streets and running red lights like a madman. It didn't help that Radiance was cussing my ass out for driving instead of waiting for an ambulance with medics that could administer CPR. She was screaming that if her baby died, she'd never forgive me. Man, it was like being in the middle of a nightmare that you can't wake up from."

Jayla pressed a hand against her chest. "Oh, my God. So, how is Lux doing? Is she still in the hospital?"

"Nah, they kept her for two-and-a-half days before they kicked her out."

"What? Why'd they kick her out?"

"As soon as Lux started feeling a little better, she started getting into feuds with the nurses."

Jayla tilted her head to the side. "How does a child get into feuds with nurses?"

Sadeeq smiled and puffed up with pride. "You don't know Luxurious. That girl has a mouth on her…gets it from her mother. Anyway, Lux said the nurses were picking on her because she was blasting music from her phone and they were upset because she kept having pizzas delivered. She said the hospital food sucked," Sadeeq explained with an amused smile.

Jayla doubted if she would get along with Lux's little grown ass, and she was in no hurry to get to know her bratty stepchild. "So, what about you and your wife? Did you at least set a date to be legally separated?"

"Nah, man, she's not letting me go."

"She doesn't own you, Sadeeq! When you're ready to leave, pack your shit and go."

"I wish it was that simple."

"Why isn't it?"

"Because she uses my kids to keep me in line. I can't tell you how many times I tried to bounce before I even met you."

"This is starting to sound ridiculous. How can she hold you hostage in a marriage if you want to leave?"

He shifted his eyes away from Jayla. "You don't understand," he mumbled, looking down at his boots.

"I'm listening…make me understand."

"Radiance constantly threatens to put my kids in the system, to keep her hooks in me."

"Put them in the system?" Jayla screeched, confused. "What the hell kind of sense does that make?"

"It don't make a damn bit of sense," he agreed. "But Radiance claims if I leave, she's going to kill herself and then she's going to leave a note claiming she took her life after discovering that I was molesting both our kids. The way she has it planned, neither one of us would have the children. She'd let them go into foster care to spite me."

"Oh, Lord, she's crazy."

"Who you telling?" he said grimly. "That's the kind of bullshit I've been dealing with for the sake of my kids." He turned toward Jayla. "But that's enough talk about my problems. I slid through so I could gaze at your pretty face and hold you in my arms all night."

"All night?" Jayla repeated.

Sadeeq nodded and then flashed a smile so brilliant and beautiful, it was blinding, and Jayla melted into his arms.

Waking up with Sadeeq lying next to her was a rare experience and a sneak preview of what it would feel like when she eventually became Mrs. Sadeeq Samuelson.

He'd told her that Radiance had taken the kids to visit her sister out of town in some rural part of Pennsylvania where the roads were really bad and they'd gotten stuck in the snowstorm.

Jayla was ecstatic that she would have Sadeeq to herself all day Sunday.

Wanting to give him a taste of how sweet their life together would be, she slipped out of bed and drove to the market while he slept. The plan was to give her man a breakfast fit for a king.

When she got back, she whipped up breakfast with a smile on her face.

Aroused by the aroma of cheese eggs, waffles, potato hash, sausage, and croissants, Sadeeq stumbled into the kitchen, rubbing his eyes. Even while groggy, his ass was fine as fuck. Absolutely adorable.

Sitting at the island in her kitchen, sharing a leisurely breakfast with her gorgeous man, was a dream come true and Jayla thoroughly enjoyed playing wifey.

"This grub tastes better than IHOP," Sadeeq complimented, chomping on a piece of crisp bacon. "I already know that when we live together, you gon' have me husky as shit."

"Hell, yeah, I'm gonna keep you well-fed." Jayla bestowed a big, loving smile on him.

"Why don't you sit on my lap and feed me some of you?" he asked in a sultry tone.

"I'll be your dessert after you finish all that food on your plate." She puckered her lips at him, assuring him that after breakfast, she was going to let him smash her to smithereens.

She hadn't prepared the hearty breakfast simply to satisfy his appetite, however. She also wanted to butter Sadeeq up before she asked him if it would be possible for him to accompany her to Bailee's anniversary party.

"Babe, my friend, Bailee is having an anniversary party next month…on the tenth. Do you think you'll be able to make it?" Jayla asked with a frown of worry wrinkling her forehead. "It's going to be a very nice affair, and I'll feel self-conscious if I have to go alone."

"The tenth?" Sadeeq thought about it for a moment. "Yeah, I can do that. We can go."

Jayla exhaled.

"Do I have to wear a suit or something?"

"Yes, it's semi-formal."

"Cool. What are you wearing?"

"I don't know yet. I have to order something." Bailee picked up her phone and pulled up Diva Curves, a trendy, plus-size website. She scrolled through numerous items before she came upon the salmon-colored dress she'd been looking at for the past week. She enlarged the photo and handed her phone to Sadeeq.

"That's pretty. You'll look real sexy in that," he said, nodding his head in approval. "It would look nice with my navy suit, especially if I get a tie to match the color of your dress."

Feeling heartened, Jayla broke into a big grin. "So, you're definitely going to go with me?"

"Yeah, I gotchu, bae. Where they having it at?"

"The Ritz-Carlton."

"Wow, so they doin' it big?"

She nodded. "It's an important anniversary, their tenth. Bailee and Trent are usually frugal. They both make good money, but they're not showy at all, so it's surprising that they're going all-out for this event."

"Well, we're not gonna let them outshine us. We're gonna do it big, too. Don't worry, I'm gon' be representing for my baby," Sadeeq said and gave her a sexy wink.

Feeling relieved, Jayla put the dress in the virtual cart and ordered it.

Chapter 9

Being banished to the guest room didn't seem to faze Trent in the least. He moved around the condo with his normal ease and comfort as if everything was good between him and Bailee. Barefoot and wearing sweatpants and a worn, yellow T-shirt that bore the name of the private academy they'd both attended during their high school years.

In the kitchen, perched on a chrome barstool in front of the marble island, Bailee was bent over her laptop, attending to the final details of the anniversary party.

She suffered through a glass of lemon-flavored water when she'd rather have what Trent was drinking, a tall glass of strawberry iced tea, and she'd kill for a handful of the buttery popcorn he was munching on. But, sticking to her starvation diet, she snacked on celery sticks and tried to convince herself that their crunch was as satisfying as a potato chip.

"Hey, Trent," she called, injecting cheerfulness into her voice that she hoped would indicate she was ready to call a truce. "What do you think about switching from daffodils to roses? I know the daffodil represents the tenth anniversary, but I've never cared much for that flower. Roses are prettier and more elegant, don't you think?"

Trent kept his gaze focused on the TV and didn't bother to glance in her direction. "Whatever," he muttered in an impatient tone that told her she was interrupting his show.

Alrighty, then. It was insulting to be spoken to so harshly by her husband. She swiveled around and hunched over the laptop. They weren't a couple who fought very often, and the rare times they did, it was always Bailee who had to be appeased before they could fall back into normal married life. Being the soother and trying to cajole Trent out of his sour mood was an unfamiliar role, and she wondered how long he was going to hold a grudge. Surely, he couldn't continue the silence much longer, could he?

Trent emitted rumbles of laughter while watching *Black-ish*, a show that he and Bailee usually enjoyed together. His gleefulness was proof that he was doing fine without talking to her.

Feeling defeated, Bailee closed the laptop and slunk off toward the bedroom. She clicked on the bedroom TV and tried to focus on CNN, but couldn't. It was the same old news. The country was going to hell in a handbasket unless someone reeled the president in, and so far, no one had been able to.

In bed, she struggled to get to sleep, hoping that the morning light would bring a fresh perspective on how to whip Trent back into shape. She was tired of the sullen stranger Trent had become and wanted her loving husband back.

When she heard Trent padding down the hallway, she sat up anxiously, but her heart dropped when he bypassed the master bedroom.

Rejection hurt. It wasn't like him to be so stubborn, and if he didn't revert back to his usual go-with-the-flow attitude, Bailee was going to have a serious meltdown.

Then, she got an idea of what she needed to do to get back in her husband's good graces. Smiling smugly, she slipped out of bed, ran her fingers through her locs, dabbed her good perfume on her cleavage, and crept out the room.

"What's up?" Trent asked when she appeared in the guest room.

Figuring she could show him better than tell him, she sidled up to the bed where he lay, wearing briefs and the yellow T-shirt. She knew Trent like the back of her hand, and if there was one thing he was weak for, it was a long, juicy blowjob.

Prepared to suck him off for all she was worth, Bailee eased onto the bed, slithered up to his crotch, and began slowly licking his scrotum through the fabric of his underwear. Her tongue work was skilled and leisurely, drawing a moan from him as she lapped like a cat slurping milk.

As she moistened the material that housed his crown jewels, his erection bulged and strained, trying to slice through the opening of his drawers. Tenderly, she caressed his throbbing dick before snaking her hand inside the slit and giving it a gentle squeeze. Trent fisted the sheet and Bailee's lips curved into a smile.

The key to winning this battle and conquering Trent was to remind him where her strength lay. Straddling him, she tugged on his briefs, gliding them past his thighs. Finally free, his dick sprang upward and then bobbed back and forth.

Bailee wrapped a hand around the thick shaft, gliding her hand from the base to the crown, enjoying the feeling of the ropy veins and the heat of the blood that pulsed through them. She ran her thumb circularly over the small slit, coaxing out droplets of creamy moisture, which she licked from her finger.

"Mmm," she moaned.

Trent sucked in a gulp of air and raised his hips, demonstrating his desire. "Get on it," he said harshly, and Bailee knew he was so ready to embed his dick inside something wet and warm. He didn't care if she sat on it or gobbled it up with her mouth.

Preferring to prolong their lovemaking session, she buried her face in his crotch, taking in deep sniffs of his musky scent as she licked him from his balls up to the smooth head. Stretching her mouth open, she sucked him into her mouth and slid her tongue along his hot flesh, moaning all the while. She cupped his ass cheeks, digging her fingernails into his flesh, encouraging him to bogart his way to the back of her throat.

She planned to suck him until his toes curled and his eyes crossed, but Trent couldn't last. With his shaft situated snuggly down her windpipe, Trent, groaning and growling, grabbed two fistfuls of her hair and yanked her head harshly as he deposited a voluminous amount of hot semen.

Taken off guard, Bailee was unable to swallow it down and the thickened liquid spilled from her lips, trickling down her chin.

She wiped the corner of her mouth with the back of her hand, keeping her eyes on Trent as he lay with his eyes squeezed shut, panting. When he finally recovered and opened his eyes, Bailee flashed him a victorious smile. She had broken down his barriers, and she was proud of herself.

But Trent didn't return her smile. He didn't invite her to lie next to him nor did he welcome her into his arms. His whole demeanor changed when he propped himself up on an elbow and stared at her through dark eyes that were empty and unloving.

A sickening wave washed over Bailee. "What's wrong?" she asked, anxiously gnawing on her lip.

"Bounce," he said, in a monotone. "I need to get some sleep."

The coldness of his words hit her like a splash of ice water in her face, and she uttered a sound of shock.

"Did you hear me? I need my space. Get the hell out of here!" His voice was a dangerous tone she'd never heard him use before. There was a hard look of contempt in his eyes as he made a shooing motion that said: *Be gone, peasant.*

"You bastard!" Deeply offended and ready to pounce, Bailee raised a balled fist.

He caught her by the wrist and gave her a deadly look. "What's wrong with you, you nut-ass broad? You got me fucked up if you think I'm gonna sit back and let you put your hands on me. Now, walk your ass on out of here, like you got some sense," he growled, his face twisted into a hateful mask with an unhinged glimmer in his eyes.

Having no doubt that her typically nonviolent and gallant husband would not hesitate to hit her back, and with great force, she unfurled her fist and lowered her arm. She quickly hopped off the bed and scrambled toward the doorway.

She gave him a fleeting glance over her shoulder. Who was that stranger who had just slid from perfect grammar and diction to 'hood vernacular? Astonished, she'd watched her husband of ten years morph from a man who was dignified and respectable into a common street thug who used frighteningly aggressive body language and was comfortable with the idea of getting physical with his wife.

The sudden personality change was scary.

And creepy.

With a shudder, Bailee rushed out of the room.

Frantic, she plopped into a chair in her bedroom, hugging herself and rocking back and forth. She didn't know what to do. She couldn't confide in her mother. Due to Trent's troubling lack of pedigree, he had not been an easy sell as the son-in-law to prominent socialite Giselle Cormier Wellington. For that reason, Bailee was hesitant to say anything that would poison her mother's mind against him.

She couldn't talk to Jayla, either. It was foolish of her to have divulged the disparaging remarks Trent had made about Jayla. Now, it would be virtually impossible for Jayla to give an unbiased opinion of what she thought might be going on with Trent.

It was obvious to Bailee that her husband was bothered by something more than her unwillingness to break their mutually agreed upon decision to forgo having children.

He seemed like a ticking time bomb, and she wondered if he needed professional help.

A dark and unpleasant feeling washed over Bailee. Feeling uneasy, she rose from the chair and engaged the lock on the door.

Chapter 10

"Jayla! What is going on with you?" Lorraine yelled into the phone.

"Nothing. But you sound upset. What's wrong with you?"

"I've been getting all kinds of calls from folks from collection agencies. They've been calling my house phone, ringing the dang thing off the hook, and getting smart with me when I tell them you don't live here. One woman had the nerve to tell me I was liable for your debt and I could lose my home."

"They're trying to scare you. Next time, just hang up on them, Mom," Jayla said wearily.

"Oh, they're definitely messing with the wrong one, trying to scare me. I know my rights, and I know that I'm not liable for any debt you rack up. But what I'm curious about is why you're not paying your bills?"

"It's a long story," Jayla said with a sigh.

"I have time. This foolishness isn't like you, Jayla. You always took pride in your good credit rating. You bought your condo at twenty-five years old—a very wise decision for such a young woman. You don't want to mess around and let those folks put a lien on your property."

"They can't do that," Jayla exploded.

"Why can't they? They sure put a lien on Mr. Lambert's house."

"Who's Mr. Lambert?" she asked dully.

"A church member. The man is over seventy years old and his trifling nephew ran up a bunch of bills in his name. The devious nephew even went so far as to open up new lines of credit in the man's name. And poor Mr. Lambert didn't know the first thing about any of it. The nephew was already locked up for some other illegal activity by the time the creditors started harassing him.

"It was a big ol' mess, and that man almost lost the home that he had paid off twenty years ago. His situation was so desperate, it was looking more and more like he was going to have to pack a few things and move into a men's shelter at the Salvation Army. But Pastor stepped in and called on all his prayer warriors.

"We prayed on Mr. Lambert's behalf for several weeks. Next thing you know, Mr. Lambert got unexpected help from the Philadelphia Corporation for Aging. They did a lot for him. With their assistance, he was able to stay in his home, but there's a lien on his property until he pays off all of his nephew's debt. And there's no way he can pay off thousands and thousands of dollars in debt—not in this lifetime."

Listening to Lorraine talk about the nightmarish ordeal of the old man at her church put a shiver of fear down Jayla's spine. Although she had visited the Fair Debt Collection Practices Act (FDCPA) website and had learned a lot about her rights as a consumer, she was nevertheless rattled by the many outrageous and intimidating methods that the collection agency representatives used in an effort to get her to pay up.

We're going to bring a lawsuit against you and when we win, you'll lose your home, your car, and we'll garnish your wages until the debt is paid in full. You have within forty-eight hours before law enforcement comes after you. And you can face up to five years imprisonment if you don't honor the agreement you signed.

"So, what did you purchase to have these folks chasing you down like this?"

"I don't want to talk about it, Mom. I'm in the process of straightening out the matter, so can we drop it?"

"No, we cannot drop it. I have a right to know why bill collectors are ringing my phone night and day."

Jayla's mind raced as she tried to come up with a believable story. "Identity theft," she blurted. "Somebody got ahold of my credit card information."

"How?"

"Uh, there's a crime ring that targets gas station and even ATM machines."

"Targets them, how?" Lorraine sounded irate, like she wanted to personally catch the members of the crime ring and dole out justice.

"Criminals today are real savvy, Mom. They use some kind of device called a skimmer. They put it outside the pump where you swipe your credit card and it's able to read all your information. I use multiple cards at gas stations, and those thieves were able to make a lot of purchases on three different cards of mine. After I found out, I tried to fight it because I knew I hadn't made all those crazy purchases."

"What did they buy with your cards, Jayla?"

"They bought all kinds of stuff online. Expensive electronics, clothes, jewelry…you name it and they bought it."

"My heavens! This is terrible. Can't they track back the purchases to the address they were sent to?"

"I tried to look into it after I found out about the purchases, but the shipments were sent to different addresses all over the country. The credit card companies aren't being helpful in finding the thieves; they're holding me responsible simply because I didn't opt to pay an extra monthly fee for fraud protection. It's a shame, but you can't win when you're up against big businesses," Jayla said, sounding beaten down.

The lies rolled off her tongue fluently and with such ease, Jayla surprised herself. Sadly, her cards had been used for electronics, jewelry, and clothes, but she had willingly handed the cards over.

"There has to be some kind of law that protects you, baby," Lorraine said sympathetically.

"I hope so," Jayla said.

"Don't worry, sweetheart. I'm going to ask Pastor to pull the prayer warriors together on your behalf. The prayers will work quicker if you come and join us in our circle."

Jayla frowned. Lorraine was always trying to finagle a way to get her to go to church. "I can't, Mom. I have two open houses this Saturday and I'll be tied up on Thursday and Friday night, getting both houses ready."

"I understand. You've worked so hard to establish yourself and it's a sin and a shame that Satan sent his thieves to try to undo all your hard work. I've been thinking long and hard about you, and what you need is a husband."

"Here, we go." Jayla was instantly irked. "You always find a way to work my single status into every conversation."

"Well, how long do you plan on going it alone in this cruel world where you're so vulnerable to thieves?"

"It's illogical to think that I would have somehow been protected from identity theft if I were married."

"Think about it, Jayla. First of all, you wouldn't have been out there pumping your own gas. You would have been sitting in the passenger's seat like a respectable lady while your husband did the work that God intended a man to do."

"You don't drive, Mom, and you have old-fashioned beliefs and gender roles. There's nothing un-ladylike about pumping gas. But that's neither here nor there," she said, starting to feel frustrated.

"I still feel that your life would run a lot smoother if you had a good man by your side. In my day, we got married right out of high school, but women today want to succeed in their careers before they commit to a relationship. When they're finally ready to settle down, they discover that their eggs have gone bad."

Jayla groaned.

"It's the truth," Lorraine insisted. "Then they turn to the fertility specialists, expecting the doctors to work a miracle with a bunch of rotten eggs."

Jayla sucked her teeth. "Oh, please. Do you realize how uninformed you sound? Eggs don't rot; they decrease in number."

"What's the difference? Whether they're rotten or there's only a few of them that're old and useless—you get the same results: infertility. You girls are doing everything a-s-s backwards," Lorraine said, spelling out the word "ass" as if spelling it instead of saying it was more acceptable and Christian-like.

"In today's society," Lorraine continued, "there're far too many middle-aged women trying to get pregnant. I'm here to tell all of 'em that that ship has sailed. They should have crossed that bridge long before they started suffering with hot flashes."

"Now you're talking age discrimination."

"I'm not discriminating. I'm speaking facts." Lorraine took a deep breath. "Frankly, I don't want any grandchildren that have to be cloned in order to come into the world. I wouldn't be comfortable with a test tube baby underfoot. I'd be too scared to turn my back on the strange little thing."

Jayla couldn't help from laughing. "I hope you're not serious,

Mom. Children that are conceived outside the womb and then inserted into their mother's uterus are not clones."

Lorraine snorted. "My point is, babies shouldn't be the product of something scientists concocted. When you tamper with the natural order of things, you're likely to get strange results. That's all I'm saying."

"Well, I'm not middle-aged. I'm far from it and you don't have to worry about having weird grandchildren." Jayla chuckled, hoping to bring some levity to the discussion. When Lorraine got on her soapbox, the conversation had the potential of quickly turning ugly.

"Yes, you're still young, but the years zoom by fast after thirty. You need to find yourself a man while you're still in your good, childbearing years. Don't wait until you're all dried up with over-cooked eggs and have to find a fertility specialist to inject some youth into your womb."

Jayla suppressed a groan. "How many times do I have to tell you that I'm not looking for a husband? I enjoy being single. I love having the freedom to live my life the way I want to. When the time is right, I'll settle down. If it doesn't happen until I'm forty, then so be it—I'm good," Jayla asserted, knowing full well that she wanted marriage and children in the worst way.

She was lying through her teeth with her little spiel about not wanting to give up the single life. But she couldn't very well tell her mother that she was an utter failure in the relationship department.

"Well, baby, I'm going to do my best to pray you out of this debt. But in the meantime, you need a concrete plan."

"You're right. I'm weighing my options. Filing for bankruptcy might be my best bet."

"I hope you don't have to do that. You don't want that mess on your record for the next seven years."

Jayla took a deep breath. Her mother was really starting to irk her, and it was time to get off the phone.

"Uh, I have another call and I have to take it. It's the lawyer I contacted regarding consumer fraud," she lied. "He thinks there might be a way to get the retailers to bear the debt. After all, they're the ones that let the transactions go through."

"That's true! It makes much better sense for the stores to eat the costs rather than you. Go ahead and talk to the lawyer, baby. Call me back and let me know what he said."

"Okay." Jayla hung up, marveling once again over her ability to lie through her teeth.

Sadly, her ability to lie convincingly didn't change her dire situation. The smart thing to do would have been to talk to the debt collectors back when they'd first started coming after her. Back then, maybe they would have set up an affordable payment plan, but she'd foolishly let too much time lapse while waiting for Sadeeq to come up with the money and pay the bills.

It was too late to get any sympathy whatsoever from the creditors. They hounded her constantly through the mail and over the phone, talking to her real greasy and making outlandish threats that often scared her out of her wits. She wouldn't be surprised if those malicious bastards started talking shit about having the rights to her firstborn.

Her life was pathetic. She was so worried that Sadeeq might get mad and renege on taking her to Bailee's party that she didn't pester him as much as she should have. He had no idea of what those hateful debt collectors were putting her through.

Her mailbox was stuffed with letters from creditors that she was too afraid to open. She felt immobilized by the intimidating letters and harassing phone calls. Blocking their numbers didn't do any good; they simply called back from a different number and became even more aggressive with their demands and abusive tactics.

Needing a break from her distressing thoughts, she logged into her fake Instagram account, and was instantly assaulted by posts from Radiance. There were pictures of a girls' night out. In the photos, she posed with two other man-looking bitches that were wearing cheap clothes.

Jayla came across more postings from Radiance: pictures of the children playing in the snow while they were upstate visiting her sister and there were pictures of the kids at home.

There were no photos of Sadeeq alone or cuddled up with Radiance. And no recent family portraits that would give the impression of a harmonious household. From the posts, it appeared that Radiance was embracing her future as a single parent.

Maybe Sadeeq had been telling the truth when he said that he and Radiance were on the verge of splitting up.

Chapter 11

B ailee's relationship with her mother had been fraught with challenges for as long as she could remember, and it worsened after her father died. Her father, thirty-five years older than her mother, was nearly seventy at the time of his death when Bailee was only nine.

Despite his advancing years and failing health, he'd doted on his only child and Bailee had adored him. Her mother experienced newfound freedom when he died and began dating men her own age, traveling the globe, and partying with an elite group of new friends. It appeared to the young Bailee that her mother was celebrating her father's death instead of mourning the loss.

Grief-stricken, Bailee felt completely abandoned. She grew up resenting Giselle and it was apparent that Giselle resented her, too. She detested having an overweight daughter and didn't bother to hide her feelings.

After years of bickering and sometimes going months without speaking, Bailee and Giselle agreed to get help. Fortunately, family therapy had strengthened their bond. They still had disagreements and occasional misunderstandings, but they'd learned how to communicate their feelings instead of shutting each other out as they'd done in the past.

One of the best things that had come out of the therapy sessions was having a safe forum to let Giselle know how much it had hurt when she criticized Bailee about her weight, making her feel that she wasn't good enough. Giselle acted surprised to learn that her dietary suggestions were viewed as criticism.

During the sessions, she also brought up how unfair it was for her mother to exhibit such contempt for Trent. Giselle had expected her daughter to marry someone from a prominent family, someone she could brag about.

Unfortunately, despite Trent's fine education and career success, he didn't fit the bill. With a father who was doing a thirty-year bid for drug trafficking and other charges, Trent would never meet Giselle's standards, no matter how much he accomplished in life.

Although neither Bailee nor the therapist could convince Giselle to fully accept Trent, Bailee considered it a minor victory for her mother to simply be civil toward her husband.

Part of maintaining their healed relationship was making an effort to carve out time for mother-daughter activities once a month. Bailee was so busy with work and organizing the anniversary party, she had come close to cancelling joining her mother at the Academy of Music to see a local ballet company perform *Le Corsaire*.

Draped in incredibly realistic faux fur and dripping in jewels, Giselle had arrived at the theater looking as elegant as ever. Despite the icy pavements and snow-slushed streets, she wore heels. The woman refused to age. At fifty-one, she could pass for thirty. She was often mistaken as Bailee's sister, which drove Bailee mad.

If fifty was the new thirty, then Giselle was the poster child. It was unusual for a mother to turn heads while the adult daughter was virtually ignored, but that's how it was with Bailee and her mother. Giselle was the stunner, the gregarious socialite getting all the attention, while Bailee was treated like the homely sidekick. The public's reaction to her mother left Bailee with a confounding mix of jealousy and pride, which over time, had morphed into a puzzling blend of hatred and love.

Living in her mother's shadow was extremely difficult, but with the help of therapy, she was conquering her demons.

Long-limbed and lissome, Giselle glided into the lobby with the demeanor and grace of a noblewoman, and Bailee stepped forward to greet her. "You look lovely, Mom," she said, feeling dumpy as she went in for a hug and air kisses.

"Thank you, darling," Giselle replied, cutting a disapproving glance down at Bailee's comfortable Ugg boots.

In the past, prior to family therapy, Giselle would have verbalized her displeasure at her daughter coming to the theater in drab work attire, but she'd learned to hold her tongue and Bailee was grateful.

Bailee planned to glam it up for her anniversary party and other pending social events throughout the year, but it wasn't her style to go full-diva with a beat face and her hair coiffed for the sake of sitting in a darkened theater.

Arms linked, mother and daughter chatted as they walked, giving the impression that they were dear friends. But as they made their way to their box seats, anyone listening closely would have realized that their conversation was stiff and awkward.

The moment the curtain rose, revealing the spectacular set, Bailee forgot about her marital problems. She was so captivated that the pressures of her job also rolled away.

The performance, a masterwork of classical ballet, took her breath away. The flamboyant costumes of glittering gold, sky blue, and soft pink were mesmerizing. The energy between the dancers was contagious and Bailee was riveted by the impressive jumps that they performed effortlessly.

At the conclusion of the amazing three-act show, Bailee found herself applauding enthusiastically and alternately wiping away tears.

"Oh, darling, you're crying," Giselle exclaimed. "I never realized you were such a ballet enthusiast. As you know, I'm a member of the American Ballet Theatre, and my contributions allow me exclusive seats, invitations to ABT dress rehearsals, private back-stage tours, you name it," Giselle exclaimed with a sweeping wave of her hand. "Misty Copeland will be performing in in a few months. Would you like to see the performance and meet her?"

"Sure, I'd love to."

"Great. We could spend the weekend in New York. Do some shopping and relax at my favorite spa. Do you think hubby will let you go?" She had spoken the word, "hubby," with affection, as if she actually approved of her son-in-law. But Bailee realized her mother's feelings about Trent hadn't changed. She was merely making an effort to acknowledge him; something she'd never done before they'd started therapy.

"I don't need my husband's approval, but I couldn't possibly go away for an entire weekend."

"Why not?" Giselle sounded genuinely disappointed.

"I'm bogged down with work. My position requires working at home most weekends," Bailee explained, struggling not to sound annoyed. Giselle was taking the mother-daughter time a bit too far. One evening per month was all that either of them could tolerate. Any longer than that and Giselle would revert back to her old programming and begin bringing up Bailee's weight and other perceived flaws.

"I think a weekend together would do us both good," Giselle insisted.

Bailee could feel a spark of defiance igniting inside her. She didn't intend to put up with Giselle's sly comments ever again. And she'd be damned if she would put up with the amount of shade her mother was capable of throwing over the course of a long weekend. "It's not a good idea, Mom," Bailee said in a tone that told Giselle to drop the subject.

"Fine, let's have dinner. I made reservations at Ruth's Chris Steakhouse."

Giselle guided Bailee outside where her hired car was waiting at the curb. During the ride, Giselle steered the conversation to ballerina Misty Copeland, and she spoke of the dancer as if they were close friends. Giselle was such a shameless name-dropper, which annoyed Bailee to no end.

"I thought I led a regimented lifestyle with my strict low-carb diet and my punishing daily workouts, but Misty is much more fanatical than I am when it comes to her body. She has a new book that details how she keeps her body lean and strong."

It took all of Bailee's strength not to roll her eyes in irritation. Giselle was a total narcissist. How could she even begin to compare her workout to that of a prima ballerina?

"I can order a copy of Misty's book if you'd like."

Misty! So, you're on a first-name basis with her, are you? "That's okay; I already have it," Bailee lied, hoping to change the subject. In a short amount of time, Giselle had reverted back to her old behavior of trying to fix Bailee.

At the restaurant, while Giselle dined on a juicy rib-eye steak and grilled asparagus, Bailee stuck her fork into a boring salad.

"It's great that you're eating healthy. Good for you, honey."

"Thanks. I'm trying to lose a few pounds for the party." The thought of the upcoming anniversary celebration made her want to gag. What a farce! Yet, she couldn't cancel.

First of all, too much money had been spent and secondly, cancelling would seem like she was throwing in the towel on her marriage, which she wasn't.

She planned to talk Trent into going to marriage counseling with her. If at the conclusion of counseling, they discovered their marriage was worth saving, then she'd consider going off the pill. However, in her heart of hearts, she felt that Trent's terrible attitude had nothing to do with starting a family. She had no idea why there was venom in his tone on the rare occasions that he spoke to her.

And she dreaded learning the truth.

Giselle inspected Bailee with penetrating eyes, and then said, "I can tell you've lost a little; your face is smaller. I wanted to mention it when we hugged earlier tonight, but you're so sensitive, I didn't want to bring up anything that might make you uncomfortable."

"I'm not sensitive to compliments. I just don't like being told how I should eat or what kind of workouts I should do." On the defensive, Bailee's voice climbed in pitch.

"Why're you getting so worked up? All I said was that I could tell you were slimming down." Giselle shook her head as if she couldn't win for losing when it came to her temperamental daughter.

A familiar tension filled the air and the two women ate in silence.

Bailee stole a glance at Giselle, admiring and envying her beauty. At a hundred and twenty pounds, she was dainty and elegant with long, slender fingers that were tastefully bejeweled. Compared to Giselle's hands, Bailee's were short and stubby.

She'd inherited her mother's delicate facial features, but her robust body type came from her father's side. Having a beautiful, swan-like mother hadn't been good for Bailee's self-esteem, but she'd fought like hell to become comfortable with her weight, even during the days when her mother used to look at her with repugnance. On many occasions when her snobbish friends were visiting, Giselle had gazed upon Bailee with embarrassment.

Bailee didn't know what hurt worse: her mother's resentment or her mortification.

Trent's love and acceptance of Bailee had been the primary reason she'd been able to experience self-love, but now that he was behaving erratically, giving her the silent treatment and talking to her disrespectfully, she was rapidly losing the confidence that it had taken years for her to build.

"I'm wearing Oscar de la Renta to your anniversary party," Giselle said, her voice cutting into the silence. "It's a white, off-the-shoulder gown made of silk brocade. It's understated and elegant—very refined and tasteful, not glitzy at all. As you know, I abhor gaudiness," she said, her lips pursed.

Bailee knew her mother's many aversions all too well. Growing up, she'd been reminded of what was tacky, gaudy, and ghetto on a regular basis.

"Who are you wearing, darling?" Giselle inquired.

"A new designer—someone you've never heard of."

Actually, Bailee's dress was being made by a seamstress in nearby Roxborough. Giselle was well aware that Bailee wasn't built for the fashions of popular designers.

"Did you love my father?" Bailee blurted, surprising herself and Giselle with a question that seemed to have come completely out of the blue.

Giselle put down her fork. "Why do you ask?"

Bailee shrugged. "Now that I'm grown—eleven years older than you were when you married him—I wonder what it must have been like to be a twenty-year-old girl married to a fifty-five-year-old man."

"It was difficult at times, but it was also thrilling. Daniel was a wealthy investor and a very powerful man. I was attracted to his power."

"Were you physically attracted to him?"

Giselle wrinkled her nose. "Not really. I had trouble getting through the physical aspect of our relationship. Though I loved his brilliant mind, his exquisite taste, and his commanding presence, I was never sexually attracted to him."

"What turned you off—his age?"

"It wasn't his age, per se. What turned me off was the way he looked without clothes." She smiled apologetically. "His body was flabby from neglect. And his big gut…" She drew her lips together tightly and wrinkled her nose as if she smelled a terrible stench.

"I see." Bailee speared a chunk of romaine lettuce and chewed miserably. Giselle was describing her body, fat-shaming her on the sly. She wondered if Trent now saw her in a new light. Was he repulsed by her extra padding and the "cushioning" (as he called it) that he used to rub and touch in a way that seemed close to reverence?

Had it all been an act? Can someone fake that kind of devotion? Bailee wondered.

Glumly, she wrapped her arms around herself. It was a movement that suggested insecurity, a demonstration of how completely unloved she felt.

Giselle looked up from her plate and lifted a brow. "Are you cold, Bailee?"

"No." She loosened her arms and let them relax at her sides.

"You don't look well." Giselle's concerned gaze scanned Bailee's face as if searching for hidden clues.

"I'm fine." She managed to choke out the words after swallowing down the lump that had formed in her throat.

After waving goodnight to Giselle, Bailee settled in the driver's seat of her car. She was glad to be alone with her thoughts. While driving, her phone buzzed and she quickly dug it out of her purse. Her eyes shifted downward and she squinted at the name that lit the screen.

She'd hoped to hear from Trent, telling her that he was sorry, but the text was from the florist she'd hired to create the centerpieces and floral displays for the party.

She didn't bother to respond to the florist's message that listed the price difference between white and red roses. She no longer cared about the flowers. Her marriage was disintegrating and the color and type of flower no longer mattered.

In the course of only a few weeks, she'd gone from someone her husband adored to someone he seemed to despise. She should have pulled the plug on the party and set up an appointment with a divorce attorney, but instead, she tried to convince herself that her marriage would miraculously survive.

The neon sign of a convenience store beckoned her like a wave from a dear friend. Without thinking twice, she swung into the lot, parking haphazardly in a rush to satisfy her cravings.

She hurried inside and the sight of all the salty and sugary snacks caused her pulse to race. She grabbed a basket and went up and down the aisles, tossing in all the snacks she'd been denying herself.

She decided that the drawers of her nightstand would make great hiding places for her goodies. With so much comfort within arm's reach, she doubted if she'd even think about the empty side of the bed.

Chapter 12

J ayla had express-shipped her dress to make sure she had it in time for the party, but on the day of Bailee's big event, the dress still hadn't arrived. Frantic, she called Diva Curves, a Miami-based apparel store, and spoke to the owner, Marisol. Marisol had given her a tracking number and guaranteed her that the dress would arrive no later than five o'clock. She'd even promised Jayla a full refund if the dress arrived late.

To save time Jayla had already gotten her hair and nails done the night before at a posh salon in Center City.

She only had one showing on her schedule, and afterward, she planned to get her makeup done, and then go back to her condo and wait for her gorgeous dress to arrive. Once she was dressed, her plan was to go downtown, check into the hotel, and wait for Sadeeq.

For Sadeeq and her to attend such a gala event together seemed to legitimize their relationship. It was possible that Bailee's socialite mother had arranged for media coverage.

She deliberately hadn't told Sadeeq that they might be photographed together for a major publication. He'd find that out later when their pictures were splashed all over the Internet. Even if they weren't photographed by a photographer, Jayla planned to slide one of the hotel staff some cash to take candid shots of them with her phone.

She'd post the pics on her fake Instagram account and tag Radiance.

Seeing her husband and Jayla all booed up would be a wakeup call to the bitch and could possibly prompt her to let him go a lot sooner than she'd planned.

Whatever happened, Jayla was sure she and Sadeeq were going to have an amazing night together.

But before any of that could happen, Jayla had to meet with Simone, a bougie young girl from North New Jersey. She and her mom were interested in buying a duplex in West Oak Lane. Simone had been pre-approved a month ago, but didn't really qualify for much.

She had one too many Nordstrom and Neiman Marcus accounts that were at their limit. She also had fifty thousand dollars in student loan debt. She paid her bills on time every month, but she was overextended and her debt-to-income ratio was so high the bank looked at her as a high-risk investment.

Unfortunately, Jayla had too many clients in the same boat as Simone, which was one of the reasons she couldn't get ahead in the housing market.

While in the midst of touring the house, Jayla came to the conclusion that she didn't like Simone. She was the kind of client that wanted more than she could afford, turning her nose up at every room they walked through.

"Are they going to repaint this kitchen?" Simone inquired, her mouth turned down in displeasure.

"No," Jayla replied blandly.

"What about the floor—are you going to put down new tiles?"

"I'm sorry, as advertised, the owner is selling this property as is."

Goddamn, do you want this house or not? It was annoying having to deal with someone who was working with a small budget and who unrealistically expected the house to be in perfect condition.

Jayla was only earning a three-thousand-dollar commission and she refused to let this bum bitch stress her out.

Jayla's constant sighs and eye rolls didn't stop Simone from asking numerous idiotic questions, such as: "Do you think the seller would be interested in a rent-to-own arrangement?"

Jayla inwardly asked the Lord for strength as she responded by closing her eyes as she shook her head, no! She was so sick of Simone, she was at the point of not caring if she sold the house or not.

But the part of her that was broke and facing bankruptcy couldn't deliberately turn down good money, and so she mustered the strength to give Simone a last-minute sales pitch.

"Don't forget, this duplex will start paying for itself as soon as you get a tenant on the second floor," Jayla reminded Simone, inserting excitement in her tone.

Simone looked over at her mother for her opinion, and then the two of them walked around the kitchen, reexamining the cabinets and other features, finding fault with everything.

As they tried to make up their minds, Jayla's phone rang. The call was from Sadeeq, and she quickly excused herself to take his call.

"Hi, baby, I'm showing a house right now. What's going on?" Jayla said brusquely. Though she was always happy to hear from Sadeeq, his call had come at an inopportune time when she was trying to close the deal.

"My ride got booted," he said glumly.

"Oh, no. Why?"

"Man, they booted it on some bullshit. I put money in the

meter, but I didn't peep the sign that said no parking during rush hour."

"Okay, but you'll still be able to make it to the party, right?" Her voice cracked with dread.

"Yeah, I'm still coming, baby. I'm trying to figure out how I'm going to get Lux home from dance class, get to the barber, pick up my suit from the cleaners on Fifty-Second Street, and then get to you by seven. I can't Uber everywhere."

Jayla could feel her level of stress escalating, but she tried to stay calm. "How much does it cost to get the car out?"

"Around fifteen hundred dollars."

"What! You have got to be kidding." Jayla unconsciously began wringing her hands.

"Owing that much to this greedy-ass city is crazy, ain't it?"

"Why do you owe so much?"

"Radiance keeps getting all these tickets and she never tells me nothing about 'em." He blew out a long breath of exasperation.

"I don't have that kind of money, Sadeeq."

"Yeah, I know. Man, my head is killing me from trying to figure this shit out." He paused and then said, "What about a rental car? If you get me a rental, I could handle my business and still get to the party on time."

Oh, my God, I can't afford to put another charge on my one and only credit card I have left that's not maxed out.

She could use her company card and make up an excuse about her car breaking down while she was on her way to the showing. Yes, that's what she'd tell the chick that ran the accounting department at work.

"Okay, Sadeeq. I can get us a car. To save time, I'll pick up your suit and meet you at Enterprise on City Avenue after I finish with this client. Take an Uber there and we'll pick out something nice when I get there."

"Okay, thank you, baby. You're a lifesaver. See you soon."

By the time Jayla hung up with Sadeeq, Simone's mother had persuaded her to think of the duplex as a starter home, and she convinced her to buy it. Jayla was thankful that the woman had closed the deal for her.

Jayla told Simone that she'd be in touch with a settlement date, and then tried to rush her and her mother out of the house. Unfortunately, they insisted on another walk-through. Though they didn't voice any more complaints, they were irking Jayla's nerves, acting as if they already lived on the property, selecting bedrooms and discussing window treatments.

Jayla kept looking at her watch, hinting for them to hurry up. "Uh, I have another appointment. I'm sorry, but I have to hurry you ladies along and lock up the house," she said with an apologetic expression. They still didn't move along fast enough to suit Jayla, but she had no choice but to grin and bear it.

After finally getting those two slow-moving bitches out of the duplex, she sped down Ogontz Avenue, weaving through traffic as she headed for the dry cleaner in West Philly.

When she finally arrived at the dry cleaner, the Korean woman that ran the place refused to give her Sadeeq's suit without a ticket. She had to waste more time getting Sadeeq on the phone, and asking him to recite the ticket number to the nasty bitch at the counter.

With the suit hung carefully on the hook in the backseat of her car, she crept along in jammed-up traffic, feeling so drained and exhausted, she wondered if it was remotely possible to look refreshed by the time the party started.

At last, she made it to the rental place and pulled into the back lot. Sadeeq was there, pointing to a navy blue Lincoln MKX.

"This jawn is lit. It matches my suit," he said, eyeballing the MKX like it was a sexy woman. "Everybody that came through the spot wanted to rent it, but I talked the agent into holding it for us," he announced, clearly impressed by his own powers of persuasion.

Jayla had hoped for something less expensive than the MKX, but she nodded glumly and then hurried into the rental office, where it was warm. Her hand trembled as she filled out the paperwork and she felt her stomach tighten when she handed over her company credit card.

After the transaction was complete, she let out a breath of relief and rejoined Sadeeq on the lot. He climbed inside, and she had to admit that he looked hot sitting behind the wheel, but she didn't have time to enjoy feasting her eyes upon him.

"I gotta go, babe," she said, giving him a quick kiss through the open window. "See you at the hotel. Oh, and please be on time."

"Don't worry about that. If anything, I'll be early." Looking adorable, he clutched the steering wheel and simulating driving, like a little boy with a brand-new toy. "We gon' turn up so much tonight, muthafuckas gon' be thinking it's our anniversary party." He puckered his scrumptious lips and blew her a kiss. "See you at the hotel, baby."

During the drive home, despite feeling bone weary and out of breath from the whirlwind of activity, Jayla also felt a sense of accomplishment. Sadeeq had access to the kind of ride that a fine-ass man like him deserved to be driving.

When she reached her condo, she smiled at the sight of the package sitting outside her door. Standing in the living room, she ripped open the box and pulled out the dress. It was perfect! She was going to look so hot tonight!

Picking up Sadeeq's suit and driving to the rental car place had caused her to miss her appointment to get her makeup done. She'd have to do it herself, but luckily, she was pretty good at contouring and had mastered the art of creating flawless, smoky eyes.

Jayla checked into the hotel. She handed the front desk clerk her credit card and the clerk handed it right back to her, informing her that the card had been declined.

Embarrassed, she went through her wallet and handed over a second card that stood a good chance of also being declined. As badly as she wanted to, she could not risk putting the hotel bill on her company card. As the clerk swiped the second card, Jayla prayed for it to go through. Feeling self-conscious, she looked around the lobby to see if anyone was paying attention to her embarrassing moment.

She said a silent prayer of thanks after the clerk gave her the keycard to her room.

Mentally and physically exhausted, she trudged to the elevator. But once she was in her room, which overlooked Broad Street, her spirits lifted.

What a beautiful view, she thought as she admired the car lights that lit up the night.

She couldn't wait until Sadeeq arrived. She intended to make sure he appreciated their view as he bent her over the sofa and fucked her in the window.

When her phone lit with a text from Sadeeq, telling her that he'd be on his way as soon as he dropped Lux off at home, Jayla was delighted that everything was finally coming together. She called room service and ordered a bottle of wine, fried shrimp, prime rib with steak fries on the side, and a slice of cheesesteak.

Room service arrived and she started eating and drinking. Wanting to save her appetite for the party, she was careful not to gobble up everything. She put the stainless steel lids over the dishes, saving the remainder of the meal for after the party.

She took a leisurely shower, put lotion on her body, spritzed herself with her most expensive perfume, and then began to apply her makeup. Afterward, she admired her work. Considering that she wasn't a professional makeup artist, she'd done a fantastic job. And it didn't hurt that she was blessed with such a pretty face.

Next, she took her new dress off the hanger and slid it over her head. The fabric was stiffer than it appeared, which caused alarms to go off in her head. On the hanger it seemed as if it was made of a stretchy material, but it wasn't. She almost fainted from lack of oxygen as she forced the constricting dress over her tummy and hips.

She looked in the mirror and almost cried when she saw her reflection. She tried her best to hold back tears. After so much advance preparation, she ended up looking like a blimp. The dress looked horrible on her, emphasizing all her bodily flaws, and making her appear fatter than she actually was.

She observed herself from different angles, hoping that she didn't look as awful as she thought. But there was no denying it, she looked like she was about to burst out of the dress, and her belly fat was not concealed; it was on full display.

An emotional wreck, she picked up the phone and called Sadeeq. "Where are you?" she shouted after the phone rang and rang and then went to voicemail. "As soon as you get this message, call me back and let me know what's going on."

She hung up and almost broke down and cried as she considered skipping the party downstairs. But she couldn't do that. If she didn't attend Bailee and Trent's anniversary celebration, she'd look like a hater...and a jealous hater at that.

She checked out her reflection again, and nothing had changed. She still looked horrible with noticeable rolls of flab on her sides, her back, and an unsightly, protruding gut.

She gave a loud groan of anguish, but then reminded herself that tonight wasn't about her. It was Bailee's night.

Jayla waited another half-hour before calling Sadeeq, again. He still didn't answer and this time her call went straight to voicemail. Not a good sign.

Already forty minutes late and not knowing what else to do, she texted him to let him know that his suit was hanging in the closet and that she'd left his keycard at the front desk.

She went downstairs and entered the ballroom feeling self-conscious and all alone. There were a lot of people in attendance, but she didn't know anyone. She craned her neck, trying to find Bailee, but couldn't find her among the throng.

She caught a glimpse of Trent and their eyes met briefly, but neither acknowledged the other. Trent was surrounded by a group of white men that were probably colleagues and clients from his firm. She wondered how many of them had heard the rumor that she enjoyed having trains pulled on her in restrooms and that she ate dick in public places.

It probably was her imagination, but it seemed that the men from Trent's firm were giving her leering looks. Feeling like she was under their lustful scrutiny, her face colored with shame as she pushed further into the ballroom.

She noticed that most of the guests in attendance were with their significant other, causing her to feel even more alone and miserable.

Throughout the hectic day, she'd been comforted by the thought of her and Sadeeq walking into the party together as a couple and turning heads. But no one was paying her any attention. The guests engaged in private conversations and laughed at private jokes; they all seemed to be part of an exclusive club, of which she had been denied membership.

A part of her was relieved that big-mouthed Chance and Tone weren't there, but on the other hand, it would have been nice to have someone to talk to.

The server approached with a tray of champagne and she grabbed two glasses and guzzled them down. In the vast room, she finally spotted Bailee, who was dressed impeccably in an obviously expensive dress that flattered her curvy figure. Bailee had always managed to carry her weight with such confidence that Jayla envied her.

When Bailee noticed Jayla, she hurried over to greet her. "You finally made it. Where have you been?"

"Waiting for Sadeeq," Jayla replied, rolling her eyes.

Bailee looked around. "Well, where is he?"

"He's on his way. But enough about him. You look amazing, girl!"

Smiling, Bailee did a quick spin. "Thanks, Jayla."

Trent approached with a distinguished-looking older gentleman who was Caucasian, as were most of the guests. Deliberately ignoring Jayla, he introduced Bailee to the man who broadcasted wealth and power in the tailoring of his suit, the glint of his watch, and the confident set of his shoulders. When Bailee, Trent, and the older man were joined by another affluent-looking, silver-haired white man, Jayla retreated into the background, giving Bailee her space to socialize with her guests.

With so many powerful, money people in attendance, Jayla should have used the opportunity to network and pass her business cards around, but she felt too insecure about her appearance to attempt to hobnob with the wealthy elite.

For the rest of the evening, Jayla sat at a table in the back of the room and tried her best to be invisible. It would have been rude not to speak to Bailee's mom, and so she got out of her seat to say hello when she noticed Giselle making her way to the restroom, dripping in blinding diamonds and wearing a phenomenal white dress that had to have cost quite a few stacks.

Bailee's dad had left Giselle a lot of bank, and Jayla wasn't surprised that the woman reeked money.

Jayla felt big and oafish as she stood next to Giselle, who was sleek and trim and ridiculously youthful. Instead of aging, the woman was going in reverse. It was no wonder Bailee had a strained relationship with her mother. Bailee was twice Giselle's size and not nearly as glamorous. That had to suck. A mother had no business looking better than her daughter.

For the most part, Jayla stayed in her seat. Sitting allowed her to watch the door as she waited for Sadeeq, and it kept the guests from noticing how tight and ill-fitting her dress was.

Thankfully, the servers supplied her with a steady stream of food and drinks, and she was happy to accept both.

When it was time for Bailee and Trent to cut their cake, Sadeeq was still nowhere to be seen. After the cake cutting, Trent's boss stood to make a congratulatory toast. Feeling alone and abandoned, Jayla almost burst into tears in the midst of the tribute.

Although she was happy for Bailee to have made it to the ten-year mark, she was so sad for herself. She couldn't believe Sadeeq had stood her up on such an important night, and after all she'd gone through to help him get there.

What was the purpose of getting him a rental car, picking up his suit, and running around like a crazy woman only for him not to show? There had to be a logical explanation. She tried her best to enjoy the party, but she couldn't. She stood up and walked to a secluded area where she could curse Sadeeq out privately, but after repeatedly getting his voicemail, all she could do was leave heated messages and type angry texts.

With her thumbs flying over the keypad, she fired off insults that matched her fury, calling him every name she could think of: bitch-ass, punk-ass nigga, broke-ass bitch.

Despite her best efforts, she couldn't hold back her tears, and she ended up rushing to the restroom to cry her heart out.

When she came out of the bathroom, Bailee and Trent were on the dance floor, looking lovingly into each other's eyes and smiling as they whispered endearing words to each other.

It was too much for her heart and her stomach to bear. The sight of the loving couple, along with too many glasses of champagne, had left Jayla feeling nauseous.

Sick to her stomach and teary-eyed, she waded through the sea of black suits and pastel dresses. It took a while to make it out of the crowded ballroom, and she felt bad for not telling Bailee goodnight. But she had to get out of there before she embarrassed herself and Bailee by vomiting all over the beautifully decorated room.

Inside her hotel room, she knelt in front of the toilet, but nothing came up. She stumbled over to the bed and collapsed onto it. With her head hanging over the edge, everything she'd eaten and drunk came up. When Jayla attempted to stand up to clean the mess, she heaved again, and this time, she regurgitated all over herself and the bed.

She collapsed to the floor, asking herself where she'd gone wrong. How had she ended up in such a miserable place with a no-good, married man? Why didn't she have true love with a reliable and successful man like Bailee had?

She managed to get up off of the floor and into the shower. And at some point while soaping her skin, she decided that she'd had enough of Sadeeq's shit. She and Sadeeq were over. Today was the last time he would disappoint her. She was not giving him any more money or helping him out, ever again. Fuck him and his entire stupid-ass family!

And fuck this hotel room, too. It was time to pack up and go home. Hell if she was going to try to get some sleep in a room that reeked of vomit and was a reminder that she'd be stood up once again.

Dressed in the tights, loose sweater, and fur boots that she'd arrived in, Jayla stuffed Sadeeq's suit in a waste bin and then checked out of the hotel.

During the drive home, she decided that she would block his number and refuse to answer the door when he inevitably came around with a handy excuse for tonight.

At home, she came up with another idea. Not only would she leave Sadeeq alone for good, but she was also going to lose weight. Not the way she usually lost—dropping a few pounds and then gaining even more back.

This time she was going to take serious steps to change her life for good.

Once the thought came to her mind she began searching online for bariatric weight loss surgeons in Philadelphia. She found a ton of before and after pictures of women and men who'd undergone the surgery. Their results were amazing and many of them looked like totally different people.

Jayla could not wait to schedule a consultation for the gastric sleeve procedure.

Once she lost the weight, she would have more confidence and be able to get and keep a good man. The prospect of finally doing something positive for herself instantly put her in a better mood.

However, her happiness was short-lived.

Her phone began to buzz with a text message from Sadeeq.

As her eyes scanned her phone, her lips pulled into a grim line.

Radiance was in an accident in the rental. I need you to come to the 18th district police station & let the cops know she didn't steal the car. Oh yeah, when you come, bring my suit with you.

Jayla gasped and covered her mouth. As a sledgehammer pounded inside her chest, her stomach lurched, but this time nothing came up.

If ever there was a time that she wanted to collapse, it was now. She wanted to hit the floor so hard that she incurred severe head trauma, leading to a coma that lasted many, many years. And hopefully when she awakened, the bullshit message that Sadeeq had left her would be nothing more than a bad dream.

Chapter 13

After binge-eating three times in the past two weeks, Bailee hadn't managed to diet down to a smaller dress size as she'd planned, but she was grateful to be able to fit into her anniversary dress without any major alterations.

She didn't have her mother's taste in couture fashion, but over the years, she'd become skilled at selecting the perfect dress based on its cut, its ability to stretch, and the way it flattered her body. She'd never be caught dead wearing anything that gaped, puckered, pulled, tugged, or felt uncomfortable.

So far, the evening had turned out perfect. The staff at the Ritz-Carlton was professional and organized, making sure Bailee's vision came to life. The guests raved about the beautiful setting and poured lavish praise over every well thought-out detail: the sumptuous food, the four-tiered cake, the rose centerpieces, and the dessert stations were big hits.

Sadly, Bailee was only going through the motions, pretending to be celebrating ten years of marital bliss. Trent was role-playing as well, lovingly embracing her as they smiled contentedly for the camera.

When they shared the first dance, Trent's lips brushed against her cheek. "You're more beautiful than the day I married you," he said, gazing at her tenderly.

Her face twitched as she struggled to keep from grimacing. With all eyes on them, and wanting to keep up appearances, she smiled back. "You're so full of shit," she said, holding her smile.

"I haven't been easy to live with lately, and I apologize. It's not you—it's work. The amount of stress I've been under is unbelievable."

She laughed gaily for the benefit of the onlookers. "And you decided to take your troubles out on me?"

"They gave the Cranston account to that little fuck, Ted Thorndale, and I'm expected to work under him. I've given the firm seven years of my life, but I can't stay there any longer. It's degrading."

"And you've decided to confide in me…because?"

"Because I need you to ask your mom to give us a loan—an advance until you get your inheritance."

"What?" Realizing that she was frowning, Bailee quickly relaxed her features and smiled.

Going along with the charade, Trent smiled back adoringly. "I want to start my own firm. I've already picked out office space, and I'm sure I can take a few of my accounts with me. I'm going to show those bastards that I don't need them for a meal ticket."

"Oh, so that's what I've been to you—a meal ticket?" She dropped the smile and narrowed her eyes, no longer caring who was looking at them.

He crinkled his brows. "I earn more than you, so how have you been my meal ticket?"

"Okay, I'll rephrase my words. All these years, you've considered the money I'll eventually inherit as your safety net." She shook her head. "My mother tried to warn me that you were after my money, but I refused to believe her."

"I was never after your money. After all, it's not like you're exactly rolling in dough. You don't have control over your father's wealth; your mother does," he said snidely.

"You're asking me for money, but I'm in the dark about why your behavior changed so abruptly. One minute you were the man I thought I knew, but after I declined your sudden and urgent baby request, you became a monster, treating me like scum. Was that your plan—to start saddling me down with kids to weaken me? Did you think that by mistreating me you could bully me into asking my mother for the money to finance your venture?" she asked in a voice that was louder than she'd intended.

"People are looking at us, Bailee. Let's discuss this after the party."

She laughed, not bothering to hide the bitterness in the sound. "I feel as if you've been playing me for all these years, and I don't give a damn who's looking." She stared at Trent, as if seeing him for the first time. The face that she used to love gazing at now enraged her.

She stopped dancing and disentangled herself. She surprised herself when her palm suddenly connected with Trent's face. The sound of the slap reverberated at the exact time that the song came to an end, and heads turned in their direction.

Trent froze. His eyes blinked in disbelief.

Feeling self-satisfied, Bailee left Trent in the middle of the dance floor, and strutted over to the bar, not caring that the guests were gawking at her. "Give me two bottles of champagne," she said to the bartender.

Discovering that her marriage had been a sham was a reason to get good and drunk.

Purse tucked under her arm and a bottle of chilled champagne in each hand, she walked in the direction of the elevator with her head held high. She'd never imagined her marriage ending, and certainly not in the middle of a crowded ballroom while in the midst of celebrating ten years.

She caught a glimpse of Giselle holding court with two men from Trent's office. Usually, Bailee felt a twinge of envy when men fawned over her mother, but not tonight. She was relieved that Giselle was distracted, permitting her to make a clean getaway.

As she waited for the elevator, guests, as well as hotel staff, cast inquiring glances in her direction.

Macy, her assistant, dashed toward her. "What happened out there? Are you okay?" Phony concern coated her words and her eyes twinkled with excitement as she waited for Bailee to explain why she'd slapped her husband.

"I'm fine," Bailee replied curtly and then hurried inside the elevator. She had no intention of satisfying Macy's or anyone else's morbid curiosity.

Despite her irritation with the entire situation, she found it humorous that Trent, who loathed public spectacles, would have to come up with an explanation for his wife's abrupt departure while suffering through the humiliation of getting slapped across the face. She laughed to herself, imagining him blaming her conduct on too much alcohol.

The one person she had expected to be right on her heels, concerned about her well-being, was Jayla. Jayla should have been rushing behind her, carrying two additional bottles of champagne, and squeezing inside the elevator seconds before the doors slid closed.

But the last she'd seen of Jayla, she was holding her phone pressed to an ear, and looking agitated.

Busy greeting her guests, Bailee hadn't been able to find out what had happened to Sadeeq. All she knew was that he was a no-show, and Jayla seemed distraught over his absence. She'd probably gone to her room to cry in private.

Bailee felt like crying, too, but she refused to. Crying was banned for the rest of the night. She planned to call Jayla and invite her to her suite so they could turn up together. Jayla was going to be stunned to learn that she and Bailee were in the same boat.

Bailee's perfect marriage was as bogus as Jayla's affair with Sadeeq. Her life had fallen apart and she should have been hysterical after learning that her husband was after her money, but she was strangely calm.

Knowing the truth had set her free. She didn't have to seek out a marriage counselor and she no longer had to rack her brain, wondering what was going on with Trent. His ploy to separate her from her assets had backfired, and he'd lost his golden goose.

Stepping out of the elevator, she recalled how she'd fought Giselle tooth and nail about making Trent sign a prenup, and now she was glad she'd listened to her. Trent would leave the marriage with only his personal belongings and his car. The condo was hers, and she planned to change the locks ASAP.

As she ambled down the hallway, her phone jangled inside her purse. She sighed and didn't bother to look at it. It was probably Giselle wondering where she'd run off to.

She'd shoot Giselle a quick text in a few minutes, telling her that she had a headache. Luckily, she didn't have to worry about Giselle leaving the party and personally coming to check on her. She wasn't that kind of doting mother and never had been. She'd take Bailee at her word, tell her to feel better, and she'd continue enjoying the party.

Eventually, Bailee would have to come clean and admit that her husband had been conning her all along. He'd played the long game, willing to wait until her thirty-fifth birthday. Of course, her mother wouldn't say the words, *I told you so*, but her silence would speak volumes. She'd never believed that her flawed daughter was loveable and she'd tried to tell Bailee so.

Inside the luxurious suite, she took her phone out of her purse.

Where are you? Giselle inquired via a text.

I have a terrible migraine, Bailee replied and then powered off the phone.

She kicked off her shoes, popped a cork, and stood in front of the window, admiring the spectacular view as she sipped champagne straight from the bottle.

She had every right to be hysterical, but she was eerily calm and accepting. There was no fight left in her. She gulped down mouthfuls of champagne, hoping for a buzz, hoping to feel something besides numbness.

Her mind backtracked to her teen years when Giselle used to Photoshop all her pictures, cropping out her lower half and making her appear to be smaller by slimming down her chubby cheeks and her chunky arms. Getting straight A's was not good enough for Giselle; she wanted a normal daughter. *I want you to be normal,* she'd said when explaining why she was shipping Bailee off to a fat camp, for her own good.

Bailee's struggle with weight had been a lifelong battle until Trent, who repeatedly told her that she was beautiful the way she was.

What's he doing with her fat ass? Mean girls used to whisper whenever Bailee and Trent walked around campus, hugged up together. Despite the haters that gave her and Trent second glances whenever they were out together, she always considered herself to be confident, smart, and amazing, regardless of her size.

She thought she had embraced her curves a long time ago, but had she? The truth of the matter was that Trent's alleged love had surrounded her in a protective bubble, giving her a false sense of security.

Now that she was without protection, where did she go from here? Back to self-hatred and disgust? Back to avoiding her naked image in the mirror?

She shook her head adamantly. She refused to be the self-loathing person she once was. She either had to get serious and lose the weight or learn how to love every roll of flab, every stretch mark, and every extra pound.

As she chugged down champagne, she wondered what was going on with Jayla.

Certain that a few glasses of bubbly would help Jayla get over Sadeeq's absence, Bailee picked up her phone to invite Jayla to her suite, so that they could drown their sorrows together.

Jayla's phone rang and rang and eventually went to voicemail.

"Where are you? If you don't call me right back, I'm putting out an APB on you," Bailee said, sounding carefree.

Her entire world had collapsed and amazingly she hadn't fallen apart. And she wouldn't. Somehow she'd find the strength to find peace in being alone.

But not tonight.

There was no reason to hide out in her room like she'd done something to be ashamed of. Deciding to return to the party and have a drunken good time, she slid her feet back into her heels and left the suite.

After making a pit stop at Jayla's room, and getting no response, she stepped out of the elevator and sauntered toward the ballroom. Stopping at the entrance, she surveyed the crowd. Drinks were flowing from the open bar and everyone seemed to be enjoying themselves. Apparently, her presence hadn't been missed.

Searching for Jayla, her eyes roved from table to table.

Suddenly, her breath caught in her throat and her heartbeat

accelerated as she struggled to comprehend what her eyes were seeing. She blinked rapidly in an attempt to adjust her faulty vision, yet there it was before her.

Renowned adversaries, Giselle and Trent, were huddled at her mother's table, engaged in what appeared to be an intensely intimate conversation. As partygoers cast surreptitious glances at the cozy pair, Bailee stood transfixed while her brain struggled to make sense of the incomprehensible scene.

The unlikely pair sat facing each other and Giselle's chair was strategically positioned between Trent's outstretched legs.

From her vantage point, Bailee attempted to read every nuance of their body language and facial expressions. It seemed to her that Trent was sulking. Bailee recognized the woebegone, puppy dog face that he'd successfully used on her too many times to count. It was amazing how he could still look so incredibly handsome with the stupid, slack-jawed look on his face.

She also recognized Giselle's expression as she attempted to crinkle her Botoxed brow. Her head was tilted to one side, which was her patent, "I feel your pain" move.

What the hell is going on? Is my mother comforting Trent?

Before the shock of that possibility could fully register, Bailee was nearly rendered unconscious by the sudden visceral blow she received.

In what seemed like agonizingly slow motion, she watched as her mother lifted a hand and pressed it against Trent's face tenderly. The purported sworn enemies locked eyes as Trent covered Giselle's hand with his own.

Speechless and doubling over as if she'd been punched in the gut, Bailee backed out of the ballroom. She quickly made her way back to her suite before she became a crumbled heap on the floor.

There was no doubt that she still loved Trent and she realized that getting over him and eventually healing from the loss would be a process, but she hadn't expected to be betrayed by her own mother.

Oh, God, please let this be my imagination. My eyes were deceiving me and I didn't see my mother and Trent flagrantly flirting. She was only being maternal. No, who am I kidding? My mother doesn't know the meaning of the word, maternal. Jesus, I don't need this kind of drama in my life.

Needing to discuss her dilemma, Bailee climbed to her feet and began pacing while blowing up Jayla's phone—to no avail.

Unable to reach Jayla, Bailee's racing thoughts returned to Trent and Giselle.

Did Trent have Giselle in his crosshairs now that he'd lost Bailee? For an opportunist like Trent, the mother was a much better catch than the daughter. Giselle's bank account was unlimited. And despite the age gap, she and Trent—two beautiful people—looked more suitable together than Trent and Bailee. No one would be whispering, *"What's he doing with her?"* when he squired Giselle around town.

Oh, dear God! Her stomach knotted painfully. The idea of Trent and Giselle involved in a relationship was too much to bear.

Giselle was such a hypocrite, always complaining that Trent was too rough around the edges to make an appropriate spouse for her daughter, but at the first signs of trouble, she was ready to snatch him up.

Where was Jayla? She tried her number again. No answer. Bailee gnawed at her lower lip.

Without a doubt, she was going to confront Giselle, and if she thought there was even an inkling of truth to her suspicion, it was possible that she might lose her mind.

Chapter 14

Jayla drove as slowly as possible to the Pine Street precinct. She'd never been involved in any criminal matters and had never been inside a police station. She hoped she hadn't broken the law by allowing Sadeeq to drive off the lot in a car that was rented in her name.

And if she had broken the law, was she walking into a trap?

Images of being cuffed and tossed inside a jail cell scared her so badly she had to pull over to the side of the road to try and calm down.

Maybe she needed a lawyer. Although he wasn't a criminal attorney, Trent came to mind. But she couldn't call him; he was still celebrating at his party. Besides, Trent would never go out of his way to help her.

All the love she'd felt for Sadeeq had turned to pure hatred after reading his text. What had she been thinking when she got involved with such a lowlife? Not only should she have run the other way when she found out he was married, she should have run in the opposite direction the moment she learned that his wife's name was Radiance and his daughter's name was Luxurious. Those names alone should have warned her that he was nothing but trouble.

But instead of following her instincts, her dumbass had stuck around because the dick was superb and the outer packaging was appealing. She'd thought she could elevate him, but instead, he'd pulled her right down into the gutter with him.

As the engine idled, she glanced in the mirror to apply lipstick, hoping a pleasing appearance would persuade the police to go easy on her, if she was in trouble. But no amount of lipstick could steady her shaky hands or disguise the pure terror in her eyes.

It occurred to her to turn the car around. Go back home and start packing her shit. She could relocate to a remote island and live off the land. She'd lose weight for sure if she had to forage for her meals.

Realistically, she wasn't built for living in a hut in a foreign land. But she wasn't built for jail, either. Her hands trembled as she gripped the gear shift and pushed it into drive.

Get a grip. You're overreacting. You did nothing wrong, she tried to convince herself as she drove at a snail's pace.

About a block away from the precinct, a dark SUV pulled up behind her and the horn began to blare. She didn't have to squint to recognize Sadeeq's SUV that supposedly had been booted. *What a fucking liar.*

He gestured for Jayla to pull into a narrow street.

Cursing and rolling her eyes, she followed his instruction. She stopped at the curb, threw the gear into park, and with fire in her eyes, she stomped over to Sadeeq's SUV. He was sitting in the warm vehicle, listening to Big Sean, and smoking an L.

He lowered the window. "Where's my suit?" His words were accompanied by a cloud of weed smoke.

"Fuck your suit; I threw that piece of shit in the trash. Now, what in the hell is going on, Sadeeq? What happened with the rental?" The idea of Radiance wheeling around in the rental while she was alone at the party made her seethe. She was so furious she didn't feel the bitter cold air—all she felt was heat.

"Yo, that suit wasn't cheap. It cost—"

"I don't give a flying fuck how much it cost," she spat.

"Look, I know you mad," Sadeeq said in an appeasing tone. "You got every reason to be pissed, but I'll explain everything later. Right now, we got to get our stories straight. I plan to tell the cops that you were showing me some houses today, and when my ride ran out of gas, you let me hold yours. I'll say I didn't know it was a rental and when my wife wanted to go to the club with her girlfriends, I told her it was okay to drive it."

Jayla shot him a look of astonishment. "You allowed your wife to drive off with the rental when you knew I was at the party waiting for you?" She searched his face and didn't see a glimmer of remorse.

"Man, that's beside the point. Right now, we gotta make sure that our statements match," he said with his face contorted in annoyance.

"I'm not lying for you! Do you realize the kind of trouble I could be in? How much damage did she do to the rental?"

He made an inarticulate, frustrated sound, as if having to explain anything to her was a wearisome chore. "I don't know, man. I wasn't there. She hit another car and the driver is in the hospital. That's all the information I have." He shrugged, nonchalant.

"Oh, my God—someone's in the hospital? Can this shit get any worse?" Jayla covered her face in horror. She was going to have to find a new occupation because there was no doubt that she was going to be fired, sued, imprisoned, and blackballed in the real estate industry.

"Man, fuck the other driver! I'm worried about my wife!" Sadeeq's voice rose to a pitch that was almost shrill. "They got Radiance locked up for car theft, vehicular assault, and a bunch of bullshit charges. I need you to talk to the cops and tell them that you loaned her the whip."

"Fuck Radiance," Jayla fired back. "I used the company credit card for the rental that you allowed your 'hood rat wife to tear up. I can't believe this shit, Sadeeq. What were you thinking?"

"First of all, who you calling a 'hood rat? And don't be coming at me with this sucka shit."

"I'll come at you any way I want. I'm in debt over your dumbass."

"Dumbass, huh?" Sadeeq gave her a deadly smile. "Okay. Well, let's keep it one hundred, you fat-ass, dusty dick licker—"

Jayla gasped.

"You put your profile up on that fat chick's website because you wanted a buff dude to fuck you and pretend like your elephant ass looked sexy. It wasn't nothing but a game and I played my part. But don't get it twisted, bitch. I ain't do all that heavy lifting in bed out of the kindness of my muthafuckin' heart. That kind of hard labor comes at a cost. You didn't give me a damn thing that I didn't earn."

Jayla was stunned into silence. The words that had shot out of his mouth were swift and deadly, like bullets entering her heart.

But it wasn't a quick kill.

She teetered on her feet, grasping at the door handle before making a slow and anguished descent to the ground.

In a show of frustration, Sadeeq made a loud groan. "Come on, man, get up off the ground and stop bullshitting. Ain't nobody got time for this."

But Jayla couldn't move. The knowledge that their relationship had never been real was devastating. Sadeeq had been using her from the very start. How could she have been so stupid?

Ashamed and distraught, tears spilled from her eyes and she prayed the ground would open up and swallow her whole.

Sadeeq got out the SUV and roughly yanked Jayla by the arm, trying to pull her to her feet. "Come on, bitch. Damn! Get the fuck up before five-o rolls up, thinking I'm out here whipping your ass."

The man she had catered to at the expense of her credit rating, her livelihood, and her pride, had callously called her *bitch* one too many times. Rage prevented her from thinking rationally and she came up from the ground, swinging and clawing. When Sadeeq tried to grab her, she bit into his hand like a wild, ravenous animal. Insane with fury, she bit into flesh and muscle and wouldn't let go, not even when her teeth began to scrape against bone.

Howling in pain, Sadeeq punched her in the head, but she felt nothing. She yearned for retribution, and the taste of his blood and his anguished screams incited her to shake her head like a pit bull, trying to bite off a chunk of his hand.

He flung her around, punched, and kicked her, but Jayla wouldn't let go. *Grimy, lowlife muthafucka* was all she could think of while her teeth were latched on to his hand.

And she was still holding on when a squad car screeched to a stop. She didn't come to her senses and release Sadeeq's mangled hand until the police threatened to blast her with pepper spray.

Mouth covered with Sadeeq's blood, Jayla was handcuffed and shoved into the back of the squad car. Despite her dreadful circumstances, it was thoroughly satisfying to look through the window and witness Sadeeq's face contorted in agony as he repeatedly yelled that he needed an ambulance to take him to the hospital.

She hadn't expected Bailee to respond to her phone call from jail while in the midst of celebrating, but Bailee had come through with a lawyer in tow, and Jayla was released on the spot. No charges were brought against her after the high-priced attorney made it clear that his client, an upstanding citizen, had been brutalized in the street by a common thug, whom she'd bitten in self-defense.

Jayla's swollen face and the knot on her head that was sustained from Sadeeq's punches were proof that she'd been assaulted.

Although it was determined that Jayla had allowed Sadeeq to drive the rental, Radiance was not authorized to drive it, and for her crimes, she was left sitting in jail. Sadeeq was charged with assault and battery and was also behind bars.

It was a great relief to learn from the lawyer that Jayla's insurance was responsible for the repairs to the vehicle, which turned out to be minor. Sadeeq and Radiance, on the other hand, were responsible for the personal injury liability as well as medical expenses incurred by the other driver. The other driver, it turned out, hadn't sustained a scratch, but had insisted on going to the hospital, complaining of whiplash.

Sitting in her living room with a bag of frozen corn pressed against the knot on her head, Jayla sat on the couch and Bailee sat next to her. Jayla sniffled through a summarized version of how badly Sadeeq had used her. When she finished, she waited for Bailee to give her a scathing lecture, but Bailee was uncharacteristically compassionate as she rubbed Jayla's back and told her everything would be all right.

"I can't thank you enough, Bailee. I'm shocked that you're not getting on my case for being such a dumbass," Jayla said, dabbing at her eyes with a tissue.

"I can't judge you, girl," Bailee said morosely.

Jayla gave Bailee a sidelong glance. "You can't judge…since when? A few weeks ago, you tried to preach a sermon about my alleged bad behavior, but this time, I really deserve it. So, go ahead, let me have it."

"I'm serious, Jayla. I've had an awakening."

"What kind of awakening?"

Bailee drew in a long breath. "For starters, my marriage is over," she admitted with lowered eyes and a tremor in her voice.

Jayla stared at her in disbelief. "Stop playing, Bailee."

"I'm serious. It's over between Trent and me. I plan to sit down with a divorce attorney in a few days."

A look of confusion appeared on Jayla's face. "What are you talking about? You celebrated your tenth anniversary last night. I watched you and Trent greeting guests, laughing and smiling for the cameras, and looking like the happiest couple in the world."

"It was a front. We were both pretending to be a devoted couple. I figured all the guests saw past the façade when I slapped Trent in the face."

Jayla gawked at Bailee. "You did what?"

"Didn't you see the scene I made on the dance floor?"

Jayla shook her head. "Sorry, Bailee, I was so consumed with self-pity, I rushed out of the ballroom while you and Trent were dancing. I was so hurt that Sadeeq had stood me up, I couldn't enjoy your happiness. In fact, I was jealous of you two," Jayla confessed in a whisper.

"There was nothing to be jealous of," Bailee admitted.

"How long have you and Trent been pretending to be happily married?"

"I thought we *were* happy, but apparently, Trent had a hidden agenda. He was after my money."

"You're kidding, right?"

Bailee shook her head. "I never suspected. When my mom forced me to present him with a prenup, he didn't hesitate to sign it. He made it clear that he could make his own money, and didn't need mine. Since my mother had arranged for the condo to be in my name only, it was my secret plan to sell it as soon as I received my inheritance and buy a big, fancy house that would be in both our names. I was looking forward to us jointly owning our next home—something in the million-dollar price range.

Jayla whistled at the amount Bailee had planned to spend.

"Of course, you were going to be our realtor."

"Stop torturing me. The commission from that sale would have made a big difference in my life. My boss and my arrogant coworkers would have been forced to show me some respect."

"Don't worry, girl, I got you. Now that my marriage is over, I'm going to sell the condo and get something nice, just for me."

"What's your price range?"

"A million…a million-point-five," Bailee said nonchalantly.

"I'll be on the lookout, but I hate profiting from your un-happiness."

"It's okay," Bailee said, wearing a sad smile. "It's amazing that I was married to that man for so long and never really knew him. For that matter, I suppose I don't think I know myself, either."

"What do you mean by that?"

"The confidence I had in my body was based on the belief that Trent thought I was beautiful."

"Didn't he?" Jayla asked, looking puzzled.

Bailee shook her head. "About a month before the party, Trent and I got into an argument. He said things that left me speechless and he looked at me in a way that made it obvious that he despised me."

"Oh, no," Jayla uttered, recalling how Sadeeq had made it clear that he had never cared for her. But never in a million years would she have suspected that Trent didn't truly love Bailee.

Bailee pressed a hand against her forehead. "I feel like my entire adult life has been a lie. My identity has been deconstructed, dismantled, and destroyed. I need help, and I'm thinking about taking some time off work. Perhaps I'll take a trip to somewhere quiet and peaceful. A place where I can do some intense soul-searching."

"Are you talking about a Buddhist retreat where you sit around meditating all day?" Jayla asked with a frown on her face.

Bailee shrugged. "I'm not sure. But I'm definitely going to a retreat that allows for intense self-analysis." She shook her head sadly. "What I know for sure is that I need to reexamine my feelings about my weight. I need to be able to stand in my own truth and honestly say that I love myself for who I am—with or without the approval of a man. If I can't do that, then I'm going to have to admit that my weight is a burden, and then do something about it."

"I know exactly how you feel. When do you think you'll be leaving?" Jayla inquired.

"I have no idea, but you'll be the first to know." Bailee rose from the couch and Jayla stood as well. After they hugged, Jayla walked Bailee to the door.

Jayla didn't have to decide whether or not she loved her extra pounds before she took some kind of action. She knew for a fact that she hated her flab, despised her cellulite, and loathed the outrageous numbers that flashed on her scale. And she didn't have to go away to a retreat to figure herself out.

She loved to eat and was incapable of sticking to a restrictive diet. Nevertheless, she'd be damned if she was going to remain fat while Bailee meditated her way to a skinny body. Oh, hell no! It was time to get serious about weight loss surgery. It was clear that the only way she'd ever be thin was to allow a surgeon to use his knife to whittle her stomach down.

Chapter 15

Bailee arrived home and Trent wasn't there. Despite his absence, the condo felt small, constricting. It had been their love nest for the past ten years, and now the place that had once been her sanctuary seemed more like a prison cell. She wished she could leave her wrecked marriage behind, pack her bags, and go away to an undisclosed destination. But she couldn't set off on her journey of self-discovery without first attending to a few important matters.

The first thing on her list was to kick Trent out. Not that he'd care, but it would feel good to say the words, *get the fuck out!*

She spent hours online looking for a divorce attorney. Of course, she could have handed the matter over to Giselle, but Bailee wanted to keep her divorce private until it was final. She was a big girl and didn't need her mother all up in her business.

Bailee thought about Trent huddled near Giselle at the party and was still baffled by her mother's overly intimate response to him. Maybe too much liquor had caused Giselle to become uninhibited and too touchy-feely with Trent. Not wanting to embarrass her mother by bringing up her uncharacteristic conduct, Bailee decided not to mention it.

When Sunday turned into Monday morning, and Trent still hadn't come home, Bailee called in sick at work. She wanted to be home when Trent arrived, so that she could see the look of shock on his face when she told him she wanted a divorce. An opportunist like Trent would remain locked in a loveless marriage forever simply because the scandal of a divorce might stand in the way of a promotion at work.

She considered calling his job to find out if he'd arrived for work but couldn't bring herself to. She didn't want anyone to misjudge her intentions and inaccurately think she was checking up on him.

Finally, around noon, while Bailee stood in front of the sink rinsing out a coffee mug, Trent strode through the front door. Prepared to confront him, she whirled around, but he swept past the kitchen and made long strides toward the guest bedroom without giving her as much as a glance.

Indignant over his unremitting bad attitude, she was also struck by his stylish appearance when he dashed past her. He was wearing clothing she'd never seen before: a Canada Goose jacket, new black leather zip boots, and a fur hat with flaps. Trent never wore hats, no matter how cold the temperature.

His new winter attire looked like it cost outrageous sums, much more money than he'd typically spend on clothes. His boots alone had to have cost at least five hundred dollars. And the jacket was definitely a grand.

What was going on? It was out of character for Trent to make sudden and expensive purchases. By no means was he a slouch when it came to his appearance, but he was a bargain shopper, not the kind of man who would spend several thousand dollars on a trendy winter outfit.

His entire identity seemed to be changing and she wondered if her husband had simply lost his mind.

From the guest room, she heard drawers opening and banging shut. The sound of hangers rattled in the closet. Curious, Bailee made her way down the hall and was stunned to discover Trent flinging clothing into several pieces of luggage.

"Where's my passport?" he grumbled, continuing to pack and not even bothering to glance at her.

She felt sucker-punched and was too shocked to respond. He was planning a trip somewhere that required a passport, and in doing so, was robbing her of the opportunity of kicking him out.

Not wanting him to know that he'd gotten to her, she went to her bedroom, retrieved his passport from a drawer, and flung it on the bed with no questions asked.

Feigning nonchalance, Bailee sauntered out of the bedroom and returned to the kitchen. Perplexed, she stood in the middle of the floor wringing her hands.

Where the hell is he going? Surely, there's too much work piled up at his firm for him to take a spur-of-the-moment vacation.

Needing to occupy herself, she stood in front of the counter and began rearranging the coffee pods in the K-cup carousel.

With exaggerated swagger, Trent strolled into the kitchen carrying his bags. From the corner of her eye, Bailee could see that his body language was confrontational.

She didn't turn around.

"You realize our marriage is over, right? I can't play this game any longer," Trent announced. "I'll be back in two weeks to clear out my things."

Stunned and sensing that Trent was about to drop an even bigger bombshell, her hand, which hovered over the coffee pods, became suspended in midair.

"Oh, yeah," Trent added ominously. "Fuck that stupid prenuptial agreement you made me sign; I'm going where the real money is.

All this time…all this *damn* time, I've been with the wrong one," he said with spiteful laughter.

She frowned perplexedly. "What are you saying, Trent?"

"I'm saying that from now on, I'll be the one who pulls the purse strings. And since I'll be in control of the money, you might as well get accustomed to calling me *Daddy.*"

"What the hell are you talking about?" she asked with mounting suspicion.

With a malicious chuckle, Trent walked out and slammed the door.

On shaky legs, she made her way to the living room, retrieved her phone, and called Giselle. "Mom, what's going on?"

"Nothing, dear. Why do you ask?"

"Trent packed his bags. He said he's taking a vacation, and he hinted that there's something going on between you two. Do you have something to tell me?" Fearing Giselle's response, Bailee's stomach tightened into a knot.

"No, why would I?"

"Mom, please. Be honest."

There was a lengthy pause that spoke volumes, and Bailee pressed a hand against her heart.

"Actually, I'm, uh, traveling to St. Croix and when, uh, Trent mentioned that he'd like to make some connections in the Caribbean, I invited him along," Giselle said in faltering speech. "Didn't he clear the trip with you?"

"Clear it with me? Mom, do you hear yourself? My husband is accompanying you on a vacation, and you're acting like it's completely normal. What exactly is going on with you and Trent?" Bailee shrieked.

Giselle went briefly silent, then she spoke in carefully measured tones. "Listen, Bailee. Neither of us wanted to hurt you, but the heart wants what it wants. You can't help who you love."

"Love?" Bailee's voice was shrill. "A few days ago, you couldn't stand Trent. Now your heart suddenly wants him? Oh, my God; this is too much for me," she said, frantically fanning herself as if the flurries of air would help her to remain on her feet and continue breathing.

"I told Trent not to tell you because I knew you were going to overreact."

"Are you nuts?" Bailee screamed. "My mother and my husband are having an affair, and I'm supposed to stay calm?" She drew in a long breath and released it, forcing herself to calm down. "How long have you two been going behind my back, Mom?"

"It's only been a little over a month—a very intense and passionate month. And I've discovered that what Trent and I have is really sacred."

"There's nothing sacred about it! What you have is immoral and disgusting," Bailee shouted.

"Calm down, sweetheart," Giselle said gently. "Listen, I'm a little unsure as to why you're so upset. Trent said that you two don't even share the same bedroom anymore. He said the marriage has been over for quite a while. He told me that you're not happy with him and he's *miserable* with you."

Bailee flinched. The way Giselle emphasized the word, *miserable*, was like a hot slap across Bailee's face.

"When you got physical with him in front of all of your distinguished guests, it was proof that he's been telling the truth. Frankly, it seems to me that I'm doing you a favor by taking Trent off your hands."

"Do you hear yourself—do you realize how deranged you sound? What is wrong with you? You were always a cold person, but you're still my mother and I would have never dreamed you'd deliberately hurt me like this. Are you going through some sort of midlife crisis, like menopause? Or are you just a heartless bitch?"

"There's no reason to make slurs. I realize that having such a youthful and attractive mother hasn't been easy on you, and I do sympathize, dear," Giselle said calmly, as if she hadn't stuck a knife in her daughter's heart. "I also realize that getting accustomed to Trent and me being together as a couple is a lot to process, but there's no excuse for you to insult me. Maybe you should take an aspirin and lie down. I'm sure you'll feel much better after a nap."

"A fucking nap won't make me feel better." Bailee yelled so loud, she could feel a vein protruding from her forehead, and she feared she might burst a blood vessel. Lowering her tone, she asked wearily, "How am I supposed to deal with something like this and not go crazy?"

"You'll be fine, sweetheart. Listen, if you think it will help, we can discuss this at length when I get back from St. Croix. We can have dinner at Romello's. You love Romello's steaks, don't you?"

Oh, my God, this is insane. My narcissistic mother steals my husband and tries to placate me with an expensive steak.

Hurt and offended by her mother's profound lack of remorse and warped sense of reasoning, Bailee gave a soft cry of distress and disconnected the call.

She paced the floor until she felt as if her legs were about to give out. Finally, she collapsed into Trent's reclining chair.

Slumped over in anguish, Bailee recollected the time of Trent's personality change. A month ago, which was approximately the same time he'd begun his scandalous affair with Giselle.

She squeezed back tears as she pictured Trent and Giselle frolicking together in St. Croix. It was completely humiliating for Trent to trade her in for her youthful-looking, but nevertheless, middle-aged mother.

Clearly, Trent was only using Giselle for her money, but that realization did not ease Bailee's pain.

Images of Giselle and Trent continually scrolled through Bailee's mind. She pictured them promenading through the airport, holding hands, kissing, feeding each other snacks, and engaging in all manner of public displays of affection. Most likely they had opulent accommodations in St. Croix with a private beach where Giselle could sunbathe nude while Trent slathered her toned body with sunscreen.

The visuals that played in Bailee's mind were painful. To rid herself of the emotional harassment, she took two Ambiens, and then ended up sleeping for thirteen hours straight. She woke up in her darkened bedroom feeling groggy and disoriented.

Remembering the betrayal brought out an anguished moan and a pounding headache.

Additionally, she was ravenous.

She clicked on the bedside lamp and noted the time. It was six in the evening and she wanted dinner and dessert, but she had no energy to cook. Nor did she want to order any cheap takeout. She wanted a good quality meal, but didn't want to sit in a restaurant and dine alone.

No doubt, Jayla would be willing to join her for a meal, but she wasn't ready to share the news of the heinous betrayal by the two people in the world she should have been able to trust the most.

Without bathing or brushing her teeth, Bailee threw on a pair of sweatpants, a bulky sweater, and a heavy coat. Car keys in hand, she ventured out into the cold night in search of food.

In the car, a song came on the radio that reminded her of her college days with Trent and, without warning, the tears began to flow. Sniffling as she drove, she told herself that along with a hot meal, two big slices of cheesecake would make her feel better.

Using her hands-free application, she called ahead to the Cheesecake Factory and ordered two appetizers, an entrée, and two slices of cheesecake. Then she changed her mind. Two slices weren't enough; she needed a whole Chocolate Hazelnut Crunch cheesecake to feel satisfied.

After the friendly voice on the other end of the phone gave her a number for pickup, she felt the tension begin to melt away. She pressed down on the accelerator, eager for the comfort that food provided. Food had always been a dependable companion and had never let her down.

Food loved her even if her own mother and husband didn't.

Chapter 16

Bailee assumed that work would take her mind off her problems, and so after taking a few days off, she returned.

"Oh, I wasn't expecting you today," Macy said when Bailee arrived at the office. "Mr. Dunham called a meeting. It's in the conference room and it starts in ten minutes. I'll call his assistant and let her know that you'll be attending the meeting, after all," Macy added.

Bailee's brows drew together. "What's the meeting about?"

Macy squinted down at handwritten notes. "It focuses on accounting, risk, and regulatory issues."

For fuck's sake! The meeting would be a snooze fest, but she couldn't dodge it. Although she really didn't feel like interacting with her boss, Fred Dunham, or any of the other banking executives, she had no choice. Even though she'd held her upper-management position for two years and had always done superb work, she felt like she constantly had to prove herself.

Fred and her colleagues were a grim bunch of uptight, older white men and they all held the belief that Bailee's age, race, and gender should have disqualified her from sitting at the same table with them.

Having to deal with their condescending attitudes often required that Bailee throw herself into warrior mode, and usually, she was ready for their persnickety old asses.

But not today.

She had intended to use work as therapy and wasn't in the mood for putting on her armor and wielding a sword. It had been her hope to spend the day working in the quiet solitude of her office, allowing lists of numbers and boring reports to numb her brain.

In her office, she took a few moments to gaze out the window and her mind drifted to Giselle and Trent. What were they doing in that moment? Breakfast on an oceanfront terrace or were they leisurely making love? Trent always woke up with a hard-on and with no reason to hurry out of bed, he was probably pressed against Giselle right now…

Forcing away the grotesque imagery of her mother and husband thrashing around in bed, Bailee bit down on her lip hard enough to draw blood.

From a desk drawer, she retrieved the thick folder that contained the quarterly report. Report in hand and with her chin up, she made her way to the conference room.

As she stood outside the double-frosted doors of the conference room, to her dismay, she could see the blurry outlines of her colleagues and it was apparent that the meeting was already in full swing.

Fred Dunham was on his feet, speaking to the executives, when Bailee crept inside the room, mouthing apologies.

With condemnation in their bleary eyes, the team of grim reapers (as Bailee referred to them in her mind) turned their gazes upon her. Feeling like a party crasher, Bailee gave the men a weak smile and attempted to quietly pull out a chair. As luck would have it, the legs of the chair scraped against the polished floor and squealed in protest, causing her to cringe and prompting her colleagues to roll their eyes heavenward.

Fred drew in an impatient breath, ran a hand down his tie, and then resumed speaking to the team. "As the fabric of banking continues to evolve and new technology players emerge in the marketplace, the GroTech Annual Summit will bring together senior executives from across the financial industry to shine a light on what is actually generating top line growth and bottom line profits through partnerships, collaborations, and investments." He gazed in Bailee's direction. "Bailee has been compiling a list of stand-out partnerships between our bank and GroTech companies and she can bring us up to speed. Bailee, the floor is all yours."

Bailee's mouth gaped open and she stared at Fred with a panicked look in her eyes. There was a long, awkward pause as she frantically rustled through the pages of the quarterly report.

Shit, shit, shit! Macy had given her the wrong information and Bailee had nothing to contribute because she'd only recently begun working on the Annual Summit.

Normally, she would have been able to easily bullshit her way out of any disastrous situation she found herself in. She'd throw out some names and numbers and fake it until she could make it, but today she felt completely exposed as unprepared and unprofessional.

She felt like a token African American who had only been able to climb up the ranks of the corporate ladder due to affirmative action policies. It wasn't true, however. In reality, she'd been hired and promoted based on merit, but instead of being quick on her feet, she began to visibly shudder.

Her teeth clattered together as she attempted to formulate a sentence.

Then tears sprang to her eyes, and in the next instance, she was sobbing openly. She apologized for her meltdown, but couldn't hold back the flow of tears.

Agony. Rage. Grief. Desolation. Those emotions erupted from her in awful gasping sobs, merging in waves so forceful, she could hardly catch her breath.

It was excruciatingly painful to be treated with such disregard by the woman who had given birth to her and the man who had vowed to love her for better or worse. She'd hoped to keep her personal problems at home where they belonged, but this blunder at work had pushed her over the edge.

Crying in the workplace was the kiss of death, and the men who sat on either side of Bailee slid their seats away from her, as if her condition might be contagious.

In the next instant, she went from being apologetic to angrily pointing the finger of blame. "This is not my mistake," Bailee yelled in frustration as she fiercely smacked the table with the quarterly report. "This is the work of my assistant, who would love to have my position," she pointed out with maniacal laughter. "She told me we were discussing accounting, risk, and regulatory issues. Obviously, she lied to me. She set me up. This is a flagrant act of sabotage!"

Completely unhinged, Bailee, who was usually dignified, had become wild-eyed, snarling like a rabid animal that was backed into a corner.

The men seated at the table had been waiting for her to fail and now that the moment had finally arrived, Bailee didn't see any point in trying to hold herself together.

Thrashing, kicking, and screaming like a madwoman, she was led out of the conference room by Fred's assistant, Claudia Kolinski, a sturdy woman whom Bailee was friendly with. In addition to Claudia, there were two other female staff members, whom Fred had enlisted with a phone call.

Alternately laughing and weeping, Bailee dug her heels in, making it difficult for the women to usher her out of the room. "I didn't fail; it wasn't my mistake. I'm always prepared and all of you damn well know it!"

Once the three women had managed to haul her out of the conference room and into the corridor, Bailee, a total basket case, slid down to the floor. With her back propped against the wall, she cried and kicked out her legs in a defiant manner usually reserved for toddlers.

She was unable to rein herself in, and helplessly watching herself implode was like having an out-of-body experience.

"Bailee, you have to get up," Claudia beseeched her. But Bailee continued kicking.

Unable to reason with her, Claudia called for the help of security.

A team of uniformed men led by the head of security, a thirty-something black man named Reuben Daniels, rushed onto the thirty-second floor, ready to manhandle the perpetrator if necessary. When Reuben saw that it was Bailee causing the ruckus, he brusquely motioned for his men to return to their posts. He also shooed the hovering female assistants away.

He got down on one knee. "What's going on, Ms. Evans?" he asked gently.

"Everyone's against me, Reuben...and I mean, *everyone!*" she bawled. "My mother, my husband, and now my assistant," she divulged, realizing that she sounded like a crazed conspiracy theorist, but unable to stop herself.

"I've been instructed to escort you off the premises, and I have to do my job. So, let's not give these people more of a show. Will you come with me willingly?" Reuben asked, holding out a hand.

Whimpering, she grasped his hand as if she'd been extended a lifeline. He gingerly pulled her to her feet and ushered her toward the bank of elevators. "Someone grab Ms. Evans' coat and her purse," he barked at a group of onlookers.

He glanced down at Bailee and asked in a softened tone, "Is there anything else you want from your office?"

She shook her head.

Moments later, Macy, unable to conceal a grin, brought Bailee's coat and bag and handed the items to her.

Reuben led Bailee down a secluded hallway. "I've decided we'll use the service elevator…for privacy," he explained.

Bailee nodded solemnly. Reuben's thoughtfulness touched her heart. He'd always treated Bailee well and was kind and courteous at all times. He seemed to regard her with pride and approval for representing black folks in her prestigious position at the bank, and she was immensely sorry that she had caused him embarrassment.

Regretting that she'd let Reuben down, a sob tore from her throat, and the sound was so guttural and pained, she barely recognized it as her own voice.

Uncomfortable with the raw emotion that Bailee displayed, Reuben's eyes shifted downward. "You're not in any shape to drive, so I'll put you in a cab," he said, his eyes trained on his polished black shoes.

Again, Bailee nodded mutely.

As her senses gradually returned, she was flooded with humiliation over her behavior. She could never show her face at First Mutual Bank again. Not ever! If she wasn't already fired, she undoubtedly had to quit. She determined that first thing tomorrow, she'd submit her resignation.

In retrospect, she wished that on her way out, she had given Macy a swift kick in the shins. Or better yet, a punch in the face.

But physical violence would have brought on an assault charge, and Bailee already had had more problems than she could handle.

The tremendous pain of the losses Bailee had suffered was un-remitting and incapacitating. There was no way to escape it. Al-though her emotions ran high at all times, causing her to cry at the drop of a hat, the upside to being jobless, husbandless, and motherless was that Bailee had lost her appetite for two days, and she hoped she'd emerge from her personal horror show as a much thinner version of herself.

With significant weight loss, maybe she'd find the light at the end of the tunnel. Maybe her life wouldn't seem so hopeless.

But on the third day, her appetite returned with a vengeance.

Bailee promptly went to the website of an expensive restaurant and selected enough gourmet food to feed an army. The total of her takeout order was three hundred and twelve dollars, and Bailee didn't bat an eye as she keyed in her credit card information. She needed the food like a drowning woman needed a life raft.

Before leaving her condo, she threw a coat over her pajamas, put on old, scuffed boots. She didn't bother to check her reflection in the mirror or tame her locs that were sticking out all over her head. Resembling Medusa, she trotted outside to her car.

Dressed inappropriately in her nightclothes, she walked boldly inside the exclusive restaurant and was oblivious to the stares that both patrons and staff aimed in her direction as she collected three large shopping bags that overflowed with steaming food containers.

Back in her car, she placed one shopping bag on the front passenger's seat and the other two were situated on the floor in the back. During the drive home, the assorted aromas pervaded her nostrils, causing her to drive with one hand on the steering wheel, and the other groping inside the shopping bag, blindly opening plastic containers until her fingers located the Parmesan Truffle Fries.

When the piping hot, cheesy-tasting fry touched her tongue, she lowered her eyelids blissfully, and then stepped on the accelerator, impatiently wanting to hurry home to begin the feast.

At home, she set out the copious amount of containers on the island and excitedly sampled one dish after another. As the combined flavors exploded in her mouth, she could feel a warm feeling slowly building, embracing her like a much-needed hug.

Chapter 17

Dodging debt collectors had taken a toll on her emotions, and Jayla no longer answered any calls from numbers she didn't recognize. Feeling like the walls were closing in on her, she didn't open collection letters, either. She was aware that inaction was not the best course of action, but she was completely immobilized by fear and needed a break from listening to and reading threats from bill collectors.

After it was clear that Sadeeq wasn't going to pay the bill, she continued to procrastinate while trying to figure out exactly what to do, and somewhere along the way, her original debt was sold to a third-party collection agency, and the amount that she owed had somehow tripled. The aggressive tactics of the third-party agency were so far out of the bounds of the law that Jayla had no choice but to change her phone number.

Mentally exhausted from everything in her life: her weight, being used and abused by Sadeeq, and owing money to everyone and their mother, Jayla drove home from work with a heavy heart. She should have never allowed her situation to get so far out of hand.

Hindsight was twenty-twenty, and she now realized that had she set up a nominal monthly payment plan, her debt would have never been sold and her credit would not be destroyed. Now that the third-party collectors were involved in recovering the debt, they had begun calling her job, which was completely embarrassing. The receptionist at work put a stop to the harassing calls at work, but not until she told all the other agents about Jayla's awful financial predicament.

With a heavy sigh, Jayla turned on her blinkers to make a left turn into the parking lot of her building. Suddenly, Mr. Murphy, from across the street, came hobbling out of his house, waving his arms, determinedly flagging Jayla down.

Annoyed, she hit the brakes and lowered her window.

His timing was so perfect, she wondered if he'd been looking out of his window, waiting for her. He was block captain as well as the president of the Community Development League, and she assumed he wanted to tell her about a new problem in the neighborhood and invite her to an emergency, problem-solving meeting.

Damn! I just went to one of his dreary, mind-numbing meetings last week! I wish he'd leave me alone.

Times like tonight, she hated that she was buying her condo. Mr. Murphy wouldn't feel the need to constantly update her on neighborhood issues if she were merely a renter.

"Hey, Jayla, how are you?" he asked, hands stuck in his coat pockets, his shoulders hunched against the wind.

"I'm fine," she said curtly. "What can I do for you?"

He smiled sheepishly. "I'm not trying to get in your business or anything, but the wife wanted me to speak to you about a problem we've been having."

She frowned in aggravation. "What sort of problem?"

"Well, we've been getting numerous phone calls from a collection agency, asking if we know anyone named Jayla Carpenter who lives on our street."

Oh, no! This gossiping muthafucka is going to tell the whole neighborhood that I'm drowning in debt.

"Now, I don't know how these people found the wife and me, but Miriam thinks we were easily located because we have a landline."

Flooded with embarrassment, Jayla groaned inwardly and ran a gloved hand down her face. "I'm sorry you're being harassed, Mr. Murphy. Those predatory collectors are using deceptive tactics. Just tell them you don't know me and tell them you'll file a complaint if they don't leave you alone."

"Well, now, we've tried that, but they keep calling. Miriam and I are debt-free and although we don't have the right to tell you how to live your life, it's not fair for us to get harassed while you're living in peace."

"What the hell do you expect me to do, Mr. Murphy?" The words came out much harsher than she'd intended, and Mr. Murphy flinched as if he'd been slapped.

He held a high opinion of himself and expected to be treated with the utmost courtesy. The simmering anger that glinted in his eyes as he regarded Jayla was so chilling, she wondered if he was going to punch her, and she considered rolling her window up.

"I've been meaning to ask you what happened to that young fella that used to come around—the one that drove the dark-colored SUV," he said in an ominous tone.

"Uh, he, um…"

"He's gone, huh?" he said with a sneer. "A few weeks ago, he was all up in them yams, but I suppose he got bored with you and moved on to the next simple-minded woman."

Indignant, Jayla lifted an eyebrow. "Excuse you!" *I can't believe this old, filthy-mouthed bastard is all in my face and insinuating that I'm a used-up skeezer.*

One side of Mr. Murphy's mouth lifted up in an evil smile.

"When you heavy-set girls start getting some self-respect for yourselves and stop letting these young, fuck boys treat you like cum buckets, you'll be much better off. Anyone can lay wood, but it takes a real man to provide for a woman and treat her right."

"You got a lot of nerve trying to lecture me like you're my father," Jayla spat. "I don't recall asking for your advice. I'm a grown woman and I pay my own damn bills—"

"Obviously, you *don't* pay your bills. If you did, we wouldn't be having this conversation, now would we?" he said with triumph gleaming in his eyes. "Maybe if you stopped giving the milk away for free, those hooligans you associate with would have no choice but to buy the cow."

"You out of line, nigga. You better kiss my ass and stay the hell out of my business." Jayla was livid and on the verge of hopping out of her car and throwing hands with the old man.

"You made it my business when your creditors started harassing my wife and me," he countered with a wide smile that revealed a set of teeth that were too white and too large to be real.

"Fuck you, Mr. Murphy. I don't have to listen to your shit." Glaring at him, she gave him the finger and then rolled up the window. Stepping hard on the accelerator, her tires squealed as she shot forward and then made a sharp, screeching right turn into her building's parking lot.

After parking, she stomped angrily from her car to the entryway of the building. As she rode the elevator up to her floor, her phone rang. She dug the phone out of her bag and observed on the screen a number she didn't recognize. She accepted the call because none of the bill collectors had her new number.

"Hello?" she said, wondering if Sadeeq had finally gotten out of jail and had somehow managed to get her number. Although she was through with him, she welcomed an opportunity to curse him out.

"Hello, Jayla Carpenter, this is Peggy from Regional Recovery, LLC—"

Jayla gasped in shock. "How'd you get this number?"

"Your neighbor, Mr. Murphy, was very helpful. But that's beside the point. You have forty-eight hours to pay your debt in full or we plan to freeze your bank accounts and send a tow truck to confiscate your 2009 blue Subaru Impreza Sedan."

"Bitch, I don't know who you think you're talking to, but I know for a fact that you don't have the legal right to freeze shit or confiscate a damn thing from me. You better use your scare tactics on someone that doesn't know any better."

Incensed, Jayla hung up. Although she had talked tough on the phone, she wasn't quite sure if the debt collectors had the power to act out on their threats. That snitch-ass Mr. Murphy wasn't shit. She'd given him her new number at the last community meeting, and being vindictive, he gave her number to the collection people.

It would be a snowy day in hell before she'd ever step foot inside another Community Development meeting. That bastard was going to miss the sweet potato pies and the expensive Starbucks hot chocolate she used to bring to his stupid meetings. *Ungrateful bastard!*

Searching for a way to feel better, Jayla pressed the Instagram icon, curious to see if Sadeeq had recently updated his page. She was hoping to see the same old pics that had been posted for the past few weeks, which would indicate he was still behind bars. But, to her chagrin, Jayla discovered she'd been blocked.

Changing tactics, she used her fake profile to view his page, but his page had been changed to private.

She immediately went to Radiance's page, and was relieved that it hadn't been changed to private.

But she instantly regretted allowing her curiosity to get the best of her.

There were three rows of new photos that depicted the Samuelson family in all their ghetto glory. One picture showed a shelf that was filled with liquor bottles of every type, along with two glitzy, oversized goblets that were emblazoned with gold letters that spelled out *His* and *Hers*.

Jayla turned her nose up at the crass display.

There was a photo of Radiance wearing a tiara and a T-shirt with the words: *Magnificent 30* airbrushed across the front. The bitch had recently celebrated her thirtieth birthday and from her big smile, you'd never dream that her ass had been sitting in the clink for the past couple of weeks.

A picture of Sadeeq holding little Nafeese touched Jayla's heart a little. The child was wearing Sadeeq's oversized ball cap and he looked so cute. But Jayla flipped when she came across a picture of Radiance sitting on Sadeeq's lap, with the caption: *Date Night*.

Date-Fuckin-Night! This bum nigga and his trash bitch are enjoying their lives like it's all good. Meanwhile, I'm in a living hell and being persecuted over bills that I didn't create.

She kicked the coffee table so hard, a bowl that was filled with decorative pinecones tumbled off and the sparkly objects flew all around the room.

Envy and rage cut like a knife. She would typically soothe those emotions with a quick run to KFC or Taco Bell, but food wasn't the answer this time. She knew with certainty that she wouldn't find any peace until she satisfied her urge for revenge.

The pocketknife in her purse probably wouldn't penetrate the way she wanted it to, so she trotted to the kitchen and took a long, sharp knife out of a drawer.

Outside, the starless sky was a brooding shade of deep purple. She hadn't intended to go back out into the cold night air, but fortunately, her anger enveloped her like a bubble of warmth.

She smiled throughout the drive from Mount Airy to Nicetown, and when she reached Glenwood Avenue, she parked at the end of the raggedy block and crept to the middle where Sadeeq's SUV was parked. The streetlights were defective, preventing any illumination of the vehicle.

Shrouded in darkness, Jayla knelt down on the cold pavement and went to work. The tires were so sturdy, she had to apply lots of pressure to get the tip of the blade inside the thick rubber. When she finally heard the sound of air whooshing out of the first tire, she felt a rush of adrenaline that gave her the energy to deflate the remaining tires.

All right, pussy, let's see how far you'll get driving around on rims.

She felt good, but the feeling of elation was short-lived. Instead of going straight home, she ended up making detours to both KFC and Taco Bell. At KFC, she bought extra crispy tenders, biscuits, and potato wedges. At Taco Bell, she bought every item on the dollar menu.

Back at home, with only crumbs left from the food she'd devoured, Jayla sank down on the sofa feeling bloated and miserable. Deeply ashamed of herself, she dropped her head in her hands and cried. The helpless sobs that emerged seemed to come from the very depths of her soul.

She hugged herself and rocked back and forth, whispering, "Why can't I be like a normal person and eat regular-sized portions of food?" Sniffling and crying, she continued her self-directed tirade. "I hate being so fucking greedy. If I don't stop binge-eating, and get some self-control, I'm going to end up being a bed-ridden bitch that weighs four or five hundred pounds and requires a crane to lift my big ass out of bed. That's not cute!"

When the tears finally stopped falling, she made up her mind to take the first step toward changing her life. Gastric bypass surgery was a drastic measure, but she felt she had no choice.

Also, there would be no more cyberstalking Sadeeq and
Radiance. Watching their lives online was detrimental to her
emotional well-being. It was finally time to do something
positive for herself. Going under the knife seemed like the
best course of action.

Chapter 18

Binge-eating and binge-watching TV series was getting old, but Bailee was stuck in an emotional rut. It was the thirteenth day of the St. Croix trip and she was glad to have a ringside seat in the living room where she'd be able to hear Trent trying his key in the lock when he returned tomorrow. He was going to need a court order and a police escort to get inside the condo.

And even a police escort might not be able to save him from an unexpected knife wound or sudden bullet to the groin.

Permanently maiming Trent was worth five years of jail time. With good behavior she'd get out in two or three, and she'd only be in her mid-thirties. Of course, as a violent criminal, she'd be unemployable. After her meltdown at First Mutual, she was already unemployable in the banking industry, so what did she care about future job prospects?

Once she was eligible to receive her inheritance, she could live off the money for the rest of her life as long as she was frugal…or if she invested wisely. Unfortunately, she didn't know anything about investing.

But Giselle did.

Remembering that Giselle was her worst enemy in the world, she realized she couldn't turn to her for financial advice.

She had no one to turn to.

Except Jayla.

Sadly, Bailee hadn't been much of a friend lately, refusing to respond to Jayla's texts or phone calls. She simply didn't have the strength to talk to Jayla or anyone else.

It was difficult enough having to interact with the locksmith, and he was the quiet type. He probably would have been more talkative and friendly if his nostrils hadn't been assaulted by the smell of rotting food that emanated from the kitchen.

The trash bin overflowed with garbage in used plastic containers that Bailee hadn't felt like carrying down the hall to the trash chute. Taking out the trash had been Trent's job and she'd be damned if she was going to trudge through the building laden down with trash bags while he relaxed and soaked up island sunshine.

If the neighbors decided to launch a complaint about the stench coming from her condo, then so be it. Bailee was at the point where she hated everyone and saw no reason to be considerate of a single soul.

No one has been considerate of me, she thought, sticking her hand into a bowl of buttery popcorn.

Too depressed and listless to continue venturing out into the cruel, cruel world to pick up gourmet meals, she'd resorted to having groceries delivered. Groceries that consisted of lots of snack food and easy-to-prepare sandwiches and frozen dinners.

A rank odor wafted up to her nose and she shot a look of disgust toward the kitchen. She'd have to call a cleaning service because she was much too lethargic to do anything about the trash or the dirty dishes that were piling up.

Escaping the funk from the kitchen, she cut off the TV in the living room, grabbed the popcorn, and moved to her bedroom.

She turned on the bedroom TV, and after situating herself in a comfortable position on the bed, she cushioned the bowl of popcorn between her thighs. She frowned when she noticed that the unpleasant smell from the kitchen had worked its way into the bedroom and was conspicuously close.

She sniffed under her armpits and grimaced at the musty smell. She swiped a finger along the crevice between her thigh and groin and took a whiff, and then nearly hurled from the overpowering stench.

Wrinkling her brows, she pondered when she had last bathed, and concluded it was on that disastrous last day at work.

Her lack of hygiene sent her running to the bathroom to take a long shower. Afterward, as if suddenly aware of her recent eating habits, she stepped on the scale and let out a yelp. She'd picked up fifteen extra pounds and was surprised that it was possible to gain so much in such a short time span.

It was clearly time to stop sulking and take charge of her life. She had to either accept her big-girl status and love the body she was in or do something about it. She knew for certain that she was inviting diabetes, high blood pressure, heart disease, and certain forms of cancer into her life if she continued to eat unhealthily and pack on more pounds.

But she didn't know how to change her compulsive overeating. Food had always been a Band-Aid for duress and anxiety. With all the stress in her life, she needed the comfort of food more now than ever. In fact, the guilt over the numbers on the scale triggered an urge to fill up a bowl with large scoops of ice cream.

Something sweet to complement the salty popcorn would make her feel a lot better.

At the rate that she was shoveling down tons of food, she was going to end up having to use a walker to drag her hefty body around.

With her future looking bleak on all fronts, Bailee decided she had no choice but to fight back. If she expected to save herself, she had to accept that she couldn't do it on her on. She needed help.

Feeling more empowered than she had in a long time, she opened her laptop and searched online for a weight loss retreat. No matter what the cost of the program or the amount of time required, she was up to the challenge of taking control of her life.

It was settled. Travel arrangements had been made. Luggage was packed with toiletries, workout wear, swimwear, and casual clothes for dining. A huge amount of money had been withdrawn from her bank account to pay the fee to a posh fitness resort in Florida that guaranteed weight loss.

Bailee was ready for the healthy getaway, and excited about the mind, body, and spirit transformation that the resort promised. She'd ticked everything off the list of necessities except water shoes for the beach, which she'd have to pick up from the mall.

Filled with hope that there might be a rainbow at the end of the storm she'd been through, she felt optimistic enough to finally return Jayla's numerous calls.

"Hey, what are you doing?" she asked when Jayla picked up.

"Hello, stranger. It's about damn time you called me back," Jayla replied sarcastically. "Where have you been? I was starting to think that maybe Trent had smoked your ass, dismembered your body, and stuffed it in a plastic container."

"My goodness! You watch too much of the ID Channel, girl," Bailee said with nervous laughter.

"I'm glad you called. I tried to contact you at work, and when I found out you were no longer employed there, I almost passed out, girl. What the hell is going on, Bailee?"

"I've done a lot of soul-searching."

"Okay. And?"

"And I've decided it's time to make some positive changes." Bailee chose not to disclose the intimate details of how horribly her life had exploded since she'd last spoken to Jayla. She couldn't bring herself to reveal the treacherous deeds of Trent and Giselle, nor could she bear to talk about her embarrassing exit from her job.

"Are you saying that leaving your job is a positive change?"

"Yeah."

"I realize you're not hurting for money, but I thought you loved having such a high-power position at the bank."

"The job was stressful, and I've discovered that I love myself more than any job. With a pending divorce and the strain of my position at the bank, my eating has gotten out of control."

"Girl, tell me about it. After all that shit that went down with Sadeeq, I've gained so much, I'm afraid to get on the scale."

"Well, I *did* get on the scale, and the numbers were horrifying," Bailee confessed. "I believe I have an eating disorder, and I can't fix it on my own. So, I'm leaving on Monday—"

"Leaving to go where?" Jayla blurted.

"An exclusive fitness retreat in Florida. And that's why I called you. I have to pick up some water shoes at the mall, and I'd like to have a last rendezvous with some good food. Can you meet me at the King of Prussia Mall around four, and then join me for dinner? My treat, of course," Bailee added, aware that Jayla was always broke.

"Sure, I can meet you there. By the way, I have some news to share, too."

"Oh, yeah. What's up?"

"I'll tell you all about it when I see you at the mall," Jayla said mysteriously.

"Cool. See you at four."

With a few hours to kill before meeting Jayla, Bailee composed an e-mail to Trent.

Trent, No need to stop by to pick up your things when you get back from St. Croix. I've changed the locks. I've arranged for a moving company to transport your personal effects to my mother's house where I assume you'll be taking up residence and enjoying the life of a kept man. Contained in your belongings will be your stupid reclining chair. As per our prenuptial agreement, all the contents of the home, including wedding gifts, will remain in my possession.

Good Luck & Good Riddance, Bailee

She could have omitted the cutting remarks and the petty insults, but she was bitter, and rightfully so. Therefore, she saw no reason to act like a mature adult or to pretend that their breakup was amicable.

Fortunately, her pain seemed to be subsiding, somewhat. The fact that she was willing to get out of the condo and socialize with Jayla was proof that she was on the road to recovery.

Leaving the shoe department at Nordstrom, Bailee met up with Jayla in the women's department. Jayla was so engrossed in browsing through the sleek and stylish garments, she didn't notice Bailee approaching.

"I think you're in the wrong department, Miss. Plus-sizes are downstairs." Bailee teasingly mimicked the crisp tone of a sales associate.

Jayla looked up at Bailee and laughed. "I am not in the wrong department, honey," she informed.

"Oh, really? Then, who are you shopping for? Do you have a new, skinny, best friend?"

"Nope. I'm shopping for myself," Jayla declared with a hand on her hip. "I'm getting clothes for the new, skinny body I'm gonna be rocking shortly. I've already started filling my closet with tiny clothes, and I want to add more."

Bailee raised a brow.

"I had a consultation for weight loss surgery, and I was approved," Jayla announced, beaming as she spoke. "That's the news I wanted to share. Girl, my whole life is about to change, and I'm so excited."

"When is the surgery?"

"In two weeks and I can't wait. My insurance is paying for everything, and I've been approved to take time off from work. My mother is going to use her vacation time, so she can stay with me and help during my recovery period. Isn't that thoughtful of her? There's nothing like a mother's love."

The shadow that fell over Bailee's face at the mention of a mother's love didn't go unnoticed by Jayla.

"What's wrong?" Jayla asked.

"Nothing." Bailee cut her gaze away from Jayla.

"Something's wrong. I know you, Bailee, and you look like you're about to cry. What did I say that upset you?" Jayla persisted.

"It's nothing. Seriously." Bailee wished she could confide in Jayla about Trent and Giselle, but it was too soon to talk about it without breaking down and getting hysterical in the mall. Maybe she'd be able to have the conversation when she returned from the retreat.

"How much weight do you think you'll lose with the surgery?" Bailee asked, changing the subject.

"I'm not sure about the approximate number of pounds, but from what I've read, I'll probably drop down quite a few dress sizes. Can you picture me wearing a size ten—or smaller?" Jayla picked up a short black dress and held it in front of her.

"Really? I haven't worn a ten since elementary school."

"Me, either, chile. But that's the goal. I've friended a bunch of chicks on Instagram who had the surgery and their before and after pictures are amazing. They got so thin after the surgery, they look like totally different people now."

"But surgery is so drastic, Jayla. Are you sure going under the knife is something you want to do?"

"I'm positive."

"When I get back from the resort, I'll have to keep up the program at home, and we could join a gym together and maybe hike on weekends."

"No, thanks, Bailee. We've been talking about working out for years, and I'm still paying off a gym membership that I rarely use," Jayla retorted. "In order for me to work out, I'd need a drill-sergeant type of personal trainer coming to my place to force me to work out."

"How about Weight Watchers then? I'll join with you when I get back."

"I tried that already, and I'm not dealing with those points and their frozen meals again. It doesn't work for me. This time, I'm taking the shortcut around all that mess and getting the surgery done."

"I can't believe you're so hell-bent on surgery? Aren't you scared? Suppose something happens while you're under anesthesia? Surgery seems like an excessive way to achieve the same results you can get on your own with a little willpower and self-love."

"Wow, you already sound like a cult member and you haven't even started getting brainwashed by the leaders of the fat farm, yet."

"It's not a fat farm. It's a healthy lifestyle retreat."

"Whatever. You lose weight your way and I'll do it my way. You can fight food urges all you want, but I'm going to let the surgeon cut my stomach down by eighty percent. After the surgery, I won't be hungry and thinking about food all the time."

"So, you're not going to eat any good food, ever again?"

"I'll still grub on my favorite foods, but I'll eat much smaller portions."

Bailee shook her head. "I'd rather adhere to a nutritionally sound diet and learn the root cause of my overeating than lie on an operating table and think someone is going to cut out the problem. Besides, what are you going to do if one of those staples pop?"

Jayla sighed. "The gastric sleeve is going to make my stomach so small, I'll get full faster, and I'll vomit if I overeat."

Bailee grimaced. "That sounds unhealthy...and really wrong on so many levels."

"I think it's great that we've both decided to make a change. I'm not criticizing your method, so how come you don't have anything positive to say about mine? You sound like a hater, Bailee."

Bailee chewed on her lip thoughtfully. "You're right, Jayla, and I'm sorry for being judgmental. It's one of my fatal flaws and something I'm going to work on. I'm happy you want to make a change, but I'm a little concerned, that's all. But, don't worry, I'll get over it."

"You'll definitely get over it when you see me rocking my new, miniature clothes," Jayla responded, swaying her hips sexily for emphasis.

"Stop it, Jayla," Bailee admonished as she quickly looked over her shoulder, hoping no one had spotted Jayla's gyrations.

"*You* stop, Bailee! You're entirely too wound up, worrying about the people in this store. I don't care what anyone thinks of me. Girl, don't let me get to twerking in front of all these uppity Nordstrom shoppers," Jayla threatened with a devilish smile while still swiveling her hips.

"Oh, no, please don't. It's time to get out of here." Laughing, Bailee tugged Jayla's arm.

"Noooo, let me go, I have to practice my skinny-girl twerk," Jayla replied, enjoying the embarrassment she was causing Bailee.

"Aren't you hungry? I'm treating you to dinner at Morton's," Bailee blurted as a last-ditch effort to get Jayla to behave.

Jayla straightened up. "Morton's? Cool! I thought we were eating at the food court, but since we're going to a high-end restaurant, I'll save my twerking routine for another time."

"Thank God," Bailee said as she guided Jayla out of the department store.

Chapter 19

"He's my godson, and I'm not going to turn my back on him when he needs me," Lorraine Carpenter asserted as she scooped a heaping portion of potato salad next to the two large fried chicken breasts on Jayla's plate.

"But you haven't seen Derek in years, Mom. He's probably not the nice church boy you used to know; he's a hardened criminal now."

"I doubt if Derek is a hardened criminal. We both know that he was falsely accused of robbing that man at gunpoint. That boy never touched a gun a day in his life."

"I know, Mom, but prison does bad things to people. It changes them, makes them corrupt."

"That's nonsense." Lorraine made a dismissive gesture and then loaded Jayla's plate with green beans. Next, she piled three fluffy biscuits on a saucer next to the dinner plate. "Besides, who am I going to cook for after you have the surgery? You're not going to eat my good food anymore."

"Don't take it personal, and please don't act like losing this weight is a bad thing. I have to do this, so I can feel good about myself."

"Aw, sweetie, there's no reason not to feel good about yourself. You're beautiful and perfect just the way you are."

"No, I'm not." Jayla shook her head adamantly. "If I'm perfect, why does my boss constantly discriminate against me and only give me the shitty listings?"

"Watch your mouth," Lorraine cautioned. "You know we don't use profanity in this house!"

"Sorry, Mom," Jayla mumbled. "But seriously...if I'm so perfect, why do men only want to get me in bed, but none of them want to wife me?"

A look of pity crossed Lorraine's face. "I thought you didn't want to settle down."

"I've been fronting so you wouldn't feel sorry for me. I'm just a piece of ass to every man I've ever cared about."

Lorraine's features quickly formed into a stern expression. "I'm not your girlfriend; I'm your parent, Jayla, and I don't want to hear another word about any fornicating that you're involved in."

"It's the twenty-first century, Mom; everybody's fornicating. The point is, I want to experience being normal for once in my life. I'm tired of dragging all this weight around and I'm tired of people looking at me and seeing someone they either despise or feel sorry for. For once in my life, I want to experience what it feels like to be admired and respected."

"It's not the outside that counts; it's the goodness of your heart."

"That sounds good in theory, but in our society, it's not true. Everyone judges me and I'm sick of it."

Lorraine gave Jayla's shoulder a squeeze. "I understand, sweetie. But I'm going to miss spoiling you with my cooking. It's one of the ways that I express love," she said, stroking Jayla's hair affectionately.

Jayla forked up a mound of potato salad. "I know, Mom."

"On the bright side, with Derek having to eat that bad prison food for all these years, I'm sure he'll appreciate all the love I put into my dishes."

Jayla released a long sigh. "I don't want to sound negative, but whether Derek was guilty or innocent of the crime, he's a convicted felon, now. Being a single woman, I think you should reconsider living under the same roof with him."

Lorraine put a hand on her hip. "I'll have you know, I changed Derek's diapers. I'm like a second mother to him. What exactly do you think my godson would do to me?"

Rape and rob you, maybe? "I don't know, Mom. It's so hard to know who to trust anymore."

Times like now, when a strong male presence would have come in handy, Jayla couldn't help missing the father she barely remembered. A firefighter killed in the line of duty, her father was only twenty-nine years old when he passed. Lorraine had vowed never to love another man again, and turned to the church for support.

Lorraine took a seat at the table. Before digging into the potato salad, she pointed her fork at Jayla. "Derek's mother was my best friend, and before she passed, I made a promise to look out for her boy. If she was still here and you needed help, Jayla, I'm sure she'd look out for you. Where's your sense of Christian duty, child?"

"I don't have faith in people the way you do. Not anymore. I've learned the hard way that people present themselves one way and turn out to be another."

"Well, you need to get prayed up like I am. With God on your side, there's no reason to fear any man," Lorraine said, now pointing a big serving spoon at Jayla. "Listen, I don't want you treating Derek like he's a criminal when he moves in here, do you hear me? We're going to welcome him into this family and help him get back on his feet."

"If you say so," Jayla said grudgingly.

"I hate to think about what that boy has been through, caged up with a bunch of animals. I intend to provide him with a home where he'll feel safe and loved, and reunite him with the church."

"When exactly is he getting out?"

"Next week."

"You're kidding. Are you going to leave him alone in your home when you come to stay with me after my surgery?"

"That's the plan."

"Mom! He could rob you blind while you're away."

"What do you suggest I do? Renege on my promise to look after you?"

Jayla frowned. "No, you can't leave me to fend for myself while I'm incapacitated! I think you should tell Derek that he has to stay at a halfway house or a shelter. Anywhere but here."

"I'll do no such thing. But I do have an idea."

Biting into a crunchy piece of chicken, Jayla gave Lorraine her attention.

"Instead of me staying at your place, why don't you stay here with Derek and me?"

Jayla winced. "Ew. I don't want to be around a strange man while I'm recuperating. Besides, I'd rather be in my own bed, around my things when I'm not feeling well."

"Why're you acting like he's a stranger when you practically grew up together?"

"I only saw Derek on holidays, and I haven't laid eyes on him since I was like fourteen or fifteen. For all we know, he could have grown up to be a serial killer."

"His mother raised him to be a good, God-fearing boy, and I've made up my mind. You'll stay here with Derek and me, and that's the end of the discussion." Lorraine leaned back in her chair and folded her arms.

Despite having to drain her meager savings account to pay a bankruptcy attorney, Jayla felt hopeful about her future. As she sat in the attorney's office signing off on paperwork, she could physically feel the burden of debt lifting from her shoulders.

"The first thing you should do after the bankruptcy is final is open a new line of credit," the attorney advised.

Interested, Jayla sat straighter. "Really? I thought the bankruptcy would remain on my credit report for seven years."

"That's true, but you'll find that some creditors, like car dealerships, for instance, will take a chance on you because they're aware you don't have any pending debt that'll prevent you from paying your bills on time."

Jayla's eyes lit up. The plain-looking Subaru she drove was not sexy at all, and it had been acting up lately. She could use a newer model car to go along with her new body, and she couldn't wait to get behind the wheel of something sleek and shiny with that new car smell on the inside.

"Establishing credit and rebuilding your credit history is a step in the right direction," the attorney continued.

You don't have to tell me twice!

Things were starting to look better and better by the second and she wondered if she could dare to dream that her good luck might lead her to a good man that didn't try to hide their relationship behind closed doors like it was a dirty secret.

What would it be like to be kissed and hugged in public, and treated like she was highly valued? All her life she'd observed other women holding hands with their man or having a protective arm around their waists as they strolled along the city streets. Yet, those simple gestures had never been extended to Jayla.

At least not in public.

But those days would soon be over, she thought brightly. She would no longer be the fat chick who was kept hidden.

She could picture herself getting engaged in the foreseeable future. Getting married. And having kids, like everyone else.

"We should have a court date in sixty days," the attorney said, breaking into Jayla's thoughts. "I'll keep you posted."

Jayla and the attorney shook hands. She walked out of the law office and emerged into the crisp air feeling like a brand-new woman, and feeling grateful for the opportunity to press the reset button on her life.

A text from Lorraine telling Jayla that Derek had arrived earlier than she'd expected sent Jayla speeding down Roosevelt Boulevard after her meeting with the bankruptcy attorney.

She drove so fast and erratically, she nearly sideswiped a shiny Mercedes, and for that error, she received a barrage of epithets from the driver.

"I'm sorry," she mouthed.

"Fuck you," the driver exploded.

Instinctually, she was about to give the angry motorist her middle finger, but she didn't have time for road rage. Not wanting to leave her mother alone with a jailbird who could potentially knock her upside her head, snatch her purse, and rape her, Jayla sped along. She only took her foot off the gas pedal when she approached red light cameras.

When she reached her mother's house, she parked hastily and dashed inside with her hand wrapped around the handle of the blade that she took out of her handbag and tucked inside her coat pocket.

"Mom!" Jayla yelled as she let herself in with her key.

"We're in the kitchen, honey," Lorraine called in a sweet, lilting voice that was usually reserved for her beloved pastor.

With a sense of relief, she removed her hand from the handle of the knife and followed the pleasant aromas that drifted from the kitchen. Seated at the table was a tall, thick, fine-ass man, the color of brick clay with facial features so strongly masculine, they could have been chiseled from stone.

His hair was styled in a trendy, high fade with a tangle of curls on top. He looked nothing like the gangly boy she remembered.

The only telltale signs that the hot, broad-shouldered, beefed-up man in the kitchen was her childhood friend, Derek Gallion, were his warm, cocoa-brown eyes, his distinctive high cheekbones, and his complexion.

"Look at you, Jayla. All grown up and beautiful." The tone of his deep voice was a rich mixture of street jargon and eloquence. His words of praise were followed by a bright smile that took his good looks to another, more extreme level of hotness.

He got up from the table and gave Jayla a big hug.

Derek's steely arms felt good around her, but she didn't want to let her guard down around him. She wriggled free from his embrace. "Hi, Derek. You've changed a lot since I last saw you."

As her eyes appraised him, she noticed her mother smiling in approval, as if she was ready to call Pastor and get the two of them hitched.

Lorraine had wanted to marry Jayla off as soon as she'd graduated college, and now, with Jayla in her thirties, it appeared that Lorraine was desperate enough to hand her over to a felon.

An easy-on-the-eyes felon, but a felon nonetheless.

"Sit down, Jayla, and let me make you a plate," Lorraine offered. Derek jumped to his feet and pulled out Jayla's chair.

"I see that being in prison didn't cause you to forget the good manners your mother instilled in you," Lorraine said appreciatively.

"No, ma'am. I'll always be a gentleman, despite being wrongly incarcerated for the past ten years."

"The injustice of it all," Lorraine said, patting Derek on the shoulder. "Don't you worry, hon. Jayla and I are going to help you put those unpleasant memories behind you, and help you move forward."

Speak for yourself, Mom. After dealing with Sadeeq, my antennae are up for con artists, and the jury is out on Derek.

"Thank you for kindness and hospitality, Ms. Lorraine," Derek said. "I don't plan to be a burden for long. As soon as I can get on my feet—"

"You are not a burden," Lorraine interjected. "You're like a member of our family, and the only thing I expect is for you to accompany me to church on Sundays and let the Holy Word fill you up with understanding and forgiveness."

Oh, Lord, here she goes. Better Derek than me sitting up in church all day!

"Yes, ma'am, I'll go to church with you," Derek responded, his head down as he dug a fork into a baked potato that was loaded with butter, cheddar cheese, and sour cream.

Jayla couldn't help feeling sorry for Derek. Her mother hadn't been able to drag her to church since she was in high school, but poor Derek, being Lorraine's captive houseguest, had no choice but to indulge her wishes and sit up in Sunday service, listening to Pastor go on and on for hours.

After the meal, Derek insisted on clearing the table and washing the dishes, giving Lorraine an opportunity to get Jayla alone in the living room. "Do you see how big and handsome that boy turned out to be? I'm telling you, he's husband material," she said, beaming.

"Slow your roll, Mom. He's straight out of prison, and we don't know what kind of damage was done to him in that place. He could be all messed up in the head. Furthermore, he was tried and convicted. So, despite his good manners, he could very well be the violent criminal the court said he was."

Lorraine sucked her teeth and waved a dismissive hand. "That's Helena's boy in there, and he's sweet as pie. You can see with your own eyes that there's nothing violent about him. It was a case of mistaken identity because they think all black men look alike, you know that."

Jayla sighed. "That's true, but he's had ten years to become an expert in the art of deception, and I'm not going to give him a pass merely because he's Ms. Helena's son...and you shouldn't either."

"Are you saying I should kick my best friend's son out?"

"No, but I am saying you should keep your eyes on him and keep your wallet and other valuables out of sight...as a precaution."

"That's ridiculous. I'm not living in fear inside my own home. Just give him a chance, Jayla, and stop treating him like a suspect."

"I believe in being cautious," Jayla said firmly.

Lorraine sighed. "I'm going upstairs to tidy up the guest room. I want you to join Derek in the kitchen and make small talk. Get to know him better."

Jayla frowned.

"Go on, now," Lorraine insisted, motioning with her hands. "Make him feel welcome, Jayla. It's the Christian thing to do."

Jayla rolled her eyes toward the ceiling and then grudgingly treaded to the kitchen.

"I heard what you were saying to your mom, and I'm sorry that I make you feel uncomfortable. It's understandable, though. Hopefully, I won't be a burden for too long," he said with hurt glimmering in his eyes.

"Derek, I didn't mean to hurt your feelings—"

He held up a hand. "Let me finish. I didn't commit armed robbery. I've never owned or even touched a loaded gun. If I could change anything, I would have never stepped foot into that Chinese store that night, but what's done is done. I missed out on being a comfort to my mother when she was sick and needed me, and that's a pain in my heart that I have to live with for the rest of my life. I'm not asking for pity; I just wish you'd give me a chance to prove that I'm a decent person. I'm not a freeloader, and I plan to pay your mother back for my room and board."

"She doesn't expect—"

"I insist, and I told her that."

"Listen, Derek, I'm sorry that I made you feel bad, but the way the world is today, it's not wise to put blind faith into anyone."

"Understood," he said morosely.

Feeling awful, she patted him on the back, and feeling his muscles beneath his shirt excited her. His hard body was a reminder of how much she missed having a man in her life. Despite his good looks and obvious strong back, she wasn't looking for anything serious with Derek.

But, she sure could use some good dick. With Derek, she wouldn't allow her feelings to get involved. She'd use him for sex the way so many men had used her.

As she imagined herself dropping over on her lunch break from work, and jumping into bed with Derek while her mother was at work, Jayla allowed her hand to meander down to his crotch.

He caught her by the wrist. "Yo, what are you doing?"

"I'm sorry, I thought…" Her voice faltered in embarrassment.

"I'm gay, Jayla," he whispered. "Can you keep that information to yourself? Being a Christian and all, I don't think your mom would understand."

Jayla nodded dumbly. Her gay-dar was completely off.

"I hope we can be close friends—like when we were kids," Derek offered.

Friends? Feeling humiliated and rejected, yet again, and this time by a gay dude, Jayla began to sob. "I feel like a fool," she admitted in a voice that cracked.

Derek gathered her in his arms. "Shh, shh. Don't cry. I'm sorry. I'm so sorry," he murmured as he patted her on the back.

Enclosed in his arms, Jayla caught a glimpse of her mother entering the kitchen. Jayla watched as her mother came to a complete stop while looking delighted and surprised at the same time.

Lorraine cleared her throat. "Sorry to interrupt you two love-birds." Her hand touched her heart. "I hoped you two would hit it off. Do I dare start dreaming about beautiful grandchildren?"

Jayla and Derek cut their eyes at each other and burst out laughing.

"Let's leave the grandkids out of it, Mom. I was just welcoming him home," Jayla said.

"Mmm-hmmm," Lorraine muttered dubiously. "I saw the sparks between you two the moment you set eyes on each other." She raised a cautioning finger. "But I insist that you two be respectful of my home. No hanky-panky while you're under my roof," Lorraine added sternly.

"Yes, ma'am. I would never disrespect your home or your daughter," Derek replied, allowing Lorraine to believe that he was attracted to Jayla, but would work hard to control himself.

Chapter 20

Bailee arrived at Gentle Breeze Wellness Center with no illusions. She was fully aware that the weight loss facility wouldn't provide her with a quick weight loss fix. Nor was it a beauty spa where she'd be pampered, either. The atmosphere was more clinical than glamorous. Her private room, for which she'd paid extra, certainly wasn't the Four Seasons, but it was comfortable and cheerful enough.

The focus of the retreat was on sustainable lifestyle changes. The structured environment, exercise classes, outdoor activities, and prepared meals would help Bailee with her journey toward a healthy lifestyle. The hefty price tag was well worth the opportunity to learn long-term weight management.

The place was exclusively for women and Bailee was glad. She didn't want a man standing on the treadmill next to her while she grunted and perspired.

During her tour of the facility, she noticed numerous signs that read: LOVE THE SKIN YOU'RE IN. She assumed the idea was to love yourself throughout the journey and not to feel that you weren't lovable until you reached your goal.

After the tour, she sat down to map out her personalized daily schedule with a perky health specialist named Susan.

Reading from a list in front of her, Susan offered Bailee the option of starting her day with morning meditation or a sunrise beach walk. Meditation sounded like a waste of time and Bailee opted for the beach walk.

"Breakfast is at seven-thirty and then there's Ultra Circuit Training in the gym, which is mandatory," Susan said.

"Okay," Bailee responded with a smile, though she suspected she'd be crying in the morning while trying to get through an hour of torture.

"At nine-forty-five, you have the option of Aqua Fit or Zumba Class."

Bailee picked the water fitness class. Working out in a pool seemed more pleasant than doing strenuous and complicated dance movements.

Susan went through the entire daily schedule, which not only included intense workouts, but also lectures on nutrition, cooking demonstrations, and counseling sessions. The grueling day ended each night at eight and, at that time, the women were free to mingle on the patio or hang out in the media/game room.

Bailee was certain she'd collapse in her bed every night at eight, too drained to socialize with the other women or sit around watching movies or TV.

Susan looked at her watch and stood. "Lunch starts in ten minutes, so I'll walk you to the dining hall. Since your day doesn't officially begin until tomorrow, you can use the downtime to either relax on the beach or at poolside. I advise you to check out some of the activities that you didn't select, just to get a feel of everything the program offers. Who knows, you might want to switch some things around."

The two women walked to the dining hall, and then Susan shook hands with Bailee and wished her well. Aside from the cooking staff, Bailee was alone in the brightly lit room. She took a seat and studied today's menu, which was a meager meal consisting of a medium-sized salad with raw almonds and a tiny portion of dressing on the side. She was offered a tall glass of water with a lemon wedge floating on top, and also her choice of black coffee or green tea with no sweetener.

Her stomach growled in protest. Desperately craving a buttery roll to go along with the healthy salad, it sank in that her stay at Gentle Breeze would not be pleasant or easy. It would require a great deal of sacrifice, inner and outer strength, and the ability to withstand starvation.

After lunch, Bailee went to her room to lie down. Tomorrow would be the beginning of a grueling ordeal, and she figured it was a good idea to relax and luxuriate while she could. She watched a movie on her laptop and then took a leisurely nap. When she awakened, she freshened up and decided to familiarize herself with the facility.

After checking out the women participating in a variety of classes, it was clear that the clientele at Gentle Breeze all tipped the scale at well over two hundred and fifty pounds. It was refreshing not to be the biggest girl on the premises as she was accustomed to being.

At her former job at the bank, she'd been surrounded by the stick-figure, size-zero young waifs who held assistant positions. Even the more mature women in upper management didn't dare carry any extra poundage, and they all appeared to be anorexic, as if they were unwilling to eat more than a few celery stalks per meal. Bailee always felt out of place with her female coworkers and colleagues, but she felt right at home at Gentle Breeze.

As she continued sightseeing, she was surprised to see a male fitness instructor. She had assumed that the "exclusively female" resort also included the staff.

Boy, was she wrong. Sitting at poolside, she observed an instructor that looked like the Middle Eastern version of Brad Pitt. He had blond-streaked dark hair, light-brown eyes, and succulent lips. He was too handsome for his own good, distracting the women with his perfectly sculpted body while they tried to concentrate on his command to grip the side of the pool and lift their left leg up and down.

"You can lift your leg higher than that, Cindy," he admonished a crimson-cheeked member of the class.

"I'm trying, Brahim," Cindy replied, frowning as she strained to get her hefty leg up higher.

Brahim was a little gruff for Bailee's taste, and she thought about switching tomorrow's Aqua Fit class to Zumba. But she had a change of heart when she thought about the high-intensity workout that Zumba required.

As Brahim barked out orders, he stood in the center of the pool. The sun beamed down and encircled him like he was a bronzed deity, and its rays seemed to highlight every detail of his magnificent physique.

Deciding that the Florida sun was hot enough without Brahim emitting even more heat, Bailee left the pool area and went for a walk around the landscaped grounds where the shade of tall trees could cool her off.

Walking along a smooth-paved path, she passed colorful flower-beds and vibrant green shrubbery. Engulfed by a sense of inner peace, she inhaled the fragrant air and smiled. Coming to Florida was an important step in rebuilding her confidence. She'd given Giselle and Trent far too much headspace, and it was now time to put them out of her mind and reclaim her life.

Lost in her thoughts as she explored, she'd walked much farther than she'd intended. The violet and tangerine hues of the setting sun glimmered through the lush foliage that lined the walkway on the grounds, reminding her that it would be dinnertime soon. She was already starving from the paltry lunch she'd been served.

God forbid if she missed dinner and ended up having to go to bed hungry.

Walking fast, she circled back, and was breathing heavily as she lumbered up a steep incline she hadn't counted on. Somehow, she'd taken a wrong turn and had ended up at the back of the building instead of the front entrance. Afraid that the door would be locked, she sighed with relief when the handle turned easily.

Finding herself in an unfamiliar corridor, she couldn't figure out how to get back to the main lobby. When she heard voices emanating from a room that was a few feet ahead, she picked up her steps and stopped abruptly when she happened upon a shocking sight.

Brahim, the instructor of the Aqua Fit class, was standing in the shadowy corridor. Brahim's back was against the wall with his eyes closed blissfully while Cindy, the rosy-cheeked member of his class, was crouched in front of him, her head bobbing as her lips stretched around his colossal hard-on.

What the hell? Bailee took off in the opposite direction, speed-walking as her mind swirled with questions. Should she report what she'd seen? Were they two consenting adults or was Brahim abusing his authority and taking advantage of Cindy?

After giving it some thought, Bailee decided to stay out of it. Cindy was an adult and not a child that needed protection. If low self-esteem had caused Cindy to feast hungrily on her instructor's dick in a darkened hallway, devouring it like it was a juicy piece of meat, then it would take a lot more than Bailee's snitching for Cindy to discover her self-worth.

After a couple of wrong turns, Bailee found herself in the familiar lobby area, and from there, she easily made her way to the dining hall.

Munching as slowly as possible on turkey breast wrapped in

Romaine lettuce leaves, Bailee's thoughts wandered to the sex act she'd happened upon. Though unethical, it was probably pretty common for the staff and clientele to hook up.

But Bailee was certain she wouldn't fall victim to the lure of hooking up with a member of the staff, no matter how intense and spectacular forbidden sex could be.

As she grew close to finishing the unfulfilling turkey wrap, her stomach still felt empty, and she concluded that it was entirely possible for her to be persuaded to suck a dick in exchange for a big, meaty, fried-oniony, dripping with oil, high-caloric Philly cheesesteak.

On the third day of intense workouts and having to subsist on rabbit food, Bailee was at her wit's end and stormed into Susan's office to complain.

"I'm hungry all the time, I'm weak, my head hurts, and every muscle in my body is sore, as if I've been taking severe beatings. I feel like a torture victim at Guantanamo Bay instead of a valued client at an upscale resort. I don't see one good reason why I should stay in this abusive environment."

Susan clasped her fingers and aimed a practiced smile on Bailee. "As you're aware, the fee is not refundable," Susan gently reminded her.

"I don't give a damn," Bailee exploded, feeling dangerously close to coming across the desk and slapping the smile off the so-called health specialist's face.

Susan drew in a long, patient breath. "It's perfectly normal for you to feel like bailing on the program. But that's not the answer. Believe me, you'll regret it and you'll be terribly disappointed in yourself if you don't complete the program."

"How do you people expect anyone to get in an effective

workout if they're weak and lightheaded from hunger?" Bailee demanded.

"You're getting twelve hundred calories per day."

"That's not enough!" Bailee snapped.

The rational part of her realized she was behaving like a brat, but starvation and pain were causing her to become unhinged. She'd been having seductive dreams about barbecued spare ribs and she yearned to sink her teeth into a hearty meal.

"Give it another day or two, and I promise you'll start feeling fuller after your meals," Susan assured her.

Bailee responded by rolling her eyes like a petulant schoolgirl. On her way out of the office, it took all of her self-restraint not to do a clean sweep of everything on Susan's desk.

Concluding that she didn't have the strength to attend Cardio Bootcamp, she went to her room and sulked. After an hour of feeling sorry for herself and debating packing her bags, she finally decided to stick it out. Imagining going home and accidentally bumping into the beautiful couple, Trent and Giselle, prompted her to stop the hysterics and pull herself together.

Propelled by the desire to morph into the best version of herself that was humanly possible, Bailee rose from the bed and checked her schedule. She'd missed Cardio Bootcamp and was already five minutes late for Butt & Gut class. Maddie, the instructor of the class, didn't tolerate tardiness. Grabbing her water bottle, Bailee rushed out of her room.

It was her hope that she'd be able to enter the class as inconspicuously as possible, but when she arrived, she was thrown off by the sight of a carob-complexioned man who was instructing the class instead of Maddie.

He looked vaguely familiar, but she couldn't recall where she'd seen him before.

Taken off guard by his sexiness, she sucked in a deep gasp that escalated into a bout of coughing. As she quickly guzzled down water, he glanced at her. It was a cursory glance at first, but then his dark gaze locked with hers, and in that moment, time stood still.

He picked up a clipboard and perused it. "Bailee Evans?"

When he said her name, her heart jumped so hard, it stole her breath. "Yes, I'm Bailee," she said, her voice barely audible.

She cleared her throat and spoke a little louder. "Uh, what happened to Maddie?"

"She had a family crisis, so I'll be taking her place for a while. My name's Hayden Charles. Why don't you grab a mat and join us, okay?" He pointed to the mats that were stacked against the wall.

Hayden announced that his abdominal workout was crunch-free and that he'd developed a program that worked the entire core to tighten the tummy.

Since Maddie had been a merciless, crunch-Nazi, Bailee was pleased to be finished with sit-ups and crunches.

But it turned out that Hayden's method of rapid leg lifts and squatting while doing side bends was not easy, either. While the rest of the class groaned in pain as they twisted their waists, touching right elbows down to their left knees, Bailee took a breather and drank in the glorious sight of Hayden.

A closely-cropped dark beard accentuated a strong jawline. His Mohawk fade haircut featured kinky curls from his forehead down to the nape of his neck, and the diagonal shaved lines that decorated his temples gave him a tribal look that oozed masculinity. Muscles bulged everywhere. Biceps, shoulders, thighs, and she couldn't help fantasizing about being grasped by his strong hands.

His eyes flitted over to her. "No slacking off, Bailee," he said, his silken voice freeing her from the trance she'd been in.

He walked over to her and knelt down. It made her nervous

when he clenched her waist to assist her with the torso twist. The intimacy made her feel awkward. Yet, at the same time, she felt a rush of heat moving through her, causing liquid warmth to moisten her crotch.

She lowered her gaze, hoping to conceal the smoldering desire in her eyes.

He resumed a standing position and looked down at her, making sure she was performing the movement correctly. "Good, good," he praised and then moved on to another member of the class.

Sweat poured off Bailee, and she wasn't sure if she was sweating from overexertion or lust. What she did know was that she wouldn't be leaving Gentle Breeze anytime soon. If she made any changes to her plan, it would be to extend her stay.

Chapter 21

Jayla was ready to trade Bailee in for a new best friend—Derek. Derek was a good listener, giving his opinion without sounding the least bit judgmental, and best of all, he'd turned out to be a much better shopping partner than Bailee had ever been.

Two days before Jayla's surgery, he'd willingly allowed her to drag him through the mall from one store to the next and didn't utter a word of complaint when he discovered what she was actually shopping for.

She'd given him the impression that she needed essential items, like a new robe, bedroom slippers, and nightgowns to wear during her convalescence, but when she meandered into Victoria's Secret and began browsing through sexy lingerie that she couldn't possibly fit, Derek was instantly supportive.

He dove right in, helping to pick out pieces he thought would look good on her when she slimmed down.

Like two best buds with similar taste, they mocked ugly lingerie that had no business being in the store and they gave each other high-fives whenever Jayla found something fabulous that was on sale.

"The food court is calling me. Wanna get something to eat? My treat, of course," she added, realizing that Derek's funds were limited.

"You don't have to ask me twice about food," Derek responded, relieving Jayla of all the bags she'd accumulated.

"Are you gonna carry *all* the bags?" she asked, pleasantly surprised.

"Of course; it's the least I can do."

As they made their way toward the food court, Jayla noticed several different women giving Derek the eye, but he was oblivious to their attention.

"The food court sure has changed in the last ten years. So many options," he commented.

"What are you in the mood for—Chinese, pizza, Subway, Chick-fil-A?" Jayla asked.

"I'll have whatever you're getting."

"Since this is the last time I get to pig-out, I want a large pizza and Chinese food."

"I'll have pizza. Thanks for treating me," Derek said.

"You're welcome. To save time, why don't you order our pizzas while I stand in line for my Chinese food?"

"Um, uh, I can't do it," Derek stammered.

"Why not?"

"I feel self-conscious about ordering food."

"What?" Jayla gave him a puzzled look.

"It's stupid, but… The day I got out of prison, while I was on my way to your mom's house, I stopped at Wawa to get something to eat. I told the dude behind the counter what I wanted and he looked at me like I was crazy. He told me I had to place my order on the touchscreen." Derek shook his head woefully. "Man, I was so embarrassed and flustered, I just walked out the store."

"Why'd you walk out?"

"I don't know shit about a touchscreen, Jayla. I've been locked up for a long time."

"Oh, I get it. Okay, well, you don't need a touchscreen here. Just ask for the pizzas."

"I'd rather not. I need you to order for me. Certain things about being out in public make me feel panicked. I don't feel like I'm socialized yet."

"No problem, Derek," Jayla said, patting his arm consolingly.

Derek made two trips to their table, insisting upon carrying all the food and the drinks while Jayla sat at the table with the shopping bags.

As Derek set the pizza boxes down, Jayla noticed female passersby, once again, checking him out.

"You got these women losing their minds over your fine self," she said as Derek fussed over her, placing napkins in front of her and putting a straw in her soda.

As he sipped orange soda, he glanced around at his admirers and shrugged indifferently.

"Would you do me a favor?" Jayla asked.

"Anything. Well, almost anything, as long as it doesn't involve ordering food," he replied, laughing.

"Would you kiss me?" she asked with a pleading look in her eyes.

He frowned in confusion. "Why?"

"None of my so-called boyfriends ever treated me like I was special whenever we were out in public. To be honest, they never acted like we were together. I never experienced any public displays of affection. I want to know what it's like."

"Never?"

"Nope. No hand-holding, no arms around me, and no kissing in pubic. That's the way it's always been, and I accepted it," she confessed solemnly.

Derek's features softened in understanding and he leaned across the small table and kissed Jayla on the lips, running his fingers through her hair for good measure.

"Your next man is going to put you on a pedestal, and he's going to shower you with plenty of PDA."

"I hope so."

"He better or I'ma whip his ass."

Jayla smiled.

"I'm serious," Derek said as he used the corner of a napkin to wipe pizza sauce off the corner of Jayla's mouth.

Jayla finished all her food, but Derek managed to eat only one slice of pizza before the large crowd of people sitting close by in the food court became too much for him.

"Are you ready to leave?" Jayla inquired, noticing his anxiety.

He nodded and began gathering the bags. Big and strong, Derek held the pizza box in his arm, clenched all the shopping bags in his hand and draped his free arm around Jayla, eliciting the envy of female shoppers as he and Jayla strolled like lovers through the mall.

Jayla drove Derek back to Lorraine's house. She went inside to use the bathroom and discovered that Lorraine was at her church's evening prayer service.

Derek brought home his partially eaten box of pizza and immediately flipped the top open and resumed eating.

Though Jayla wasn't the least bit hungry, it was a force of habit to check the fridge and freezer. She discovered four containers of Ben & Jerry's and smiled as she unsealed the plastic from her favorite flavor.

"What kind of work were you doing before you got popped?" Jayla asked as she scraped around the rim, quickly filling the spoon with the delectable treat.

"I worked for my mom's church," Derek said.

"Doing what? Choir director? Let me find out you have musical abilities," she said jokingly.

"Nah, nothing like that. I worked with a construction team, rehabbing houses."

"Your church rehabbed houses?"

"Uh-huh, and then sold them at affordable prices. The church helped improve declining areas by providing low-income housing."

"That's great. So, what exactly was your role with the construction team?"

"At first, I was just the cleanup guy. Then I worked my way up to a painting apprentice. Over time, I learned everything from putting up drywall to roofing, carpentry, plumbing, and running electricity."

"Really? With your skills, I could get you a job with one of the contractors that works for my employer."

"Don't you have to be bonded?"

"Oh, damn. I forgot about your record. But I'm sure there are plenty of contractors that hire ex-cons. I know for a fact they're not that particular about who they hire, as long as the person can do the work. I've seen contractors with workers who can barely speak English, and I'm pretty certain those dudes don't have green cards."

"I think people are more willing to hire an illegal for cheap labor before they'll hire a black man with a criminal record."

"With your skills, you could work for yourself. Flipping houses is the way to go. Contractors are taking over the real estate industry, buying cheap properties for cash, fixing them up, and selling them for a nice profit."

"Where would I get cash?" Derek asked.

Jayla stuck her spoon in her ice cream and interlocked her fingers thoughtfully. "I could persuade my mother to use some of her retirement savings to invest in us."

"Us? How far do you plan on taking our little scheme? It's one thing to trick Ms. Lorraine into thinking I'm straight, but I'm not comfortable with hitting her up for money."

"As long as we pay her back, with interest, what difference does it make?"

"We can't ask her to risk her life's savings on something that's not a sure bet."

"It is a sure bet," she insisted. "It won't be easy, and we're gonna have to grind, but the end result will be worth it."

Derek looked downward, obviously unconvinced.

"Aren't you tired of losing, Derek? I know I am. I'm the low man on the totem pole at work. I'm good at what I do, yet my boss thinks so little of me, I'm not even offered the listings of African American clients—unless they're low-income. It burns me up that I'm rarely considered for high-end properties."

Derek listened quietly as he chomped down on a slice of pizza. Jayla noticed that he kept one arm near the pizza box, as if safe-guarding it from thieves. Being on high alert for food snatchers was probably a practice he'd picked up in prison.

"You did hard time for something you didn't do," Jayla reminded him. "The only thing the system is going to give you is paltry handouts, and you deserve so much more after all they took from you. I don't think I could do this on my own, but together, we'd be unstoppable."

He looked at her searchingly. "You think so?"

"Damn, right."

Mulling over Jayla's words, Derek chewed his food. He didn't say anything, but she could tell by the hint of a smile on his lips that he was beginning to warm up to the idea.

"At first I didn't understand why the universe would play with me like this. It didn't seem fair that a fine-ass, eligible bachelor, with no kids was staying with my mom, but I couldn't have him because he's gay. Now, I get it."

"Oh, yeah? Care to enlighten me?"

"I have a real estate license and you have contracting skills. We're both in a financial rut and we're both pretty disillusioned with life right now. But by combining our strengths, we can be a force, Derek. And we can make a lot of money."

"Do you really think Ms. Lorraine will help us out?"

"Yes, but she's convinced that we're into each other. In order to get her to invest in us, we'll have to make her believe that we're an official couple."

"I don't know about—"

"Don't worry, we'll tell her the truth as soon as the money starts rolling in. Once she starts getting a hefty income from our new enterprise, I guarantee she won't give a damn that we're only platonic friends."

"I like your plan, but I'm not licensed," Derek divulged.

"Who cares? I know how to forge paperwork. Don't even worry about your credentials—I got you."

Derek's shoulders seemed to visibly relax with the news that there was a realistic way for him to earn a living. Since he wasn't computer savvy, Jayla had been helping him fill out employment applications online, and he'd also been attending job fairs once a week, but so far, he hadn't had any luck finding a job.

She began swiping the screen of her phone. "I'm checking out foreclosure listings. We should have some numbers in mind before we approach my mother about the money."

Derek looked pained. "Jayla, your mom has been good to me, and I hate the idea of coming at her with a con."

"We're not conning her. Would you feel more comfortable if you knew that she is loaded? I mean, loaded! Her so-called retirement savings came from my father's life insurance policy, and she got another huge lump sum in survivor benefits from The National

Fallen Firefighters Foundation. She invested some of the money, and believe me, she won't starve to death by giving us a loan."

"Wow, I didn't know that."

"That's because she lives damn near like a pauper. All I got out of the money was a college education."

"Isn't that enough?" Derek asked.

"Not really. My mom could have raised me in a nice home in a safe neighborhood with a great school system, but she wouldn't touch the money. Don't get me wrong; she's a good woman, but she's a miser. The way she holds on to a dollar is like an illness, almost. And it's time for her to be a little generous with me, don't you think?"

Derek held his hands up. "I'm not getting in the middle of a family issue."

"Anyway, I'm not asking her to *give* me anything. I'm asking for a loan. It's not immoral to borrow money."

"You're right."

"So…are you on board with my plan?"

"It doesn't seem like anyone is gonna hire me, so I guess I don't have a choice."

"I wish you were a little more enthusiastic."

"Just because I'm not jumping up and down doesn't mean I'm not excited." Derek placed a hand over his heart. "Inside, I'm ecstatic, but I'm a little cautious about showing it. From past experiences, things don't tend to work out for me."

Jayla gave Derek a sympathetic smile. "That was the past, Derek. Trust me, this is going to work, and our lives are going to change. We'll talk to my mom about the money the night before I go into surgery. She'll be so afraid that something's going to happen to me while I'm under, she'll agree to anything."

Derek shook his head. "That's cold."

"Whatever. As soon as I finish recuperating, we're going to purchase our first fixer-upper and then—" Jayla abruptly fell silent, pushing the ice cream away and shaking her head as if it had suddenly gone sour.

"What's wrong?" Derek asked, concern wrinkling his forehead.

"There's a slight problem with my mom being an investor… she's going to want us to be legally married."

Derek frowned. "You're pushing it now, Jayla."

"Don't worry; it won't mean anything. It'll be a marriage of convenience," she assured him. "We can easily get a no-fault divorce if either us wants to get out of it."

Derek exhaled loudly. "Okay, but let's not bring up the subject of marriage if Ms. Lorraine doesn't say anything."

"Deal," Jayla said, reaching for the ice cream container and scooping out the last spoonful. "I wonder if I'll still have ice cream cravings after the surgery. I hope not. It would hurt me to my heart to yearn for it, but not be able to tolerate it."

"We'll find out in a few days."

"I know, right? I'm so excited."

Derek had taken on the habit of catering to Jayla, and he dutifully removed the empty ice cream container in front of her and tossed it into the trash bin. He opened the freezer and retrieved another pint of Ben & Jerry's, which he set in front of her. "Being that you only have a few more nights of sin, you might as well eat up."

"Truer words were never spoken," she said as she pulled off the protective plastic wrapping, lifted the lid, and stuck the spoon in.

Chapter 22

The Butt & Gut workout was deceptively rigorous. The movements had been slow and languid, giving the impression of a gentle workout. But the next morning Bailee woke up feeling like she'd been in a car wreck. Her abdominal area burned as if on fire and her buttocks pulsated with searing pain. The muscle soreness in her limbs caused her to wince as she threw off the covers and eased her legs off the bed.

Grimacing, she walked stiffly to the bathroom. Even the act of lowering her body down to the toilet seat was excruciatingly painful.

Working out today was unthinkable, and she concluded that she needed to be treated in the infirmary with painkillers, cold packs, and a therapeutic massage.

Hunched over, she moved feebly toward the desk, like she'd been stitched up and stapled after abdominal surgery.

Deciding to send Susan a quick e-mail to let her know she was too beaten up to attend classes, she pulled out the chair and gingerly sat down.

She powered on her laptop and before she had an opportunity to compose the e-mail, she noticed a message from Jayla that was dated the day before and had the word URGENT in the subject line. Bailee quickly opened it.

Hi Bailee, You won't believe what I heard today! While eavesdropping on two coworkers, who were kicking it in the breakroom, I learned that none other than Trent Evans is looking for commercial real estate to open up his own boutique law firm. According to the realtors, he is willing to spend top dollar for the perfect space, and they were pissed that he gave his business to our rival agency.

Knowing Trent's hating ass, he probably wanted to make sure I didn't make any coins off him.

Girl, I'm nosey as hell and have so many questions. Why did he leave his prestigious firm and where did he get the resources to start a business? I know you sent him packing with only the clothes on his back, so did he have some money saved up or do you think he took out a huge bank loan? If so, you need to make sure you're not liable to help him pay it back. After all, you are still married to him.

I realize talking on the phone is against the rules, but please shoot me an e-mail to let me know if you were aware of Trent's new venture.

Btw, how are you making out on the fat farm? Say the word, and I'll overnight you a big, greasy hoagie. Lol.

Love you, Jayla

Bailee closed the e-mail and groaned.

Of course, no one other than Giselle was financing Trent's law firm, and Bailee wished she didn't know about it. Jayla hadn't meant any harm in relaying the message, as she still didn't know about Trent's relationship with Giselle. But, it was unfortunate that Bailee's peace had been shattered by learning what her mother and her husband were up to.

She'd hoped to be able to put them out of her mind while she was over a thousand miles away, but obviously, that wasn't going to happen. Feeling more determined than ever to stick to her workout schedule, Bailee decided she wouldn't give up. She'd take a hot bath with Epson salt to soak away the pain.

Before logging out of her e-mail, another message caught her attention. It was from Gentle Breeze with the subject line: *Amp Up Your Workout.* She gave the message an eye roll, wondering how the facility had the audacity to suggest that she intensify an already brutal workout schedule.

Her first instinct was to delete the message without opening it, but curiosity got the best of her.

Dear Members, This is a reminder that the trainers at Gentle Breeze are available for personal workout sessions at the rates and specified times below. Remember, slots fill up quickly, so sign up right away!

Bailee perused the rates and let out a whistle. The personal training sessions were by no means cheap, but apparently, many of the women at the retreat were willing to spend the extra money for one-on-one sessions with their favorite trainers because there were hardly any slots left.

Although she would have gladly swiped her credit card for the thrill of being able to sit and stare at Hayden's handsome face and concrete body for an hour, she simply didn't have the physical strength to add another workout session to her routine.

She wondered if rosy-cheeked Cindy had paid extra to give Brahim, the Aqua Fit instructor, a blowjob, or if their clandestine time together was free of charge.

Fat chicks were always doing the most for male attention, she thought cynically. But then again, with the way society viewed curvy women, it was understandable why they often allowed themselves to be pushovers for men.

But what kind of an excuse did a model-thin beauty like Giselle have? Giselle had traded her morals and scruples, betrayed her own daughter, and opened up her wallet for the affection of a man.

Bailee would have never imagined that Giselle, an elegant woman with impeccable taste, was anything except poised and self-assured, but judging from her recent behavior, it was clear that low self-esteem plagued women of all walks of life and all shapes and sizes.

Bailee had always berated herself when her diet was out of control. But the rare times in her life when she had controlled the quality of the food she fueled her body with and had adhered to an exercise regimen, her self-worth had drastically improved.

Perhaps a personal training session wasn't a bad idea. With the bizarre family situation she had to contend with, she could use all the extra help she could get. Without a second thought, she clicked on Hayden's name and then provided her credit card information.

"Hi, there," Hayden greeted Bailee. He presented a slight smile, but wasn't overly friendly. "I noticed you struggling in class, and I plan to help you improve your technique and perfect your form, so you can get maximum benefit from the class."

Bailee nodded. For some reason, even Hayden's voice sounded vaguely familiar.

"Before we start your workout, we're gonna begin with a five-minute warmup on the treadmill, starting at a good pace and using the incline to get your heart rate going." He motioned to the treadmill and Bailee climbed on. He pushed buttons and Bailee found herself instantly trotting to keep up with the speed.

She'd gotten extra cute for her session, wearing a lime-green stretch top and green and black moisture-wicking Lycra tights, and a new pair of white sneakers. She'd hoped to chat a little and prance around daintily in her new gear before getting sweaty, but Hayden wasn't having it.

It only took a few moments for Bailee to feel sweat trickling down the back of her neck, and before the five minutes were up, she was breathing heavily, which wasn't cute.

"Okay, let's continue to get that heart rate pumping with some jumping jacks and pushup jacks to get those muscles warmed up to prevent injury." He pulled a stopwatch from his pocket.

Bailee groaned. "Jumping jacks? Seriously?"

"You can do it," Hayden assured her.

"I hate jumping jacks. And I've never done any kind of pushup in my life."

"You'll be fine. I'll help you through it."

After ten jumping jacks, Bailee could no longer sustain the jumping aspect of the exercise, and Hayden had to modify the movement for her. She made it through only three pushup jacks before collapsing onto her chest, panting.

Again, Hayden was encouraging, assuring her that with practice, her strength and stamina would improve.

"Okay, we're done with the warmup. You can take a water break before we get into the full body workout. To get you familiar with the routine, we're only going to do one set and ten reps for each exercise."

Thank God!

Bailee suffered through basic squats, lunges, and deadlifts without toppling over in defeat. Hayden moved her along to ten repetitions of the bent over row, which weren't too bad, but she didn't actually begin to enjoy herself until the bench presses.

As she lay flat on the bench holding dumbbells, he straddled the end of the bench with his crotch area near the back of her head as he assisted her, touching her elbows and upper arms, making sure she was using the proper form. She deliberately held the weights improperly to feel the sensation of his large hands grasping her arms. They finished with the large muscle groups sooner than she preferred and it was time to move on to core and abs.

Down on the floor, using a mat, Hayden demonstrated the plank. It looked simple but hurt like hell after Bailee moved into the position. After a few more core exercises, he introduced a series of hardcore abdominal exercises that nearly reduced her to tears.

At the conclusion of the workout, Bailee curled into a knot and groaned without inhibition.

"Come on, it wasn't that bad," Hayden chided.

"Uh-huh, it was horrible. You tried to kill me," she lamented as perspiration trickled down her back, her chest, and her face.

"Stop exaggerating," he said, chuckling as he picked up her hand towel from the mat and gently mopped the back of her neck.

The gesture, totally innocent, caused a tingle that ran down her spine.

"Take a deep breath and sit up." He took her by the hand and helped her to a sitting position. "Drink," he said, offering her the bottle of water she'd brought with her.

Gasping for breath, she chugged down water. His warm, chocolate eyes studied her with concern. "You okay?" he asked.

She nodded.

"Good. We have to finish up with stretching."

"No, I can't do anything else. You're so sadistic." Bailee was partly kidding, but mostly serious.

"Stretching helps improve flexibility, helps reduce muscle fatigue; plus, it's great for stress relief."

"I can't do anything else," Bailee insisted.

"Okay, I can compromise. We'll do passive stretching."

"What's that?"

"It's a form of static stretching in which an external force exerts upon the limb to move it into different positions."

Bailee stared at him blankly. Not only didn't she comprehend fitness jargon, but she was also lost in his dark, brown eyes. She was captivated by the shape of his lips, imagining them pressed against hers.

"I have no idea what you just said," she said dreamily.

"In other words, passive stretching is an assisted stretch. I'll do most of the work. Lie flat on your back," he said, motioning with his hands.

She did as he said, allowing him to manipulate her tired arms, pulling, stretching, and twisting them into a series of positions. She had expected the movements to be painful, but they were surprisingly soothing.

At the end of the session, he pulled her to her feet. "That wasn't so bad, was it?" he asked, displaying a gleaming smile.

"It was brutal," Bailee responded, while realizing she'd be back for more of his inhuman treatment.

Chapter 23

On the morning of her surgery, Jayla was a nervous wreck. She entered the hospital terrified of all the things that could go wrong. She was aware of all the possible risks and dangers the gastric sleeve could present, but the biggest risk was death. Although her doctor had assured her that there was only an eight percent chance of dying, she couldn't help thinking about the possibility of meeting an untimely demise.

She signed in at admissions and prayed that she wouldn't be that unlucky one in a thousand. It would be just her luck to expire on the operating table while trying to cheat her way to being skinny. She imagined the people attending her funeral, shaking their heads and thinking if she hadn't been so vain and so lazy, she'd still be among the living.

It was hard to sleep last night, and after trying for hours, she was on the verge of calling Bailee to cry on her shoulder and share her innermost fears, but she remembered that Bailee wasn't allowed access to her phone while she was at the weight loss retreat spending a fortune to sweat and starve all day.

Perhaps it was good thing that she couldn't reach Bailee. Knowing

Bailee, she'd say something like, "You're beautiful with or without surgery, but if you're having second thoughts, you should postpone the surgery. Maybe you'll feel better if you at least make an attempt to do it on your own."

Considering Bailee's imaginary advice, Jayla thought about rescheduling the surgery, but then decided against it. She'd already taken the time off from work and wouldn't be able to get any more time in the foreseeable future.

By the time she had finally fallen asleep, she was convinced that surgery was her best option, but now she was feeling unsure again.

Her first instinct was to get something to eat to calm her nerves. A buffalo chicken pizza would've been perfect. She was about to head down to the hospital's cafeteria when she remembered she wasn't allowed to eat anything before surgery.

Her stomach grumbled in protest and she was dangerously close to slipping away from the admissions desk to go and sneak one last, glorious meal. The nurses and other hospital staff weren't paying her any attention, so who would know?

Realizing that pizza wouldn't be available at that hour of the morning, she crept toward the elevator with the taste of breakfast food in her mouth: crispy bacon, scrambled eggs with cheese, buttermilk waffles with lots of syrup and butter, and a heaping portion of greasy hash browns.

She jabbed the down button, and then decided that it wasn't worth the risk. Hungry and depressed, she returned to her seat and waited to be transferred to surgery.

When her name was called and she was rolled on a gurney to a room where she'd be prepped for surgery, Jayla felt very afraid and very alone.

Lorraine had worked the overnight shift and wouldn't be able to get to the hospital until Jayla was already in surgery. Derek had an early morning appointment with his probation officer, and she had no idea what time he'd get to the hospital.

At last, the big moment had arrived. As she lay on the operating table, Dr. Winslow cracked jokes about carving her a new, svelte body. She wanted to smile but was so busy reciting desperate prayers in her mind, her expression was as grim as someone taking their last mile.

After being told to count backward, she only made it to number four and then everything went black.

Hours later, she woke up feeling groggy. The first thing she did was pat her body, hoping she'd lost a discernible amount of weight on the operating table, but her body felt the same.

Her tummy was wrapped in bandages, and oddly, she didn't feel hardly any pain in her abdominal area. For some reason, she was thirsty as hell and her throat hurt so badly, it felt like it was on fire.

She asked one of the many nurses that came in and out of her room for pain medication. The nurse told her she'd have to wait until she'd been seen by her doctor, and then assured her he'd be making his rounds shortly.

A half-hour later, Dr. Winslow entered her room with a team of doctors. He viewed her chart and asked how she was feeling.

"I feel okay, but my throat hurts and I'm dying of thirst," she said, attempting not to cough.

"Let me take a look."

Opening her mouth wide was agonizing and trying to stretch out her tongue was out of the question. She felt ridiculous with her tongue sticking out limply, but it was the best she could do.

"Thirst and a sore throat are common after the endotracheal tube has been removed post-surgery," Dr. Winslow explained. "I'll let the nurse know you can have a cup of broth. Drink it slowly or you'll feel nauseous. Also, you should be able to take in a few sips of water."

Jayla nodded.

"You need to eat four to five small meals per day and try to get in at least an hour of light exercise," he said as he examined her incision. "Okay, everything looks great. I'll see you in two weeks." He added some notations to her chart, and then proceeded out of the room with the other doctors following closely behind.

When a breakfast tray was delivered, Jayla drank the broth slowly as the doctor had advised. Next, she took sips of water and concluded that it was the best water she'd ever tasted.

There was oatmeal, scrambled eggs, and cherry Jell-O on the tray. She ate the Jell-O, but she had no desire to eat the rest. For the first time in her life, she was completely satisfied with a light meal. It was a new and incredible sensation.

It was truly the beginning of a brand-new life.

After being given a sample weekly menu, a suggested exercise regimen, and a prescription for pain medication, Jayla was cleared to go home. The way the hospital staff had rushed her out of her room seemed a little insensitive. Due to the shortage of hospital rooms, she didn't have the luxury of relaxing in bed until Derek showed up to drive her home.

When she spoke to him on the phone, he said he was still on the bus, only ten minutes away. But he was taking forever.

Lorraine would have definitely been more prompt, but she couldn't make it because there was some mix-up with the schedule on her job, and her vacation time had been denied.

In the lobby, sitting in a stupid wheelchair while the nursing assistant who was looking after her, took one cigarette break after another, was torturous. She felt weak and dizzy and couldn't stop squirming around trying to find a comfortable position. If Derek had any idea of how badly she wanted to be at home in her bed, he'd hurry the hell up.

The nursing assistant checked on her briefly and then returned outside, where she gabbed on her phone. Jayla glared at the clock. If Derek didn't show up in the next five minutes, she was going to leave the hospital on her own. She'd abandon her car in the garage and take an Uber home.

When the automatic doors parted and Derek strode through, carrying a colorful bouquet of balloons, Jayla smiled inwardly. On the outside, she frowned and rolled her eyes.

"Hey, skinny girl," Derek greeted her cheerfully.

"Don't skinny girl, me. You got a lot of nerve making me sit here all this time," she complained.

"My bad. I made a quick stop to get these," he said, handing her the balloons.

"Thanks," she muttered.

"How do you feel?"

"Terrible. The doctor wants me to walk around, but all I want to do is get in my bed." She grimaced as a sharp pain shot through her.

"You okay?"

She shook her head. "I need my prescription filled, right away."

"Okay, let's get out of here."

The nursing assistant returned inside and seeing that Derek had arrived, she told Jayla to take care and went on her way.

Jayla grasped the armrests of the wheelchair and stood upright. When the room suddenly began to tilt, she tried to ease herself back into the wheelchair. She felt lightheaded and experienced an overwhelming urge to burp, but couldn't.

"What's wrong?" Derek asked.

"Nothing. I just felt like I needed to—" Before she could finish the sentence, she vomited. Globs of the cherry-colored Jell-O she'd had earlier were all over her shirt. She was so embarrassed, she could have cried.

Surprisingly, Derek didn't shrink back in disgust. "Stay right there, I'll get paper towels." He darted to the restroom and quickly returned with wet paper towels.

While Jayla sat helplessly in the wheelchair, he took charge, cleaning her up and then searching through her bag for a clean top.

The kindness he bestowed upon her, she'd never experienced with any other man, and she was so grateful that he was taking care of her.

Derek took Lorraine's place and stayed with Jayla at her place.

The recovery period at home was much more difficult than she had imagined, and she wouldn't have been able to make it without Derek's assistance.

She continuously vomited after ingesting any kind of food—no matter how small the portion. If that wasn't bad enough, there was also the discomfort of needing to belch, and the constant pain from the incisions was making her miserable.

She chided herself for taking the easy way out. Why didn't she simply go on a diet like Bailee had? She could have gotten a trainer at the gym. She could have tried Weight Watchers, again.

Even though she wasn't eating much of anything, she didn't look like she'd lost anything. She couldn't help thinking that the surgery had been a huge mistake.

She looked at her overweight body in the mirror and her eyes filled with tears.

"Some new life," she grumbled aloud.

After a week, the pain subsided and the side effects of the surgery weren't as bad. The depression lifted and Jayla was ecstatic when she noticed her clothes beginning to loosen.

By the time her two-week, post-op surgery rolled around, she felt good enough to drive herself.

At Dr. Winslow's office, she looked down in disbelief as the numbers on the scale swiftly moved downward. When the nurse informed her that she'd lost forty pounds, Jayla's eyes grew wide. "It used to take months to lose only fifteen pounds…this is incredible," she excitedly said to the nurse.

Dr. Winslow entered the room. "Congratulations on your weight loss."

"Thanks. My clothes are getting baggy, but my body doesn't look any different."

"Are you getting any exercise?"

"Not really. I've been in too much pain to work out, but now that I'm feeling better, I can start walking slowly around the building where I live."

"Cardio activity is good, but you need strength training, also. Do you have a gym membership?"

"Yes, but I don't like people watching me when I work out."

"You have too many excuses, Jayla. If you want to see good results and if you want to get healthy, you have to put in some work," Dr. Winslow said firmly. "The weight will continue to come off for a while, but then you'll reach a plateau. Even though your stomach is only a quarter of its normal size, you're not immune to regaining the weight you've lost. Surgery is not magic. You have to do your part."

"I understand, and I'm all in. I'm going to do my part," she said amiably.

During the drive home, she couldn't stop grinning over the fact that she was down forty pounds. Her first thought was to go shopping for some new clothes, but she decided to wait until she lost even more weight. If she lost forty that quickly, there was no telling how much she'd lose if she started going to the gym with Derek.

On second thought, the gym was out of the question. All of that sweating and grunting was not her style. Being realistic, a brisk walk around the block was all she'd be able to endure.

She glanced in the rearview mirror and noticed that her face looked a lot smaller and she had to admit that she really looked prettier. She considered snapping a picture and texting it to Sadeeq to let him see what he was missing. But she suppressed the urge to contact him. She was too good for that bastard. She was moving forward, and from now on, any man she got involved with would have to bow down to the queen.

Chapter 24

Spring had finally arrived, and along with the change of season, Bailee had also experienced a metamorphosis. So far, she'd lost thirty-eight pounds. Though she'd hoped to lose a lot more, she was grateful for the small changes in her body.

From eating right and working out, there was definition in her arms and shoulders. Her thighs were a lot firmer and no longer rubbed together. The most noticeable improvement was her snatched waistline.

Although she'd expected to see more drastic changes in her body, she didn't regret spending the money or the grueling work she'd put in at Gentle Breeze. One of the important things she'd learned was that striving to become unrealistically thin and subscribing to deprivation diets would only bring short-term results. She learned that the cornerstone of a healthy lifestyle was to replace processed food with real food whenever possible and to exercise on a regular basis.

Jayla, on the other hand, had experienced incredible post-surgery weight loss, and her weight was still falling off at a rapid rate.

It wasn't fair! Jayla hadn't spent any money or exerted any energy.

All she'd done was lie on a table and sleep while a surgeon's knife did all the work.

A part of Bailee was envious of Jayla's quick weight-loss procedure, while another part of her was proud that she'd personally selected a method that involved willpower and determination.

Looking in the mirror and scrutinizing herself, she noticed that her collarbones were visible and her butt had lifted considerably. Her lower legs were shapelier than she would have ever thought possible.

Despite her disappointment in the numbers on the scale, she was down two dress sizes. Clearly, she was losing inches, which some considered more important than losing pounds.

Throwing on her robe, she tied the sash and picked up the remote. She excitedly scrolled to QVC, where someone was hawking watches. It would be another ten more minutes before Hayden's new activewear segment came on.

And it would be two hours until they met for dinner near the QVC studios, outside of Philadelphia.

For the past month, Hayden had been the only thing on her mind.

The sparks between them back at the retreat in Miami couldn't be denied, but they both had enough self-restraint to not act on their attraction while Bailee was a guest at Gentle Breeze.

Although Hayden looked extremely familiar, it wasn't until she was halfway through her stay at the resort when she finally placed him. Hayden was the "Workout King," a well-known exercise guru who had initially achieved fame on YouTube and now sold millions of workout DVDs. He was only temporarily filling in for his good friend, Maddie, at Gentle Breeze.

"Clearly, we have a connection; let's see how far we can take it," Hayden had said on her last night at the retreat.

"Let's stay in touch and hopefully, we can get together when I'm in the Philly area next month," he added.

After she returned home, they communicated frequently through texts, phone calls, and FaceTime, but she longed to see him again in person. He was a frequent visitor in her dreams, he unsettled her waking thoughts, aroused her body with just the memory of him. The only time she didn't think about him was when she was sweating through her rigorous workout at the gym.

And now, the idea of a candlelit meal with Hayden sent butterflies fluttering around in the pit of her stomach, and the notion that she was going to see him live on TV in a few minutes gave her butterflies.

As she waited for Hayden's segment, she kept busy by laying out her wardrobe choices on the bed. She looked admiringly at a merlot-colored, wrap dress that hugged her slimmed-down body in all the right places, and also revealed a peek of cleavage. Spiky heels that she normally would have avoided, now gave her a sexy and powerful feeling, while also accentuating her shapely legs.

While selecting jewelry, she was torn between cultured pearls and a simple diamond pendant.

"Welcome to QVC, Hayden. I have to ask what the goal is for your activewear line?" the QVC host asked.

Hearing Hayden's name, Bailee yanked around and faced the TV. Excited, she scrambled to turn up the volume.

Damn, he's fine. Hayden was a hunky piece of delectable eye candy, and he looked super fit in a red T-shirt and navy sweatpants.

"My goal is to inject comfort and fashion into fitness attire," Hayden responded to the QVC host in the smooth voice that Bailee had come to know so well. "The HaydenWear collection is all about inspiring women to feel strong, confident, and empowered. It's also about layering and being able to mix and match. The line was designed to be attractive, affordable, and functional. It includes petite sizes, plus sizes, and everything in between so that *every* woman can rock a stylish outfit when she sweats it out at the gym. Ultimately, HaydenWear is for *all* active women on the go."

Sitting at her vanity and applying makeup while watching Hayden through the mirror, she loved the fact that he didn't limit his fitness apparel only to tall, waif types.

Observing Hayden in high definition was thrilling. She stood up and walked to her lingerie drawer without turning her head away from the TV. While fixated on Hayden, Bailee slipped into a pair of lacey panties and bra.

Tonight was finally the night to taste those juicy lips of his... and hopefully savor a lot more than a kiss. There was no point in being coy; she was feeling confident enough to get naked with Hayden and take it all the way.

Inside a quaint restaurant in Kennett Square, Pennsylvania, Hayden stood up to greet Bailee.

She looked into his intense, dark eyes and then drank in the perfection of his face: clay-brown skin, high cheekbones, thick eyebrows, and strong jawline. His manly good looks were intensified by the driving force of ambition that burned inside of him.

"Congrats on selling out everything on the show," Bailee said.

"Couldn't have done it without the entire QVC team. They're top-notch, and really supportive," he replied modestly as the waiter set menus before them.

Bailee perused the vast list of food choices. After completing nine nutrition classes at Gentle Breeze, she didn't need any advice on what to order. The words *protein*, *green vegetables*, and *limited carbs* were indelibly etched in her mind, and she wasn't tempted in the least by anything that was doughy or saturated with any kind of creamy sauce.

"How're your workouts coming along?" Hayden asked.

"Fine. My trainer pushes me to the point of nausea before he allows me to quit."

"That's good. Hopefully, you don't have an appointment with him tomorrow."

"Actually, I don't, but why is that a good thing?"

Hayden briefly fell silent as the waiter poured their wine. "I have an open call scheduled for female models," he said after the wine was poured. "However, after seeing how good you look, I think I should cancel the open call. You have the perfect face and the perfect body for my fitness line."

"Me? No way!"

"Yes, you. You're perfect."

"But I'm not even in shape. I'm getting there, but I'm not there, yet."

"You're on a journey that women from all walks of life can relate to. You'll be generously compensated, and working with me will keep you busy while you're between jobs."

"I don't know what to say."

"Say yes."

"Okay. Yes, I'll do it," she said exuberantly, although nervous about the idea.

He raised his wineglass. "Let's drink to that."

Their glasses clinked together and Bailee took a big sip. "I'm scared, Hayden. Being a model for a fitness line is absolutely insane. Are you sure I'm the right person?"

"I'm positive. You're a woman who's living your life fearlessly. Celebrating the body you're in right now and not waiting to achieve what society views as perfection. I love the fact that you own who you are as you embrace a healthier lifestyle. My brand isn't only for women who have achieved their goals, but also for those on the journey of self-love and self-awareness. Women like you, Bailee."

Bailee felt herself flush. She was at a loss for words and was grateful that the waiter chose that moment to distract her with a steaming plate of sea scallops and grilled lemon-broccoli.

She'd been so wrong about Trent, had misjudged his intentions for over ten years, but this time, she wasn't looking for a fairy tale. She no longer believed in happily ever after. She would simply enjoy the moment with Hayden, whether it lasted a week, a few months, or a lifetime.

After the meal, Hayden invited her back to his hotel, and Bailee didn't hesitate.

She drove behind him, both excited and anxious. Trent had been the only man she'd ever been with, and she was as nervous as a virgin soon to be deflowered. They parked their cars and held hands as they entered the hotel.

Alone on the elevator, he leaned close until she felt his lips brush against her face. He pulled her into him and kissed her, his fingers twisting into her hair. His lips coaxed her mouth open and her whole body hummed with electricity. She wrapped her arms around his neck at the exact moment that the bell dinged, announcing their arrival on Hayden's floor.

If she were a bolder woman, she would have pushed the emergency button and spread her legs for him right then and there. But she settled for being walked backward to his room with his hot hands all over her, sliding beneath her dress, rubbing her ass, and stroking her nipples until they were taut with need.

She could feel his hard-on pressing against her ass, and never had she been so certain of what she wanted.

She wanted him.

Inside her.

Hot and slick. Deep and hard.

So deeply embedded, she'd be at his mercy, unable to move or do anything else except shudder and gasp.

Somehow he managed to get the keycard out of his pocket and opened the door without missing a beat as he whispered, "I want you," softly in her ear. He caressed her hip before his hand crept lower and began fondling her ass.

The momentum built to a slow burn and then traveled through her system, settling in her center, turning her insides to liquid heat that could not be contained.

Inside his room, there was no reason for any more small talk. They'd made enough polite conversation back at the retreat in Florida, over the phone every night since she'd been back, and throughout dinner tonight.

Bailee was hot, wet, and ready and she had nothing more to say.

One glass of wine shouldn't have disoriented her, yet her mind felt fuzzy. Her senses jumbled and slowed down as his fingers skillfully unzipped her dress while his tongue deftly explored her mouth. It was possible that she was drunk on lust, she decided as she tottered unsteadily in her heels, and then kicked them off, and leaned against his hard body for support.

"I've been waiting so long for this moment. Never wanted anyone so much," Hayden murmured, desire oozing out with each word.

"I…" She wanted to express her emotions, but the words stuck in her throat. All she could do was shiver, bite her lip, and squeeze her eyes shut as her dress fell away from her body and dropped to the floor.

She'd expected to be under the covers, stripping off her lingerie discreetly, but he began to make love to her while she was standing in the middle of the floor, completely exposed. Wearing nothing except lace undies, all of her imperfections were on prominent display.

"You're beautiful," he whispered, his hungry gaze quieting the negative self-critique that was running in her mind. As he unhooked her bra and released her voluptuous breasts, his large hands cupped them gingerly at first, and then began kneading the soft orbs, murmuring indistinctly as he lowered his head and latched onto a rigid nipple.

As his hot tongue swirled around her areola and his teeth nipped at the delicate flesh, sharp sensations cut through her system, a confusing mixture of pleasure and pain. Her nipple felt so sensitive, she clasped the sides of his head, intending to pull it away, but found herself holding his head in place.

It had been so long since her body had been touched like this; a sudden wave of dizziness caused Bailee to stumble, but Hayden's strong arms held her upright as he carefully guided her toward the bed.

"It's your night, babe. You don't have to move a muscle. The only thing I want you to do is lie back and enjoy yourself."

Hayden took control and she tried her best to relax, but couldn't. He pushed her breasts together and alternately suckled each nipple, making it a point to be gentle as he lavished and lathed her pebbled flesh with the utmost care and attention.

Her body tensed when he peeled off her panties and showered her tummy with kisses that trailed down to her smooth mound. She purred low in her throat as he parted her labia with his fingers. The purring grew louder when he began licking her fat clit, stoking a fire within her loins. Nectar trickled out of her slit and she squirmed with desire, spreading her legs for him, as wide as possible.

At first, he slowly snaked his tongue between the folds and leisurely lapped the juices that spilled from her. Then, as if invigorated by the taste, he began stabbing mercilessly into her scorching hot opening. His lips engulfed her swollen clit while his tongue flicked at the sensitive tip, causing her to writhe as she twisted the bed sheets inside her fists and chanted his name.

Her entire body was enflamed. "Hayden," she whimpered breathlessly while alternately rocking her hips and thrusting her pelvis.

The pleasure he was giving her was so intense, she couldn't take much more. She was going to come in his mouth if he didn't stop, and she wanted to feel his dick inside her when she experienced her first orgasm with him.

"Stop," she whispered, her ass lifting upward, her hips grinding into his face. "Stop," she repeated, more urgently. While her mouth pleaded for him to stop, her wet pussy and undulating body silently begged for more.

And he obliged her. His rigid tongue tunneled into her, poking and stabbing mercilessly into her silken insides.

"Baby," he murmured, and the word was hot and tickly against her splayed labia, inciting Bailee to buck and thrust with wild abandon.

A sharp spasm ripped through her body and she grimaced and groaned through clenched teeth as he tongue-fucked her ruthlessly. Unable to stop the onslaught of torturous pleasure that rocketed through her system, her thighs clamped against his face.

Her orgasm was like a silver bolt of lightning ripping through her with a force that caused her to shudder and thrust wildly.

"Mmm," Hayden murmured, drinking in every drop and then licking her slit clean.

Chest heaving. Panting. Gulping in air. Bailee tried to catch her breath so that she could return the favor. She desperately wanted to pounce on Hayden and swallow his dick whole. She tried to struggle upright, but she couldn't move.

She had come so intensely, there seemed to be an aftershock of little grenades and missiles continuing to detonate inside her pussy, keeping her incapacitated.

Hayden tore off his shirt and Bailee caught a glimpse of his ripped abs. She wanted to reach out and stroke his six-pack, but in her weakened state, all she managed to do was imagine the feel of them.

"You don't have to move," he reminded her. "I told you, it's your night."

She nodded or at least tried to, but her satiated body was limp and spent. When he came out of his pants, revealing a mountainous bulge in the center of his briefs, she feared that in her current state of paralysis, she'd be extremely dull in bed.

Naked in the dimly lit room, Hayden's body looked as if it were made of concrete. The only thing that let her know he was a living and breathing human being and not a beautifully muscled sculpture was the way his dick began stretching and pulsing inside his loosely closed fist.

Bailee's mouth watered at the sight of him stroking his gorgeous dick. She wanted desperately to relieve him of the task of self-gratification, but he wasn't within her reach and she was still too weak to inch closer to him.

Sensing her need, he straddled her supine body and began rubbing the engorged head of his dick all over her neck and breasts, and she felt a sticky ooze streaking her chest. He dragged the pulsing, heavy flesh over one breast and then the other.

Her back arched and her nipples tightened into hard pearls as he lightly rubbed the head of his dick against them, smearing them with a glistening coat of pre-ejaculation.

He'd awakened her secret longing and she refused to be shy. "Put it in my mouth," she rasped in a desperate tone.

"No."

"Please."

"No," he insisted as he continued to haul his thickened meat over her plump tummy, leaving drippings in her navel before continuing the trek downward. And when he finally reached her pussy, he ran his dick up and down her creamy slit until her clit worked its way from beneath the hood and stood upright, bold and rigid.

Pre-cum seeped out and saturated the hardened nub, and once again, Bailee began gyrating. Never had she wanted a dick as badly as she wanted Hayden's right now. Her pussy wept with need, but he continued to slide it up and down the satiny entrance.

"Fuck me," she pleaded. "I'm ready for you."

"No, you're not."

"My pussy needs you."

"You're not wet enough," he replied, slipping the head into her tight opening.

"Oh, God," she gasped as her pussy tried its best to gobble him up.

"Slow down, baby. There's no rush," Hayden said, feeding her only half-inch increments at a time.

"Give it to me," she demanded, almost angrily, hitching upward and seizing more than she was being offered.

Hayden chuckled lightly. "I always say, everything in moderation, but I forgot that your pussy's not on a diet. Is it hungry, babe?"

"It's starving."

"I'm gonna feed it as much as it wants," he promised, easing in another inch.

"I need more. Give me more," she pleaded in a harsh whisper, her face contorting as she bit down on her lip.

"Throw those pretty legs around my back," he instructed and Bailee eagerly complied. After wrapping her legs around his back, she locked her ankles together, forcing him to plow deeper. Once his dick was embedded to the hilt, Hayden began thrusting so vigorously, his ball sac slapped against her flesh.

"Damn, this pussy is tight," he growled as he provided long strokes, filling her with a rock-hard dick that was ridged with pulsating veins.

Although his girth and width were much more than she was accustomed to, her vagina easily stretched and accommodated his size. With pleasure cresting, a sheen of perspiration glistened on her forehead.

All rational thought and reason escaped her as Bailee became lost in the sensations. The dual stimulation of hard-thrusting dick meat accompanied with throbbing veins that pressed against her soft, cushiony walls was almost more than she could bear. The wet lips of her vulva tightened around his shaft, squeezing it and pulling it deeper into her warm depths.

"It's so good," she said hoarsely. "Oh, yes, yes, yes," she crooned, her pelvic rolls rhythmically keeping pace with his forceful thrusts.

Excitement glimmered in her eyes as her inner muscles began to involuntarily contract, and her walls, like a python, squeezed his dick unmercifully, forcing liquid heat to gush out and splatter her insides.

As she released with a shudder and a soft scream, his mouth found hers and their tongues intertwined.

Chapter 25

Jayla approached the hostess desk with Derek trailing closely behind her.

He looked around in wonder at the environment as if he were inside an exclusive eatery instead of an ordinary chain restaurant.

After checking in and receiving a buzzer, Jayla and Derek took seats on a bench in the crowded waiting area.

"I've been dreaming about the Olive Garden for ten long years," Derek said. "When I was locked up, the food in the commercials used to make my mouth water."

"I've never liked the food here, so I guess it's a good thing that I don't have much of an appetite anymore. Otherwise, I'd be upset that you insisted on coming here."

"Are you gonna make me eat alone?" he asked with a hint of hurt in his voice. "You know how self-conscious I get in restaurant situations."

"I'm not hungry," Jayla maintained. "Furthermore, I'm pissed that we're here instead of sticking to the plan to check out some of the properties we plan to bid on."

"Foreclosed houses aren't going anywhere. We don't have the money yet, so what's the rush?"

"I hope you're not getting cold feet about our venture."

"No, not at all. I just got hyped when I noticed that we were approaching Olive Garden."

Jayla shook her head in bewilderment. "Who gets hyped over Olive Garden, though?"

"I do. But I don't expect you to understand."

"I definitely don't understand," Jayla said, tugging on her skirt.

"You're skinny now. You don't have to constantly adjust your clothes," Derek remarked.

"I'm far from skinny."

"You're getting there, though. With all the weight you lost, you look like an entirely different person."

"You think so?"

"Definitely."

"Even though my weight is falling off like crazy, I'm so accustomed to my clothes hitching up, it's a reflex for me to constantly tug on the back of a jacket, a dress, or a skirt. To be honest, I shouldn't even care how I look inside this dump." She made a face. "If you want really good Italian food, I can take you to Luigi's in Cherry Hill. The crap they serve here is nothing but a bunch of pre-cooked frozen mess."

"I'm looking forward to eating a whole lot of their pre-cooked frozen mess," he said, sounding defensive.

Realizing that Derek's irrational Olive Garden request had something to do with him being locked up for so long, she decided to go easy on him and not complain too much.

"By the way, my mom's so happy about us being a couple..." Jayla made air quotes around the word, *couple*. "She's been telling everyone at her church that I've finally found my perfect mate." Jayla rolled her eyes to the ceiling as if she didn't share Lorraine's desire for her to be permanently hooked up with Derek.

Derek looked pained. "I hate deceiving your mom and I feel bad for you."

"Why do you feel bad for me? I've been having fun playing the part of your girlfriend."

"I'm sure it gets annoying playing the part of a beard. Hopefully, you'll meet your true soul mate one day soon."

"I honestly don't mind being your beard."

"Good! A big part of your beard-duty is to make sure I never have to eat alone."

"Here we go again," Jayla said with a sigh. "Maybe you need to see a therapist to help you adjust to the outside world."

"I'll get it together, eventually. In the meanwhile, I know you don't have much of an appetite, but can't you sip a little soup or something, so that I don't feel as if all eyes are on me?"

"Oh, God. All right! I'll make a sacrifice and eat this gruel just for you," Jayla said.

"Gruel? There must be something wrong with your taste buds. From what I remember, the food here is banging."

"My taste buds are fine, but with my stomach shrinking and all, I've had to be a lot more selective about what I put in my mouth."

"Hmm, you didn't seem selective about what went in your mouth when ol' boy from Tinder slid through the other night."

"Is that shade?" she asked, laughing.

"No shade. I'm just saying…"

"Were you eavesdropping on us?"

"No! But y'all were loud as fuck. I heard ol' boy saying, 'Suck it, baby. Yeah, that's right, take it all the way to the back of your throat.' He was talking so much shit about your head game, I was tempted to burst through the door and get in on the action. Of course, I would have accidentally stuck my dick in his mouth instead of yours," Derek said with a sly grin.

Jayla laughed. Although she accepted Derek's homosexuality, a part of her couldn't help thinking that he was a big hunk of male gorgeousness that was completely going to waste by playing for the other team.

Still, the best part of their arrangement was the fact that she had gained a dear friend. On the strength of friendship, she had confided her deepest and darkest secrets to him—secrets she had never even told Bailee—and Derek had listened compassionately and without judgment.

After he helped her get through her recovery, she convinced him to leave the strict rule of her mother's Christian home and move in with her, where he'd be more relaxed.

Growing weary of sitting up in church with Lorraine every Sunday, Derek didn't require a lot of convincing to move in with Jayla.

To throw Derek off and keep him from discovering her true feelings for him, Jayla had increased her Internet dating.

It seemed like a cruel, cosmic joke for her to have gone to such an extreme to lose weight only to end up falling for a man who could never be hers.

Despite her remarkable weight loss journey and amazing trans-formation, she still didn't feel like she was good enough, and her continued promiscuous behavior with jerks she'd met online was proof that she was a long way from being emotionally healed.

"I'll be glad when I stop feeling self-conscious in restaurants. When the time comes when I feel I'm ready to start dating, I'm going to have to have my act together," Derek confided.

"Are you interested in anyone in particular?" she asked, injecting false cheerfulness into her tone.

"No one at the moment. But I'm sure the perfect person will come my way, eventually," he said wistfully. "Anyway, if you weren't here with me, I probably would have entered the place and then walked straight into the dining area and took a seat without waiting my turn."

Jayla laughed. "Stop playing. You would not have done that."

"I'm not kidding. I wouldn't have known any better. I don't remember all the social etiquette rules. I'm always worried that I'm going to embarrass myself out in public, and that's why I'm so grateful for you," he confessed with a look of vulnerability that Jayla found endearing.

The buzzer went off and Derek and Jayla followed the hostess into the dining area.

Before sitting down, Derek warily eyed the tabletop tablet like it was an ancient enemy. "When did they start this shit? Damn, you're gonna have to place my order for me."

"You better get used to the e-order trend," Jayla said as she took a seat. "Little toddlers and preschoolers know how to operate these Ziosk tablets, so if you want to eat, you're gonna learn today."

Reluctantly, he studied the screen and within minutes, he was tapping on a number of colorful images of fancy drinks, bread, and appetizers.

"You need to chill with the appetizers! You're not going to have any room for your entrée," Jayla cautioned. "Besides, gluttony is a sin."

"You should know," he fired back. "Not too long ago, you could eat me under the table. I watched you gorge on anything that wasn't nailed down, and I never criticized you."

"That's true," she admitted. "It seems like such a long time ago. I don't know who that greedy bitch was," she said, laughing. "It seems inconceivable for me to ever stuff my face the way I used to. Now, I only eat to satisfy my hunger, and I'm rarely hungry... thank God!"

The breadsticks arrived and Derek began munching on them.

"Mmm, these taste better than I remember." He looked up and suddenly flashed a smile as he fluttered his fingers at someone seated at another table.

"Who are you waving at?" Jayla asked.

"A cute little girl. She's sitting with her brother and her parents. They look like the perfect family," he said wistfully.

Jayla leaned forward and whispered sternly. "You can't be waving at random kids, Derek. Do you want people to think you're a pedophile?"

Offended, he turned up his nose. "Why would anyone think that?"

"A grown man fluttering his fingers at a random child is not cool. If you don't want that child's parents calling the cops, you need to stop being all Joe familiar."

"The child waved at me first. I was only being polite," Derek said huffily.

"Rule number one to being properly socialized: do not be overly friendly with children you don't even know."

"Damn, since when can't you be friendly anymore? As Ms. Lorraine would say, 'This world is quickly going to hell in a handbasket.'"

"It's true—the world is in a sad state, but when you think about it, it's a good thing that people are more aware of the behavior of child molesters."

"I resent being called a child molester," he whispered angrily.

"I'm not referring to you, specifically. I'm talking about child molesters in general…and all the other predators out here that falsely represent themselves," she explained.

A shadow fell over her face as she thought about her ordeal with the online predator named Niles.

Oblivious to Jayla's sudden, gloomy mood, Derek promptly moved his water glass and the breadstick basket over to the side when the server arrived with plates of steaming food.

He sliced his chicken parmesan and speared a piece. "Mmm, this food is banging," he said. "I don't understand why you don't like it." His face suddenly brightened with a wide smile as he looked adoringly at the children seated at the table directly across from theirs.

"What the hell did I just tell you?" Jayla exploded. "You're gonna get us kicked out of here, acting like a pervert."

"The little boy smiled at me and I smiled back. Since when is friendliness acting like a pervert? Kids know a good person when they see one."

"All right, but if the father pops off and comes over here, ready to throw hands, don't say I didn't warn you."

Derek narrowed his eyes, scrutinizing the family. "The father looks way too dignified to get rowdy up in here. In fact, if he wasn't married, I'd be all over his fine ass." Derek's tongue darted out, subtly moistening his lips seductively.

"Are you flirting with the father? You know what…you really don't know how to act in public. Get up, Derek!"

He frowned and leaned back resentfully. "Get up for what?"

"We're switching seats, so that the kids won't keep smiling at you. Plus, I want to make sure you don't try to sneakily push up on their father."

"I'm comfortable and don't feel like moving," he protested. "Nor do I feel like jostling all these plates and platters all around."

"You don't have to move anything. Everything on the table is yours. The only thing that has to move is my bowl of soup, and since I don't even want it, it can stay where it's at." Jayla stood up.

Derek responded with a sigh that was sharp and impatient, and then reluctantly followed suit. After Derek and Jayla switched seats, she glanced at the family that was seated opposite them and her eyes grew wide with surprise.

"What?" Derek swiveled around to see what Jayla was looking at.

"Don't stare," Jayla whispered harshly.

Derek hastily turned and faced Jayla. "Do you know those people?"

Clearly distressed, she covered her mouth and nodded.

"Who are they?"

She removed her hand. "I don't know the kids or the woman, but I know the man. I know him very, *very* well. But I don't want him to recognize me." She reached inside her purse and slid on a pair of sunglasses. She propped her phone up on the table against the bread basket and hit the video-record feature.

Stealthily, she situated the bread basket, so that the phone was facing the so-called "perfect" family.

Walking fast to the car, Jayla was outraged. She held up the phone for Derek to look at the video that she'd recorded. "Look at this shit. Both of those kids are calling him Daddy, and the chick refers to him as hon!"

"What's the big deal? They're his wife and kids?"

"No, they are not! I can't wait for the shit to hit the fan," she said as she uploaded the video and hit SEND.

Chapter 26

Bailee stared dreamily out the window as the Amtrak train glided along the tracks. She was headed back to Philadelphia and Hayden was on a flight to Miami. He had to meet with his team to prepare for the Hayden-Wear launch party that was scheduled for next week.

The photo shoot in New York had gone much smoother than Bailee could have imagined. The photographer, Antonio, made her feel completely at ease, constantly reassuring her and telling her the camera loved her. She'd been in New York with Hayden for three magical days and three lustful nights, and she hadn't told anyone of her whereabouts.

Actually, no one except Jayla had noticed or cared that she was incommunicado.

There'd been a number of texts and missed calls from Jayla, but Bailee hadn't responded. Jayla wasn't the type of person she could blow off with a quick summary of her passionate love affair or the new profession she'd stumbled into. She laughed to herself as she imagined Jayla's shocked reaction when she learned that Bailee was the face of HaydenWear.

Jayla would want a detailed report and Bailee simply didn't

have the time to devote to a long, drawn-out conversation with her. At the moment, all she wanted to do was reminisce about the tender moments she and Hayden had shared. She'd talk to Jayla at length when she got back to Philly. And she'd make up for neglecting her by inviting her to the HaydenWear launch party.

Jayla would love the opportunity to show off her slimmed-down body at a glamorous Miami-based event, but Bailee couldn't help worrying that Jayla might possibly drink too much and decide to give a blowjob to the bartender, or the DJ, or a server, or one of the cleaning crew.

Feeling an instant twinge of guilt, she chastised herself for having such a low opinion of her friend. Jayla wouldn't do anything like that. Jayla had denied the disgusting rumors, and obviously Trent had lied on her. End of story.

She smiled as she glanced down at her carry-on bag that rested on the empty seat next to her. She had originally packed light, but now the bag was bulging at the sides, filled with all twenty-two pieces of Hayden's line. He wanted her to get familiar with his apparel and had insisted that she take the entire collection.

Although they'd only been apart for approximately ninety minutes, she already missed him. Her lids fluttered closed as memories of this morning drifted through her mind. Hayden's hard-muscled body snuggled close, and the heat of his growing erection warming her flesh and tantalizing her until her hips involuntarily began a slow, sensual swivel that soon escalated to a swifter more urgent pace.

It was going to be difficult getting through the upcoming week without waking up to the sensation of his hard body pressed against hers. He'd invited her to join him in Miami, but she declined, not wanting to wear out her welcome.

But now, a sense of yearning that was so intense it was palpable, had begun to engulf her, and she regretted not accepting his invitation.

Needing a distraction, she fished her phone out of her purse and checked her messages. There was a text from Claudia Kolinski, her former boss's executive assistant who had been summoned to escort Bailee out of the conference room on the day of her meltdown.

Claudia was the last person Bailee wanted to hear from, and she scoffed when she read the woman's message, inviting Bailee to lunch so they could catch up. Bailee interpreted, "catch up" as a polite way of asking, "Have you recovered from your meltdown? Have you found new employment? And what exactly caused such a dignified person as you to turn into an unhinged lunatic?"

She deleted Claudia's text and then blocked her, ensuring that she never heard from the nosey bitch again.

There were over a dozen texts from Jayla and most included selfies of her wearing skintight dresses and jeans. Jayla was so infatuated with her new body, she'd brazenly stripped down and posed in a two-piece swimsuit.

Jayla's weight loss was incredible and she looked amazing in her clothes, but with her flabby thighs and the way her gut was hanging, she truly wasn't swimsuit ready. She needed to hit the gym and tone up before strutting around half-naked.

Instantly regretting her catty thoughts about Jayla, Bailee reminded herself of Gentle Breeze's slogan, "Love the skin you're in."

She reviewed her e-mails and let out a sigh when she came upon correspondence from her divorce attorney. Trent had been slowing the divorce down by trying to make Bailee liable for his credit card debt and car loan balance. Being a lawyer, Trent knew all the loopholes, and he and his attorney cleverly pointed out that marital debt had not been included in the prenup, and they wanted Bailee to pay up.

She sighed as she moved the distressing e-mail to the saved file to view later.

There was an email from Jayla with a video attachment. She opened it and tapped on the video. Since Jayla loved ratchet videos from WorldStarHipHop.Com, Bailee was expecting to see a neighborhood brawl or a side chick getting beat down or savagely choked out by an irate baby mom, but instead there was a video of two kids and their parents eating at a restaurant.

At first, she didn't understand what she was looking at. It was as if her eyes were playing tricks on her. Confused, she started the video at the beginning and squinted at the two young children and their parents. The mother was a stranger to Bailee, but the man that the kids referred to as "Daddy," was none other than Bailee's husband, Trent.

When the train pulled into Thirtieth Street Station, Bailee texted Jayla to find out her whereabouts. Jayla said she was showing a house on Federal Street and sent the address.

After retrieving her car from the garage, she drove to the Point Breeze section of South Philadelphia. While waiting for Jayla's prospective buyer to leave, she sat in the car, repeatedly watching the video of Trent and his secret family. Each time the video concluded, her trembling middle finger would tap the screen, playing it again.

The pain from each viewing was like taking a bullet to the heart.

Although she could never get over the betrayal of Trent and Giselle's relationship, she'd been on the path to healing. Unfortunately, the discovery that Trent had been leading a double life throughout the course of their marriage had opened up a fresh and bleeding wound that cut deep into her soul.

Were the two kids really Trent's? How was that possible? When did he have time to build a family?

Squinting, she stared at the screen, inspecting the children's faces. Her heart fluttered as she looked closely at the little girl's face and detected eyes that were exactly like Trent's. The boy was a dead ringer for Trent. He had his exact pecan-tan complexion, the shape of his nose, and his unmistakable smile.

Bailee examined the children's mother, wondering if they'd met before. The woman didn't look even vaguely familiar. Was she someone from Trent's office? A client, maybe? Who was this woman who had given birth to two children by a married man?

The moment Bailee noticed Jayla's client leaving, she bolted from the car and raced up the stairs of the charming blue and white home with built-in flower boxes outside the windows.

"Jayla!" she called as she opened the entry door that led to a sun-filled living room that had gleaming hardwood floors and trendy, exposed-brick walls.

"Hi," Jayla said, emerging from the kitchen and beckoning Bailee. The kitchen was ultra-modern, featuring a granite breakfast bar, and sleek, stainless steel appliances.

"I was fixing coffee. Do you want some?" Jayla asked.

"No thanks." Bailee took a seat on a stylish, lime-green leather stool in front of the breakfast bar.

"Water, juice, or tea?" Jayla offered as she poured black coffee into a mug.

"Nothing, I'm good," Bailee said impatiently. "I want to know everything you know about Trent's double life. I want to know why you never told me and why you finally decided to send me the evidence."

Jayla placed a hand on Bailee's shoulder and gave it a squeeze before sitting on the leather stool next to her. "First of all, I would have never kept a secret like that from you. I didn't know Trent was leading a double life."

"When did you find out?"

"Derek and I were at Olive Garden recently, and there were two kids at the opposite table who kept smiling and waving at him, and he kept smiling and waving back. Derek's naïve in a lot of ways, and he doesn't realize that it's not cool to be overly friendly with other people's kids. Anyway, I suggested we switch seats. When I took his seat, I glanced over at the table and saw Trent sitting there. Hearing him being called *Daddy* by the kids was a shock to my system."

"What did he say to you?"

Jayla shook her head. "He didn't recognize me, due to the weight loss, and I put on sunglasses to make sure he didn't. Then I sneakily propped my phone up and began recording."

"I don't understand how he found the time to maintain a second family," Bailee said tearfully. "Those kids looked to be at least four and five years old. How the hell is it possible that he fathered children five years ago and kept up a relationship with their mother?"

"What about all those overnight business trips he used to take?" Jayla suggested.

Bailee nodded. "Yeah, and those late Tuesday nights when he was supposed to be entertaining clients." She groaned. "How could I have been so blind? And what kind of woman would accept a part-time relationship with a married man?" Bailee blurted and then looked away in embarrassment. "Sorry. No offense, Jayla."

"None taken." Jayla gave a shrug. "Don't blame yourself. Trent's side chick was in it for the long haul. She wasn't polished like you, Bailee. She looked like a 'hood bitch to me. For a woman like that to get her clutches into an educated, hard-working professional is a major come-up for the next eighteen years. Trent is probably the best thing that ever happened to her. As long as he takes care of her and her kids, I'm sure she's been willing to play her part and not make any waves."

"This is sick. Trent worked so hard to improve his circumstances. Why would he start a life with someone who's not up to his level, education-wise or professionally? What on Earth do they have in common?"

"With Trent's background, being from the 'hood, too... Well, I hate to say it, but he was probably more comfortable with his baby mom than he was with you."

The truth hurt and Bailee flinched from the pain.

"But maybe there's a silver lining in all of this," Jayla said.

Bailee sucked her teeth. "I doubt it."

"Maybe exposing Trent's deceit can help you with the divorce. You said he was trying to force you to pay his debt. Hopefully, there's an infidelity clause in the prenup that will exempt you from being responsible for the fucking bills he racked up while trying to take care of two households."

Bailee gnawed on her lip. "I wonder where his family lives. What his baby mom drives and whether or not his children attend private school."

"We're gonna find out," Jayla said adamantly. "I read that it's hard to prove what constitutes cheating." She paused and shook her head ruefully and then suddenly, broke into a grin. "But...with the damning video, you have tangible proof that the cheating bastard doesn't deserve a goddam penny from you."

"Actually, I've had proof that he's a cheat for quite a while," Bailee admitted glumly.

"What kind of proof?"

"Nothing that pertains to the children or their mother. There's something I haven't had the heart to tell you."

"Do you wanna fill me in?"

"Trent is involved with my mother. They're living together, and my mom is serious about the relationship."

A look of confusion crossed Jayla's face. She held up her hand and waved it in the air. "Whoa. Wait! What?"

"You heard me. My mother and my husband were having an affair during my marriage and then decided to go public with it."

"But I thought your mom couldn't stand Trent."

"I thought so, too. Stupid, gullible me."

"But…all this time that you and Trent have been separated, you never said a word to me. Why not?"

"I couldn't talk about it. It was too painful. And I was too ashamed to admit that my own mother had callously stolen my husband. But, in light of the secret-family drama, I suppose she's in for the surprise of her life. And she deserves it," Bailee said bitterly.

"Fuck this coffee; I need something much stronger," Jayla announced, placing the coffee mug on the counter. She got up and crossed the kitchen in long strides. Yanking open the fridge, she took out a chilled bottle of wine with a colorful label that was a display of modern art.

"I was going to celebrate with this expensive vino after I sold this house, but I need it now," Jayla said, holding the attractive wine bottle up for Bailee to see. She retrieved a corkscrew from a drawer and opened the bottle. "Would you like a glass?" Jayla asked.

"Sure, a drink will probably help me get through the ordeal of telling the disgraceful, heartbreaking story that I'm about to share with you."

Jayla poured the dark red liquid into two glasses and handed one to Bailee. Bailee swirled the wine, sniffed it, and then took a sip. "What time is your next buyer scheduled to arrive?"

Jayla checked her watch. "Not for another hour and a half."

"Good. Plenty of time for me to open a vein and start bleeding all over again."

"I'm so sorry that you were hurt and betrayed like this. Your mom has to be the most self-centered and non-maternal person in the world. And Trent..." She shook her head. "I don't even know what to say about him. It's no secret that I disliked him, but I never doubted his love for you."

"Yeah, he was pretty convincing. But, now you know that he's a deceptive opportunist. He's a womanizer and it's within the realm of reason that he's also a psychopath."

"Did you suspect he was seeing your mom?"

"Never! They acted like they despised each other and I bought into the ruse.

"Geez. So, how'd you find out?"

"At our anniversary party, I saw my mother comforting Trent after I'd slapped him on the dance floor. I thought it was strange, but didn't give it much thought. After the party, Trent didn't come home for several days. When he finally showed up, he told me he was leaving me for my mom, and he made it clear that he was only interested in her for her money."

"Wow," Jayla uttered.

"When I confronted my mother, she acted entitled to my husband. She told me she was in love with him and seemed to expect me to understand."

Jayla smacked the top of the granite counter. "That dirty bitch has a lot of nerve. She's nothing but a high-class ho."

Bailee chuckled and then said, "I don't know why I'm laughing. You're the only person who can make me laugh during the most serious situations."

"I wasn't being funny; I'm dead serious. Giselle is always on her siddity shit, but all this time, she's been lurking in the shadows, sucking on her son-in-law's dick. Now, that's taking hoe-ishness to a whole other level."

Bailee snickered again. "I don't know why I took so long to tell you. I should have known you'd bring levity to the situation and make me feel better."

"I'm not trying to amuse you, Bailee. Your mother needs her ass kicked and—" Jayla stopped abruptly. She leaned in and eyed Bailee intently. "If you want somebody to bust her kneecaps and mess up her face, say the word and I got you," she said, speaking in a hushed tone.

"Since when did you become gangster?"

"I'm not gangster! Surely, you didn't think I was referring to myself. Oh, hell no, I'm way too cute and too civilized to be attacking somebody with a tire iron, but Derek, on the other hand…" She let her words trail off ominously. "Put it this way, after being locked up for so long, he's no stranger to violence."

"No, I don't even want to go there. Nothing violent or illegal. Trent and my so-called mother are not worth it."

"You're right; that bitch named Karma is going to take care of your mom without your having to lift a finger." Jayla drained the remaining wine from her glass. "I'm curious, though, are you going to tell your mom about Trent's baby mom and his two little crumb snatchers?"

Bailee smiled ruefully. "No."

"Why not?"

"My mother thinks she knows Trent better than I do, and she could be right because apparently, I didn't know him at all. But she had the gall to describe their illicit liaison as sacred. Can you believe that?" Bailee said, shaking her head incredulously. "So… in response to your question, I'm not going to tell her anything until I feel the time is right. And when it's right, I'm going to let her know all about Trent and his secret family. I'm curious to discover how sacred she'll consider their relationship after she finds out that he cheated on both of us."

Chapter 27

Jayla entered her condo and was greeted by the scent of garlic and onions. She could hear the sounds of Derek moving around in the kitchen, opening cabinets, clanging together pots and pans. She dropped her briefcase on the floor, removed her jacket, and hung it on the coat rack.

She strolled into the kitchen, and the sight of Derek hovering over the stove, wearing jeans and a tank top that exposed his beefy arms, stalled her steps and nearly took her breath away.

It was a sin and a shame that she was stuck in the friend zone with such a big, fine man.

Unconsciously, her tongue flicked against her lips. "Something smells good. What are you making?" she asked, purposely keeping her voice steady and devoid of lust.

Derek looked over his shoulder and grinned. "I found out from your mom that you love lemongrass and garlic shrimp over noodles. I found a recipe online."

Jayla looked at Derek, blinked, and sat down. "*You* found something online?"

"Yeah, I finally broke down and upgraded my phone." He turned toward the countertop and picked up a sleek Android. "They showed me the basics at the phone store, and I googled the Thai recipe. Cooking Thai food is a lot easier than I would have thought."

"Aw, that's so sweet, but I'm not hungry."

"I'm not trying to hear that. I'm gonna keep it a hundred, Jayla. Ms. Lorraine is worried that you're going to dwindle down to skin and bones and get sick as a dog. I gave her my word that I wouldn't let that happen. It's time for you to start following the doctor's orders and eat a lot of small meals every day."

Though Derek's tone was quiet, it was surprisingly firm. His body language was dynamic and masculine, giving Jayla the impression that he wouldn't hesitate to beat her ass and force-feed her if he had to. The way his muscles tensed was somewhat threatening and extremely attractive at the same time, and Jayla found herself growing slightly moist between her thighs.

Damn, damn, damn. Why does this motherfucker have to be gay?

He catered to Jayla throughout the meal, placing napkins in front of her, adding ice cubes to her iced tea, and even pouring Equal into the drink and then stirring it briskly. It felt good being cared for in such a genuine way, but she wished Derek was capable of seeing her in more than a sisterly way.

They were as intimate as lovers, minus the sex. They often cuddled together on the sofa while watching TV, they played video games together, he rubbed her feet when she complained about having to walk around in heels all day, and they enjoyed the same kind of music—old school—and were both anxiously waiting for Janet Jackson to lose her baby weight and get back on tour.

Jayla ate slowly, chewing the shrimp thoroughly in order to get it down. "This is delicious. It tastes like it was prepared by an authentic Thai chef."

Derek smiled appreciatively. "Glad you like it. By the way, how'd it go with the house in South Philly today? Any offers?"

"Not yet, but I'm not worried. The houses in that area are going like hotcakes. Gentrification is no joke! It's unbelievable that those small row homes are selling for up to five hundred thousand." She made a scornful sound. "And the only reason my boss gave me that listing is due to my weight loss. I suppose I look presentable enough to show houses that will bring in a decent commission." She angrily speared a piece of shrimp with her fork. "I can't wait until I start working for myself on a full-time basis." She let out a breath of frustration. "Anyway, I'm showing the house again tomorrow and I know I'll get a sale. To be honest, I have to blame myself for today because I wasn't into it and my pitch was a little off."

Derek's thick brows knitted together. "Oh, yeah? What was wrong?"

"After all this time, Bailee finally decided to open the e-mail with the video that I sent her."

"Oh, shit!"

"She came by the house while I was between showings."

"Was she was fired up?"

"Not exactly. It was more like she was extremely hurt and downhearted."

Derek nodded in understanding. "Even though their marriage was already over, it couldn't be easy for her to find out what he was into."

"And there's even more to the story." Jayla shook her head gravely.

"Spill it. I'm all ears."

She took a deep breath and let it out. "Trent was cheating on Bailee with her mother."

Derek frowned. "Huh?"

"You heard me. Her mom unapologetically stole her man."

"That's fucked up."

"Tell me about it. But don't feel too sorry for Bailee. Believe me, she always lands on her feet. After she got over the shock of Trent's secret life, and after she bitched about him and her mom, she politely informed me that she's involved in a passionate love affair with Hayden Charles."

"Who's that?"

"You know Hayden Charles, he's the hot-as-hell workout dude—they call him the Workout King. He sells millions of workout DVDs."

Derek shrugged. "I've been locked up, so how would I know who's hot and who's not?"

"I keep forgetting that you lost ten years." Jayla pulled up a YouTube video on her phone and handed it to Derek.

As Derek viewed Hayden's video, she studied his face to see if she would detect a glint of lust in his eyes. Braced to feel the painful sting of jealousy, she sat on the edge of her seat.

"I never saw or heard of him, but he's got a sweet hustle."

"I know, right?" Jayla said, relieved that Derek didn't appear to be attracted to Hayden. "Do you want to meet him?" she asked with a sly grin.

"Sure. Is he in Philly?"

"Nope. He's in Miami and Bailee invited us to celebrate with them. She's covering our airfare, hotel, food—everything!"

He questioned her with his eyes. "Celebrate what? Are they getting engaged?"

"No, it's not that serious…at least I don't think it is. He's having a launch party in Miami for his new fitness clothing line and—"

"Oh, wow. That brother's about his business; he's not bullshitting at all," Derek interjected, clearly impressed.

"You and I are not bullshitting, either. In fact, day after tomorrow, we're going to bid on a property and then we're going from bar-to-bar until we find my Uncle Gator. He's a hot drunken mess most of the time, but when he's sober, he's a hard worker. He knows how to throw up some drywall and he can follow instructions on anything you need him to do. In time, you'll have a whole team of workers, and we're going to be flipping houses like crazy."

"I wasn't comparing our business venture with what Bailee's man has accomplished. Why're you taking it personal?"

"I'm sorry if it sounds like I'm being defensive." She sighed. "It's just that Bailee stays winning. Even when she's down, she has a knack for getting up and leaving me in the dust. It's bad enough that she was born with a silver spoon in her mouth, but back in college, she consistently made the dean's list. And then, Trent put a ring on it two seconds after we graduated."

"And that worked out well," Derek said sarcastically.

"Yeah, but you have to understand…all my adult life I've been single, working for commission, and always struggling financially. Being a big girl was yet another burden. Meanwhile, Bailee didn't seem encumbered by her weight. She had a happy marriage, or so I thought. And, she had a high-powered job and an inheritance to look forward to."

"So, you've been jealous of her all these years?"

"Sort of. And the secret jealousy made me feel so guilty because she's my girl."

"You're only human, but you need to work on the jealousy thing. It's not healthy."

"I know, it's not cool at all. I thought we were finally going to become equals when we shared our weight loss journey together. In my mind, being equals meant we'd both be single at the same time as we navigated the dating world with new bodies and a new outlook on life. But Bailee is already romantically linked…and with a celebrity, no less."

Derek scowled. "Calling a fitness trainer a celebrity is a stretch, don't you think?"

"He's very well known, but that's neither here nor there. Bailee told me that Hayden chose her to be the face of his brand. My girl, who is such a brilliant mathematician that she could get a job anywhere, is now entering brand-new territory and is about to take the fashion world by storm." Jayla shook her head. "Some people have all the luck."

"It's workout wear, not high fashion," Derek said, attempting to lessen Jayla's envy.

"You know what I mean. She's going to be representing plus-size women. With the kind of luck Bailee has, her modeling career will blow up bigger than Ashley Graham's."

"And what's wrong with that? After the hell she's been through, you should be happy for her instead of bitching and complaining."

"You're right, but I can't help how I feel." Brooding, Jayla put her fork down and grimaced as she touched her stomach. "I can't eat anymore; I'm full."

Derek rose to his feet and removed her plate. "Do you have room for dessert—a half-scoop of frozen yogurt?"

She shook her head glumly.

"You need to let it go, Jayla. It's not cool to harbor resentment and jealousy toward your closest friend."

"Don't you think I know that," she whined. "I'm a horrible person. But I'm sick of being the friend who's a charity-case. I just want Bailee and me to be equals."

"You *are* equals. Nobody is better than anyone else, no matter how much they have in their bank account. You're letting your insecurities get the best of you, and if you don't watch it, the negative chatter in your head is going to ruin a good friendship."

"I keep my emotions in check. Bailee has no idea that I'm jealous of her."

"Don't be so sure. Emotions have their own energy and sometimes speak louder than words," he said wisely.

"What can I do, Derek? It's not like I can control the way I feel."

"Sure, you can."

"How?"

"Every time the green monster called envy rears its ugly head, think about how good Bailee has always been to you and replace that negativity with gratitude."

She sighed. "I'll try."

"Don't try—do it. Believe me, you'll feel better."

"A hot bath will make me feel better," Jayla said as she pushed away from the table. "Thanks for making dinner." As she headed for her bedroom, she attempted a smile, but didn't quite pull it off.

Lying across her bed and feeling lonely and dejected, she logged into her Tinder account, hoping a quick hookup would improve her mood. As she perused profiles, Derek tapped on her bedroom door.

"Come in," she said tonelessly.

Derek stepped inside her bedroom and Jayla didn't bother to look up as she stared at the screen, swiftly scrolling through a myriad of male faces.

Derek looked at her and shook his head. "You said you wanted to take a bath, but I should have known that was an excuse to sneak off and hunt down some dick."

"Why do you care?" she snapped.

"I care about you, Jayla. Every time you get with one of those clowns from your dating app, you end up depressed, moping around, and talking about how much you hate yourself."

"I *do* hate myself." Jayla let her phone slip from her hand and tumble onto the bed.

"Don't say that."

"It's the truth. I expected my life to drastically change after the surgery, but it didn't. It's still the same."

"Maybe you need counseling."

"Fuck that! I need a man with a strong back and a dominant personality."

"No, you don't. You need someone to love and cherish you."

"That's never going to happen, and I might as well be true to who I am."

"The woman who allows men to treat her like shit is a personality you invented because you didn't feel worthy of love."

"Apparently, I still don't. Bailee has her knight-in-shining-armor and I don't have anyone."

Derek sat on the bed and stroked the top of her hand with his fingers. "You have me." He leaned in and planted a delicate kiss on her cheek.

She leaned away from him. "I don't want your pity, Derek. You don't want me; you're into men."

"Yes, but I'm also into you. And not just in a sisterly way." He squeezed her hand tightly and then moved it downward, allowing her to feel the effect she had on him.

Having Derek offer himself to her was a dream come true, and in her moment of need, she no longer cared that he was offering his body out of pity for her. She sucked in a deep breath as he unzipped his pants and released his dick. Her hand wrapped around the thick shaft and gripped it without hesitation.

"You don't have to leave home for dick anymore, baby. I got you," he said softly. "From now on, anytime you're down, you can ride my dick…okay?"

"Okay." Her voice came out in a whimper, and then a sound of lust escaped her throat as she stroked his dick, her hand moving up and down slowly, from the tip to the base. A dribble of cum seeped out of the engorged tip, and she took that as her cue to lower her head and encircle the head of his dick with her lips. Before pulling the meaty shaft fully inside her mouth, she licked the drippings and moaned at the sweet and salty taste.

After lapping up all the pre-cum, she ran her tongue along the underside of his shaft, and then pulled him in so deeply she could feel his hot flesh pressing against the back of her throat and his nut sac brushing against her face.

The grunting sounds emanating from Derek encouraged her to bob her head up and down while putting immense suction on his throbbing erection. The fingers that had been entangled in her hair began moving downward, pulling up her dress and tugging down her panties. In a matter of moments, she found herself splayed out on the bed with Derek on top of her, slowly penetrating.

"Is this what you want, ho?" he asked in a gruff voice that surprised her.

"Yes," she responded, so aroused that her body began undulating at an accelerated speed.

"Are you gonna keep going online looking for strange dick?" He yanked her hair painfully. As he slammed his dick inside her, Jayla's hips rose up to meet each forceful thrust.

"No more strange dick for me...I promise," she said, panting between each word.

"From now on, I'm gonna punish this pussy every time you even think about logging into a dating app."

"That's what I need. I need to be punished and manhandled," she said breathlessly.

In response, he held her legs open and pumped dick into her until she could no longer speak comprehensibly.

Next, he flipped her over so that she was riding him. Then, he stretched an arm out and suddenly slapped her ass with such force that Jayla yelled at the top of her lungs as a powerful orgasm took her by surprise, causing her to collapse on top of him.

Chapter 28

I t was a magical night.

The audience was filled with buyers from Nordstrom, Kohl's, Macy's, and other major retailers. The hottest trainers, top photographers, and stylists were in attendance, and a few recognizable celebrities had also made their way to the event.

To kick things off, dancers dressed in HaydenWear tights and sports bras performed choreographed routines on the runway. The dance segment was intended to demonstrate the brand's flexibility for women with active lifestyles. Following the dancers, ten models emerged on stage in succession, revealing the remaining twenty pieces of the line.

At the conclusion of the runway show, a montage of the pictures filled the projection screen that served as a visual backdrop for the program. The entire montage was pictures of Bailee that had been taken at the New York photo shoot.

Bailee was immediately bombarded by photographers and fashion editors. They all asked for her management team's contact information.

"I don't have a management team," she told everyone, and within minutes, her purse was filled with business cards.

Needing a moment to gather her wits, she excused herself and made her way toward Jayla and Derek. Although she'd heard a lot about him, it would be her first meeting Derek in person.

As Bailee approached, Derek began applauding. "Bravo! Bravo! You looked amazing on screen and you look even more amazing in person," he exclaimed good-naturedly.

Jayla introduced Bailee and Derek, and Bailee liked him instantly. She thought he and Jayla made a stunning couple, and he seemed attentive as a boyfriend, but Jayla had told her that he was gay.

"Can I get your autograph?" Derek asked Bailee teasingly.

"Stop making me blush," Bailee said, her face visibly flushed. "I'm not used to so much attention. It's supposed to be Hayden's night—not mine." She noticed Jayla holding a rainbow-colored cocktail and she suddenly felt thirsty. "Your drink looks good; I need one of those," she said, looking around for a server.

"I'll get you one," Derek offered. He spotted a server on the other side of the room and squeezed through the crowd to get to her.

Alone with Jayla, Bailee grinned at her. "What'd you think about the show?"

"In one word, awesome! I think I'm going to start working out at the gym to have a reason to rock HaydenWear," Jayla said with a big smile. "And you looked phenomenal, girl. I felt so proud seeing you splashed across that huge screen." She leaned in and gave Bailee a quick hug. "I'm really happy for you. And this party is everything."

"I'm glad you're having a good time. What about Derek? Is he enjoying himself?"

"Oh, yeah, but our night won't be complete until we meet the Workout King!"

"Oh, I'm sorry. There's been so much going on, I totally forgot to introduce you." Bailee gazed around the room and spotted

Hayden in the midst of a group of people. "As soon as he gets a free moment, I'll introduce you. By the way, Jayla, you look amazing, too. You look like you lost more weight since I saw you in Philly. Girl, if you don't watch it, you're going to completely disappear."

"Everybody keeps saying that, but the way I see it, you can never be too thin," Jayla retorted.

"Be careful, okay? Make sure you're getting proper nutrition."

"Chile, as long as I look good, what do I care about proper nutrition?" Jayla waved a hand, blowing off Bailee's advice.

There was no point in expecting Jayla to respond reasonably, and so Bailee changed the subject. "Is it my imagination or are you and Derek a little more than friends? If I didn't know better, I'd think you two were a couple," she said breezily.

"Oh, I've been meaning to tell you. We're a thing now."

"You are?" Bailee creased her brow. "But…he's gay, right?" she asked in a whisper.

"It turns out, he's bi," Jayla replied, lifting her shoulders in a "go figure" gesture. "He considered himself straight until he went to prison. Being that he grew up in there, most of his sexual relationships have been with men. But that was more out of necessity than his true preference."

"Jayla!" Bailee said, sounding both exasperated and condescending at the same time.

"We're happy," Jayla interjected. "He gets me. And we're in love, so don't judge."

"All right," Bailee muttered, keeping her cynical thoughts to herself.

Derek returned with Bailee's cocktail. As the three of them chatted, Bailee noticed that Derek seemed really into Jayla, brushing her hair out of her face, encircling her waist with his arm, and constantly smiling at her. Bailee couldn't remember ever seeing Jayla being so supported and cared for by a man. She told herself that it didn't matter what his sexual orientation was as long as he was good to her friend.

Eventually, Bailee made eye contact with Hayden, and she beckoned him with a smile and a wave.

As Hayden drew close, Bailee noticed a glint in both Jayla's and Derek's eyes. They were both giving him unmistakable looks of lust. Confused, she looked from Derek to Jayla, but they didn't return her gaze; they were both too busy checking out Hayden to pay her any attention.

What the hell?

Not wanting to betray her inner turmoil, she struggled to keep her expression neutral as she introduced Hayden to Jayla and Derek. Hayden and Derek gave each other dap, and Bailee watched Hayden like a hawk, making sure Derek didn't attempt to whisper in her man's ear.

"It was nice meeting you both," Hayden said. "Now, if you don't mind, I have to steal Bailee for a while and introduce the face of HaydenWear to an editor from *Self* magazine."

Bailee had been ducking the journalists and fashion editors that had attended the launch, but the weird vibes that she was picking up from Jayla and Derek made her uncomfortable, and she was glad to take Hayden's hand and be led to the opposite side of the room.

Crowds parted for Hayden and as he and Bailee moved smoothly through the throng of guests.

She noticed the runway models milling about and socializing. Oddly, as beautiful as they all were, there seemed to be a vacant look in their eyes that only brightened when they gazed at their reflections in the many mirrored walls of the venue. A few of the models glanced at Bailee uncomprehendingly as if wondering why their starvation diets and countless hours of spin classes had not earned them the honor of being the face of HaydenWear.

"Why weren't there any plus-size models in the show?" Bailee asked Hayden.

"Plus-size models are a minority in the fashion industry, and now that top designers are putting them in their shows, those that know how to walk the runway are in such high demand, we weren't able to book any of them for my show. But I'll be better prepared when I expand the line."

"Are you planning to expand already?"

"I have to if I want to stay in the game. We've already started preparing for the next campaign," he said.

"That's fast."

"The industry moves at a fast pace," he replied. "Ah, there's Rowena." Smiling, he led Bailee toward a tall, older woman with close-cropped silver hair.

Bailee's mind was a million miles away as Rowena discussed featuring her in an upcoming issue of the magazine.

Tears welled up from deep inside her as she thought about how, in another life, the fashion spread would have undoubtedly won Giselle's approval. Accepting that her mother's approval no longer mattered, she blinked away the moisture from her lashes and fixed a smile on her face as she gave Rowena her undivided attention.

After lovemaking, while drenched in sweat and bliss, Bailee rested her head on Hayden's chest.

"We've both been working so hard, I think we should enjoy a relaxing day at the beach tomorrow," Hayden said lazily as his fingers sifted through Bailee's locs.

"Sounds great except I forgot to pack a swimsuit."

"That's not a problem. We can pick one up."

"Picking out a swimsuit is not that simple. I'll end up trying on one after another, searching for something flattering to my body type, and I'll be exhausted before we even get to the beach." Bailee let out a sigh, dreading the hunt for a bathing suit and wished she'd remembered to pack one.

"Don't sweat it. We don't have to go to the beach. How'd you like to take an airboat ride through the Everglades?"

She made a face. "Are you inviting me to ride through swamps—with alligators?"

"It'll be fun." He gave her a wicked smile.

"I'd rather suffer through the ordeal of trying on bathing suits."

"Then it's settled. We're spending a peaceful day at the beach."

"You're so conniving," she said, playfully jabbing him in his side.

Hayden chuckled as he caressed the curled hair on her temple. "You haven't said much about the magazine spread. How do you feel about it?"

"Good."

"Good? Is that it? Rowena went to a lot of trouble and had to move things around to include you in the September issue."

"And I appreciate it…"

"But?" Hayden removed his arm from around her and sat up. "Something's bothering you. What is it?"

"I don't want you to think I'm ungrateful, but my background is in finance, and although it's flattering to be the face of Hayden-Wear, I realize that modeling is not all that stimulating. It's not the kind of work that'll keep me satisfied for long."

"Are you ready to return to banking?"

"No, not at all. I was thinking about a collaboration. I want to help you enhance your brand with a plus-size line. I realize your current line is supposed to be all-inclusive, but to me, it seems as if you threw some larger sizes into the mix, as an afterthought."

"It was well planned, not an afterthought."

"It was a little absurd to have all those skinny models on the runway and then feature me as the face of your brand."

"Everyone loved the idea of a plus-size model representing the brand. Why do you think Rowena was so enthusiastic?"

"I get your vision, but why not create workout clothes that are strictly for bigger women? I'd love to work with you on an exclusive plus-size line that includes swimwear. My vision is a line that promotes body positivity and empowerment for women who are not built like twigs."

"I like the idea."

"Good! We could call it HaydenWear 2.0 or...um, how about HaydenWear Fierce?"

"I like both names, but I have to tell you that although your proposal sounds good in theory, it takes money, and I'm already up to my eyeballs in debt. Pulling off your idea would require lots of investors. You wouldn't believe how difficult it is to get investors interested in new ideas."

Bailee thought about all the numerous connections she'd made during her years in banking and she felt inspired. "I used to work directly with CEOs of big companies as well as smaller upstart, tech companies that make more money than they know what to do with. I'd love the challenge of going after money. I have no doubt that I can bring in investors."

"I'll tell you what. You work on the money aspect and I'll work on lining up designers to work with us on a limited-edition capsule collection of the plus-size line."

"Really?" Bailee hadn't felt this excited over a project in a long time.

"HaydenWear Fierce, huh?" Hayden said, nodding in approval.

"Or HaydenWear 2.0," she reminded him.

He nodded. "They're both catchy, but I'm leaning toward Fierce. Yeah, I really like it!"

"And I *really* like you," Bailee said, cupping his face and kissing him.

Remarkably, all it had taken was a little pillow talk to upgrade her position from employee to partner. Feeling sexually satisfied and emotionally fulfilled, she drifted off to sleep in Hayden's arms.

Chapter 29

"Are you nervous about tonight?" Jayla asked Derek.

"No. But, since it's our last night here in Miami, I'd rather hit up some of the clubs instead of following through with your idea."

"It's important to me."

"I know, babe. I just wish you could have stayed off that dating app while we're on a free vacation."

"I told you the deal. It's a special opportunity that I can't pass up. Anyway, it's the last time I'm going to degrade myself or allow anyone to degrade me." She gazed at Derek sincerely. "I promise that after this, I'm through with online dating."

"I hope you stick to your word because what you're asking me to do is a crime that could send me back to prison." He swallowed. "But I'm all in because I love you, Jayla."

"And I love you, too. Although the average person wouldn't be able to understand our relationship, it works for us, and that's all that matters."

"Exactly," he said, gazing down at the sleazy lingerie she had packed in her overnight bag.

Jayla picked up a see-through negligee and held it up to her.

"It's surreal that I can fit into this tiny outfit without ripping it open at the seams. Even my shoe size has decreased a whole size," she said with pride as she added a pair of hooker heels to the top of the pile of provocative clothing.

It was going to be a sleazy night and she'd selected a cheap, disreputable hotel for the tawdry rendezvous.

Despite having the thin body she'd always dreamed of and despite having a man that adored her, Jayla still battled with low self-esteem, and tonight she would embrace her inner slut in the hope of making peace with the past.

Tonight would be risky because the dude from Tinder stated that he wanted to handcuff her and treat her like scum. Being treated like scum was something she had grown accustomed to in her former, fat life, but being handcuffed was taking her secret shame to the next level of debauchery.

The danger involved in her latest escapade caused her heart to pound. What she had planned was much more risky than blowing a bartender in a crowded ballroom or letting a pack of horny dudes run a train on her in the bathroom at her best friend's wedding.

Those acts had been decadent and immoral, and she'd lied through her teeth when Bailee had confronted her about her sexual antics. She had no choice but to lie; she couldn't admit to those skanky actions and expect Bailee to understand. Bailee had no idea of how low Jayla could go. She'd probably cry for her if she knew about the strange men Jayla had asked to ejaculate on different parts of her body. Bailee would probably beg Jayla to get professional help if she was aware of how much Jayla craved humiliation.

Although she couldn't share her shameful secret with Bailee, she'd told Derek everything about herself, and although he reluctantly agreed to assist her in her final escapade, he didn't judge her.

As she stuffed an assortment of bondage toys inside her bag, excitement streaked through her and a shiver ran down her spine.

She stroked the straps of the pink suede flogger, wondering if she'd have the nerve to let her date put it to use. There was no reason to be afraid since Derek would be on standby to fuck dude up if he got out of hand.

She zipped up her bag and looked at Derek. "Are you ready for this?"

"Not really, but I got your back. If shit goes south, text me, and I'll be right here, tearing the door off the hinges."

"You won't have to do that, Derek. You have a key," she reminded him with a smile.

"Tearing down the door was just an expression. I know how to enter a room discreetly."

"Good, because the last thing we need is for someone to complain about a disturbance and get the police involved."

"The cops are the last people I want to see. Trust, I'll be as quiet as a cat burglar when I punch dude in the throat."

Jayla laughed at Derek's comment as she critically observed her reflection in the mirror. She noted how different she looked from the woman who had been dogged out by Sadeeq and so many others before him.

At last, she had a body that matched the face that everyone said was so pretty for a fat girl. Yet, she was still unable to accept that she'd transformed into the total package: an attractive, educated, and sophisticated woman that any man would be proud to take home to Mama. Deep down inside, she was still a fat girl, unacceptable in the eyes of a society that worshipped skinny chicks.

"Did you pack everything you needed?" Derek asked, breaking into her thoughts, nudging his chin toward her jam-packed overnight bag.

"Yep, everything I need is in there."

"After tonight, you're going to stop playing around with these low-life dudes from dating apps and we're starting a new life together. Do you hear me?"

Jayla nodded. "Yeah, I hear you," she agreed in a voice barely above a whisper.

"I'm not convinced that you're ready to change your ways." Derek folded his arms. "Listen, I'm going to be there for you tonight because I know it's important to you, but after this, I'm not going along with any more of your self-deprecating behavior. It's okay to get freaky, but not at the expense of your self-worth. Letting dudes treat you like a scraggly-ass ho could get you hurt. Or killed," he added ominously. "It's not cool, Jayla."

"I know. I already said this is the last time," she said in an aggravated tone. "After tonight, no more giving away ass and top to random men. The purpose of tonight is to give myself closure and to officially say goodbye to the fat chick inside my head."

"You want to blow an L before we get into it?" the man asked.

"No, I'm good, but you can go ahead," Jayla replied.

Stretched out on the bed, he sparked up and then leisurely began massaging the dick print that was visible the moment he walked into the motel room.

He looked at Jayla leeringly. "Come over here and rub on this big dick while I get lit."

Jayla sat on the bed next to him and obeyed his command. "Is this how you like it?" she asked softly as her hand glided over the hard mass of passion that swelled beneath his pants.

"I'd like it better if you stick your hand inside my pants and grip my jawn in the raw."

"Okay," she responded breathily. She could feel his eyes on her as she unbuckled his belt and lowered the zipper of his pants.

"I don't know why you look so familiar," he said. "Feels like I know you from somewhere." With his forehead wrinkled in thought, he drew in a cloud of smoke and held it in his lungs. "Were you on Facebook Live about a couple months ago, sucking on a dildo?"

"No."

"My bad. It was a fat bitch that favored you a little. In this secret group on Facebook, there was this fat bitch that would suck on a bunch of different sized dildos just to get attention and to feel loved. The bitch was eating up rubber dick. She was on some Kardashian shit without the money or the banging body," he said, laughing scornfully at the recollection.

"Did you ever communicate with the, uh, fat chick?"

"Yeah, the bitch stayed up in my inbox, trying to get some dick action."

"Did you give her some dick?"

"What's it to your nut-ass? Why're you asking a thousand and one questions like you're my woman," he said, frowning up his face, obviously peeved. "Besides, I'm not trying to live in the past. Tonight is about you being my personal slut. While I'm on some chill shit, relaxing and whatnot, I want you to lick my balls. Don't be rushing through it, though. Do it nice and slow. You feel me, slut?"

"Yes," she said dreamily, noticing how her pussy had started twitching the moment he called her out of her name and had started giving her commands. Not once had he complimented her looks or her sexy lingerie. To him, she was a bum-bitch with low self-esteem, and her attractiveness didn't matter. Since this would be the very last time she'd allow anyone to treat her like dirt, she planned to put her whole heart into the moment and enjoy her last hoorah as a skeezer.

He set the weed in the ashtray and took off his pants and then his drawers. He settled into a relaxed position and widened his legs into a V-shape, motioning her to maneuver into the space he'd provided.

Lying on her belly, Jayla slithered up to his crotch, and as he hand-stroked his burgeoning erection, she tongue-bathed his nuts.

"Mmmph! I'm ready to bust that ass wide open, you dirty ho. But I want to restrain you and have some fun beating up on that stank pussy for a while." He grabbed a handful of her hair and yanked her head upward. "Did you bring the handcuffs and the whip?"

"I brought handcuffs and a flogger," she said in a trembling voice.

"That'll work. I'ma beat the shit out of that whory pussy, and make sure it's decorated with thick, red welts before I put my dick in it," he promised and the gruffness of his voice caused Jayla's clit to throb.

Both aroused and disgusted, it was clearly time for her to text Derek, so he could save her from her own twisted desires. The freak in her yearned for the full range of sadistic torture that her brutish date had promised to deliver. If it were up to her, she wouldn't leave the room until every orifice was filled with cum and every inch of her body was covered with handprints and whip lashes.

She was sickened by herself as she lathered his balls generously. Overcome with lust, she squeezed her thighs together as he called her vile names and pulled her hair so hard, she felt strands being ripped from her scalp.

He smacked her upside the head. "That's enough nut sucking. It's time to wrap those juicy lips around my joint." He clutched his dick at the base and aimed it at her mouth. "Open wide," he said jeeringly. "And if you suck it right, I'll let you bury your face between my ass cheeks."

Despite her numerous perversions, eating ass was where she drew the line, and she was reminded of why she hated her date so much. She made a move to get to her phone, but the moment she tried to get to the other side of the room, he leapt off the bed and grabbed her by the wrist.

"Going somewhere? I know your dirty ass didn't ask me to come to this fuckin' skeezy motel so you could waste my time. Now, get on your hands and knees and crawl for this dick. You know what it is. You know that my dick runs shit," he boasted, leering at her as he fisted his hard-on. "Crawl over here and lick this ass, while I jack off," he demanded.

Her lips quivered as she lowered herself to the floor. The threat of being forced to lick an asshole sent her hurtling back to reality, remembering the real reason she was there.

Her connection with Derek was amazing, and he didn't need a text to know she was in trouble. Heeding her silent cry for help, Derek's movements could be heard outside the door.

"What the fuck is going on in there?" Derek inquired in a voice that was a low rumble of rage. Then, he stuck his key card in the slot.

"Who the fuck is that?" the man asked, his eyes narrowing as he focused on the opening door.

Derek came barreling in. Standing at six feet five inches and weighing two-hundred-and-twenty pounds of solid muscle, his eyes glowered with rage.

He was an intimidating sight as he took long strides toward Jayla. "What the fuck do you think you're doing, Jayla? You didn't think I could track you down, did you? You sneaky-ass bitch."

"Please, Derek, calm down. I can explain," Jayla cried out, playing the part she'd rehearsed on the way to the motel.

"Don't tell me to calm down." He turned his fiery gaze on the man, who was wearing a shirt but no pants or drawers and was trying to shield his dick that had gone limp with his hands.

"I don't know who you are and I don't know what's going on, but I think I should be on my way," the man said, his eyes bouncing around the room nervously.

Derek reared back in indignation. "You don't know who I am?

Well, let me inform you, muthafucka. I'm her muthafuckin' husband, nigga. Who the fuck is you?" Derek asked, stalking toward the man.

"Yo, I don't even know this broad. She contacted me online. Begged me to meet her here. She got serious issues, man. She wants a nigga to call her names and handcuff her and shit. I was only giving her what she asked for, but I'm really not even into that kind of freak shit," the man explained as he tried to creep over to the chair where he'd tossed his pants and underwear.

"Whoa, whoa, whoa! Hold up, nigga! You ain't going anywhere—not until we get some shit straight." Derek pulled up his shirt, revealing the handle of a gun that jutted out of his waistband.

Jayla hurried to Derek's side. "Let him go, babe. You know how your temper is, and uh, the last thing we need is another body on our hands."

The man's eyes nearly bulged out of his head at the words, *another body.*

"I'm sorry, okay, babe?" Jayla continued. "I'm dead wrong for cheating on you, and I'll make it up to you at home. I'll do anything you want, but please don't shoot him." Jayla's voice trembled as if she were sobbing, although she hadn't shed a single tear. As the big showdown unfolded, she was improvising and was quite pleased with how believable she sounded.

"Nah, you should have thought about this nigga's safety before you decided to spread your legs for dude. He ain't going anywhere," Derek asserted, shaking his head grimly. "I'm feeling some kind of way—like this nigga is challenging my manhood."

"Yo, I don't even know you. I don't know anything about you, so how am I challenging your manhood?" Mounting fear was evident in the man's voice as he stood in place, still shielding his privates with both hands.

"I can't believe you asked this fool to handcuff you, baby. You ain't never asked me to tie you up or nothing," Derek said, feigning emotional pain.

Jayla dropped her gaze. "I'm sorry. I was too embarrassed to let you know about my fetishes."

"Well, I'm not too embarrassed to let you know about mine. We gotta be honest with each other. It's the only way our marriage is gonna last."

The man gave a sigh of relief. "I'm happy to see you lovebirds working everything out. Now, if you don't mind, I have somewhere to be."

"Nigga, shut the fuck up. You violated my wife. You handcuffed and disrespected her and now it's your turn."

"My turn for what?" The man's face twitched and contorted as he attempted to make sense of Derek's outrageous threat.

"Where's your handcuffs, nigga? You about to get a taste of your own medicine."

"I don't have any handcuffs. Your wife is the one who brought the bondage equipment. I told you she likes that weird shit."

Derek fixed his narrow-eyed gaze on Jayla. "Give me the handcuffs."

"If I give them to you, will you handcuff him to the headboard and then just leave? I really don't want to be involved in any more violence, honey."

The man grimaced. "Yo, ain't nobody handcuffing me to a muthafuckin' thing. Now, if you crazy muthafuckas don't mind, I'd like to put my clothes on and get up out of here."

"You think your hands are bulletproof?" Derek asked in a low, deadly tone.

The man looked down at his hands that were concealing his goods. "Uh…"

"I didn't think so. If you make another move without my permission, I'ma shoot your dick off."

The man flinched.

Jayla shook her head. "No, baby, if you shoot his dick off, he'll bleed to death, and we're gonna get in trouble if we keep burying dead bodies," Jayla complained.

"We ain't gotta bury nothing. Use your head and think, baby. All we need is some gasoline and a remote spot in the woods... that's all we need to get rid of evidence."

"You're right," Jayla said, her expression hardening as she looked at the man.

The man shook his head. "Oh! Okay, I get it. This is a setup. Y'all working together to rob me. Well, I don't have much cash on me, but we can go to an ATM if you want."

"I don't want your money, man. I want some ass," Derek boldly proclaimed.

The man reared back in indignation. "Come again?"

"I didn't stutter." Derek nodded toward Jayla's overnight back. "Get your toys out of the bag, baby. It's playtime."

"Wait! I'm not into any gay shit," the man protested.

"But you're into rape, right, *Niles*," Jayla interjected, emphasizing the man's name as she handed Derek the handcuffs and a gag ball.

"Niles? Where'd you get that name? I told you my name was Fred," Niles said in desperation.

"Yes, you did tell me your name was Fred, but I never forget a face. I especially don't forget the face of the scumbag that raped me and made me lick his ass. You've probably been raping women up and down the East Coast, but you're gonna learn today what it feels like to be a victim."

"Please," Niles whined. "I thought you looked familiar. You used to be a fat bitch, right? You told me you wanted to be treated like dirt."

"When you were in Philly, I gave you clear instructions on what I would and wouldn't do, and yet you forced me to do some foul shit that I was against."

"I'm sorry." Niles darted his eyes at Derek, who began stripping off his clothes.

"Too late," Jayla said, putting a collar around Niles's neck and attaching a chain leash to it. "All right, lil' doggie, I want you to get to licking my man's ass."

Derek handed Jayla the gun and then got on the bed. Lying on his back, he pulled his legs up, presenting his open asshole. "Tongue it, bitch," he implored.

Tears rolled from Niles's eyes and he gagged repeatedly as he served Derek tongue.

Jayla snapped plenty of pictures, making sure to get clear shots of Niles's face as he alternately licked ass and sucked dick.

By the time Derek started lubing up his condom-covered erection, Niles was pleading for mercy.

"Shh!" Jayla whispered. "Calm down. You're too tense. Relax and let my baby find the G-Spot in your ass. I guarantee you that by the time he finishes pressing his big dick against your prostate gland, you're never going to want pussy again."

"Nooooo!" Niles screamed into the pillow as Derek slowly worked his dick into his ass. At this point, Jayla was filming a video with Derek wearing a leather hood that concealed his face, while Niles's face was completely exposed.

"Do you want this to play in the secret group on Facebook Live with your screenname attached?" she asked.

Groaning with pain, Niles shook his head.

"Okay, then. I want you to calm down, relax your ass muscles, and enjoy the ride. You ol, bitch-ass nigga," she added snidely.

Chapter 30

Jayla's plan to invest in real estate was virtually impossible as long as her mother continually changed her mind about loaning her the money. One day, Lorraine was enthusiastic and on board with the idea, and the next day, she'd have a change of heart. She engaged in weekly prayer meetings with her pastor, beseeching the Lord to help her reach a sound decision, but the weeks kept passing without Lorraine receiving any answers from above.

Jayla blamed the pastor for the long delay. She believed he was filling Lorraine's head with doubt because he wanted the money for the church…or to line his own pockets.

It wasn't until the beginning of summer that Jayla was finally able to extricate a sixty-thousand-dollar check from Lorraine's tightly closed fist. Jayla and Derek had to commit to a wedding date and promise to give Lorraine at least three grandbabies before she handed over the money.

Jayla and Derek were en route to Ridley Township, Pennsylvania, a suburb that was approximately twenty minutes away from Philadelphia. With Derek behind the wheel of Jayla's old Subaru, the car coughed along as Jayla stared down at her phone, perusing the online listing of foreclosed properties.

Their mini vacation in Miami was over and Jayla felt it was time for them to get busy building their empire. At the top of her wish list were new cars for both her and Derek. Something flashy and fast for Derek and something elegant for her. She'd worked so hard selling houses, but she never seemed to get ahead. It was well past time for her to get a major break in life.

After finally getting revenge on the scum bag Niles, she felt vindicated and renewed, and that transformative feeling had miraculously removed the dark cloud that had hung over her for far too long.

With a sixty-thousand-dollar cushion, she was confident that taking on the role of real estate investor as opposed to merely being an agent was a surefire way of taking her destiny into her own hands and achieving financial freedom.

She looked up from her phone and glanced at Derek. "Before we get on the Blue Route, I want to shoot through West to check out a property."

"Where in West?"

"Dearborn Street. It's a little side street near Fifty-first and Arch."

Derek scowled. "Damn, babe. That sounds like the heart of the 'hood."

"You're right, it's a bad neighborhood, and judging by the picture on Google Maps, the entire block is a total disaster. Most of the houses are boarded up."

"Okay, I'm stumped. Why are we wasting time looking at property that no one would want to buy?"

Jayla smiled deviously. "Let me explain something. The rate of gentrification has been crazy in in the Southwest neighborhoods that surround University of Pennsylvania and in North Philly near Temple University...also in the Point Breeze section of South

Philly. I personally sold a house for big bucks in that neighborhood. After eavesdropping on a private conversation at work, I discovered that certain parts of West Philly, particularly east of Market Street, are slowly being revamped."

Derek arched his brow. "Let me guess…you want to get in on the ground floor."

"Exactly. I missed out on all the other emerging neighborhoods, but I won't miss out this time."

"But isn't that risky? No matter how well you fix up a house, who would want to buy it if it's on a rundown block?"

"High-risk, high-reward," Jayla said knowledgeably. "But if it makes you feel better, I discovered that right around the corner from the rundown blocks is a cluster of really elegant Victorian houses that were restored. They're occupied by high-income residents. The guys I eavesdropped on were talking about a developer who's planning to buy all the cheap property in the area, including Dearborn Street. That's why I want to have a look. Maybe we can beat the big guy at his own game." Jayla gazed at Derek with excitement glinting in her eyes.

He stared back at her impassively, his expression unreadable.

"Say something. What do you think?" Jayla asked.

Derek's brows lowered. "I don't like the plan."

"Why not?"

"It puts us at the mercy of the developers. We won't be able to make any money until they decide to get shit popping in the neighborhood. What happens after we finish renovating the crib? I'll tell you what'll happen," he added without waiting for Jayla to respond. "We'll be stuck with a house that we can't sell until the rest of the block is fixed up. I don't think it's right to play with your mom's money like that. We promised she'd get her investment back in a reasonable timeframe—not somewhere in the far-off future."

"Let me worry about my mom. I know how to handle her. Listen, if we're smart, we'll buy as many raggedy-ass houses in that area as we can get."

Derek yanked the steering wheel to the right, causing the tires to squeal as he pulled over to the curb without warning.

Jayla gasped. "What the hell is your problem?"

"*You're* my problem! You sound crazy and I'm not feeding into your delusion. I put up with a lot from you, but you got me fucked up if you think I'm gonna go along with every half-baked scheme that enters your head. We need to stick to the plan and find something in the suburbs that we can easily fix up and flip real quick. All this other shit you talking sounds like a pipe dream, and I'm not with it," he said firmly.

It wasn't like Derek to throw a fit, and being unfamiliar with his aggressive side, when he wasn't role-playing, Jayla softened her tone. "I need you to look at the big picture, Derek. *Please!* We can do a whole lot of work and end up making only a small profit... or we can do the same amount of work and make a *huge* profit. Take a deep breath and calm down, okay? I just want to see the property. It can't hurt to take a look at the house."

Derek gave a deep sigh before merging back into the flow of traffic.

When they were close to the address on Dearborn Street, Jayla directed Derek to make a detour on Fiftieth Street. She pointed to a cluster of refurbished homes that sat like a lovely oasis amid the crumble and deterioration of the area.

"Wow! This is surreal," Derek said, gawking at the charming Victorian-style houses that were surrounded by beautiful cherry blossom trees in full bloom and paved with natural stone walkways that led to elegant front doors.

"Do you see all this amazing opulence that's sitting smack in the middle of a neighborhood that's gone to the dogs?" Jayla said excitedly. "Do you think the buyers would have invested in these properties if they didn't have inside information that the neighborhood would soon be revitalized?"

"You have a point."

"Uh-huh, I sure do," she responded boastfully. "Do you still think I'm crazy?"

"Like a fox," he said, breaking into a smile.

"Are you ready to go around the corner and check out the property on Dearborn Street?"

"Let's do it."

They arrived on the deserted block that was comprised almost entirely of vacant, burned-out, dilapidated, and boarded-up houses.

"This shit looks worse than I imagined," Derek muttered as he parallel-parked between a portable Dumpster and a yellow-booted car.

He remained in his seat with the corners of his mouth turned down in disapproval as he observed the surroundings. Jayla unsnapped her seatbelt and hopped out of the car without hesitation.

Derek got out of the car and caught up to Jayla as she peered through a front window that was hazy with dirt and grime.

"From what I can see, the place is falling apart," Jayla said. "There's an ancient-looking carpet with all kinds of stains that'll have to be pulled up, but hopefully, we can restore the wood flooring underneath. A fresh paint job, crown molding, and new light fixtures will make the front room pop." She squinted as she scrutinized the room. "I can see some old, moldy wallpaper that definitely has to be removed. If we're lucky, thieves didn't get inside and yank out the plumbing."

Derek took a quick peek through a second window. Wearing a screw-face, he took several steps back and folded his arms across his chest. "Do you seriously want to waste our time on this dump?"

"Why're you being so pessimistic? Come on, let's go have a look around back."

"For what?"

She could feel her patience waning, but she kept her voice even-toned. "We need to see as much as we can before we bid on the property. That's the thing about buying foreclosures at auction. You can't see what you're getting until you've actually bought it."

"Buying something without inspecting it first is crazy, babe."

Jayla smiled awkwardly, but didn't comment. She had no idea why Derek was being so difficult. She wondered how long it would take him to come around and see things from her perspective. Eager to get a look at the kitchen, she made her way to the back of the house by trekking through the breezeway that was overgrown with weeds and littered with trash.

Trailing behind her, Derek cursed under his breath as he stepped over broken glass, beer cans, and a soiled Pamper.

The tiny backyard, a forest of foot-high grass, thorny bushes, and thick brambles was practically impenetrable. Fearing snakes and God knew what else, Derek and Jayla treaded carefully.

When they reached the backdoor, they discovered it was hanging off its hinges.

Frowning, Derek observed the rotting wood on the broken door. He moved closer to Jayla and placed a protective hand at the small of her back. "This is a fucked-up situation, babe. Any mofo from off the street could come back here and walk right on in."

"I know," she muttered, shaking her head. "Knowing that the door is broken, I'm really scared about stolen pipes, especially if they were copper."

"Fuck the pipes; we need to get out of here," Derek said. "There's no telling how many squatters are up in this bitch."

As if struck by a wonderful idea, Jayla's eyes suddenly brightened. "Since we're here and the door's not locked, it would be a shame not to go inside and check out the premises," she said, selecting her words with care.

Derek scoffed. "You expect me to go in there?" He shook his head adamantly. "That's out of the question. I'm not entering those fucked-up premises…not without a hazmat suit."

"Derek." She spoke his name warmly as she brushed her fingers against his hand cajolingly. "I don't know why you're acting so squeamish. You used to rehab houses for a living, so you should be used to houses like this."

"The houses my mom's church fixed up were salvageable residences. They weren't condemned property like this piece of shit. We worked on houses that needed reasonable repairs and cosmetic updates, but this place is beyond repair. You don't need to go inside to realize this place would be better off being torn down and rebuilt from scratch."

Jayla didn't say a word. She folded her arms and stared at him. "What?"

"You're not very observant. Didn't you notice that portable Dumpster…the one you parked behind?"

"Yeah, what about it?"

"That presence of that Dumpster means that somebody has already bought one of the godforsaken cribs on this street and they've started clearing it out. If that's not proof that something is happening in this neighborhood, then I don't know what is."

Derek gazed at Jayla thoughtfully.

Jayla's eyes lit up with enthusiasm. "This house is going for only fourteen thousand. If we set our budget at twenty thousand for repairs, we'll make out like fat rats. The key is to picture what the property could become instead of focusing on the shape that it's currently in."

"I can't envision anything except the shit show that's right before my eyes."

How would you feel if we drove down this block six months or a year from now and it resembled that classy Victorian-style enclave that's right around the corner? Also, how would you feel if you discovered that the raggedy-ass property you're turning up your nose at was selling for three or four hundred thousand?"

"I'd feel sick to my stomach," he admitted.

"That's what I'm saying. So, let's not talk ourselves out of an opportunity to rake in piles of money. It's time to step out on faith, babe," she said pleadingly.

"All right. Fuck it. Let's do this." Derek carefully pulled the decayed door away from the rusted hinges and propped it against the house before he and Jayla crept inside.

The kitchen smelled bad, like a mixture of rotting food and cat urine. There was greasy, peeling wallpaper, dated appliances that were filthy, and overflowing bags of trash were scattered about the downstairs.

Derek twisted his lips in disgust and Jayla covered her nose.

"What do you want to investigate first, the basement or upstairs?" Jayla asked in a voice that came out muffled from behind the hand that covered her nose and mouth.

"There're probably rats, bats, flying cockroaches, and a family of vagrants down in the basement. I'm not ready for all that, so let's check out the upstairs first."

They climbed the creaking stairs with Derek leading the way and Jayla holding on to the back of his hoodie. He reached the landing and stopped in his tracks.

"Goddamn!" he uttered in a voice filled with absolute shock.

"Oh, no. What is it?" Jayla asked, dreading his response. Unwilling to face the carnage, she buried her face in Derek's back and pictured ceiling-less rooms that opened to the elements and were a haven for all sorts of flying creatures. "Oh, God, don't tell me the roof caved in. I can't take it. I'm going back downstairs."

As she turned halfway around, Derek took a firm hold of her arm. "Where do you think you're going? You forced me to come inside this godforsaken house, and now you're gonna see this."

Jayla squeezed her eyes closed, unwilling to look at the disaster that awaited her. It was her fault that they'd wasted so much time in this falling-down house, and now she wanted to abandon the mission and check out another listing that was located two blocks over.

She tried to dig her heels in, but Derek pulled her forward. "Don't be skurred," he joked. "Open your eyes, Jayla."

Her eyes slowly fluttered open. She gasped when she saw that the upstairs was completely renovated. The bathroom was a stunning masterpiece that included a glass-encased shower with floor-to-ceiling mosaic tiles and chrome faucets. There was marble flooring and the double vanities had marble countertops.

The remaining two bedrooms were painted with new baseboards and light fixtures. There was a short, curved stairway that led to the attic, which had also been transformed into a cozy bedroom.

"Someone put a lot of money into renovating the upstairs," Jayla said in a whispery, awe-filled voice.

"What do you think happened?" Derek asked.

"Who knows? The previous owners could have lost the place after taking out a big loan. Or maybe somebody got sick or died before they got around to fixing up the downstairs. Their loss is our gain, and it's a miracle that no one stripped this place down. Oh, my God, I'm so excited, my heart is pounding," Jayla said, touching her chest. "This place is being auctioned for only fourteen thousand because no one knows about the upstairs. Do you realize how much time and money we're going to save?"

"When is the auction?" Derek inquired, his level of excitement matching Jayla's.

"Tomorrow at ten. We have to make sure no one is living in the basement, and then secure that back door to protect our property," Jayla said, talking fast and excitedly. "Babe, this is a sign that the tide is finally changing, and it's finally our turn to have a good life."

They stood in the hallway admiring the renovations and Derek put an arm around her. "You get extra points for your determination. I won't ever doubt you again. Tell me what you need me to do and consider it done."

She had every right to be perturbed by the way Derek had doubted her intuition, but she wasn't. His apology was sweet. The way he bit on his lip when he was feeling contrite made her cunt clench, and she found herself growing very hot and wet.

"You acted like an asshole, but I'll forgive you if you make it up to me tonight in bed," she said, twirling her hair. Then she gave him a sly smile that told him she had something decadently salacious and deliciously dirty in mind.

And she knew that Derek would be more than willing to give into her desires.

"I got you," he assured her, his eyes darting down at his crotch that had instantly begun to swell at the promise of a long night of good fucking. "All I have to do is make a quick phone call to James."

James was the pastor's son, who, behind closed doors, was much more freaky than holy.

A shiver ran through Jayla as she envisioned three heated bodies entwined and thrashing together in her king-size bed.

All she could think of was two sets of wandering hands, two laving tongues, her trembling body covered in warm kisses, and the thrusts of two hard dicks, filling her body, and fucking into her soul.

Chapter 31

For months Bailee had gone back and forth to Philadelphia to pitch her business plan. From a list of forty potential investors, she received a firm "yes" after meeting with the eighteenth name on her list.

Although Hayden was impressed by the speed in which she'd secured funding, Bailee had expected it to happen sooner. Despite the ungraceful way she'd exited her job at the bank, she was still confident in her ability to wheel and deal in the world of finance.

With the money hunt out of the way, she was able to focus on the creative end of the enterprise. She became obsessively passionate about HaydenWear Fierce and painstakingly infused each unique piece with her vision.

At Hayden's leased office space in Miami, she worked long hours. Alongside the designer Hayden had selected, she picked out flattering styles and supportive fabrics that would inspire workout confidence for the line's target market.

She was in Miami much more often than she was in Philadelphia, and Miami was beginning to feel more and more like home. She and Hayden had an amazing connection and he had brought up the subject of living together more than once, but Bailee wasn't ready for that level of commitment.

Trent was dragging his feet on the divorce, and she was still in recovery mode over the avalanche of shock, hurt, and betrayal that accompanied the breakup of their ten-year marriage. Additionally, she was on a personal journey of self-discovery, and it seemed wiser and healthier to let her relationship with Hayden develop at a cautious speed.

She had grown weary of living out of a suitcase, and decided it was time to get out of the hotel and start looking for a place she could call home. Trying to hold on to her Philly condo seemed pointless, and she was ready to let go of everything associated with her old life.

At seven-thirty in the evening, Bailee prepared to wrap up an eleven-hour day. The muffled sound of music, grunting, and groaning that emerged from the far end of the hall told her that Hayden was still going strong, rehearsing with a group of attractive and physically fit women he'd selected to join him in his next Workout King DVD.

Deciding not to interrupt him, she headed for the elevator stairs and pulled out her phone to send him a goodnight text. She hoped to see him later on, but was careful not to appear pushy or needy. Her tendency to lean on a man for emotional support and validation was the reason she was determined to live alone and experience being single before attempting to take the relationship to the next level.

The moment the elevator doors opened, her phone buzzed against her palm. She looked down and saw "Mom" on the screen. Startled, she took a few backward steps before turning around and walking toward the stairs.

Ensconced inside the stairwell, where there was privacy, she took a deep breath before taking the call.

Instead of hearing, *Hello, Bailee,* in Giselle's cool, aristocratic voice, she heard a shriek that was similar to the sound of a wounded animal, and the pained cry was interspersed with frantic, indecipherable words.

"What's wrong, Mom?" Bailee asked. She was so sincerely concerned, her heart began to pound. No matter how deceitful and unmotherly Giselle had been, hearing her in distress sent jolts of alarm throughout Bailee's system.

"I can't understand a word you're saying. Calm down and talk to me," Bailee implored her while strongly suspecting that Giselle's lamentations resulted from the discovery of Trent's double life.

"He's gone, Bailee. Trent's gone."

"Where'd he go?" Bailee asked calmly.

"It happened so suddenly," Giselle said, gasping and crying.

"What happened? Is he gone—like in dead?" Bailee's heart tightened in her chest. She was infuriated with Trent, but she didn't wish death upon him.

"No, he's not dead, but I wish he were," Giselle hissed. "I gave that bastard everything. I funded his new law practice. He said he wanted to drive something luxurious that would give him the appearance of being successful and established while making his clients feel pampered when he took them to lunch, so I bought him a new Mercedes."

Bailee inhaled sharply but didn't say anything.

"Then, when he complained about needing his space, I bought him a beautiful home in my upscale neighborhood."

"What? Mom, are you kidding me? The cheapest houses in your area cost several million."

"Don't you think I know?" Giselle snapped. "It's cruel of you to judge me when I'm down. I'm going through too much to fight with you, Bailee."

"I'm not fighting you. What else is going on?" Bailee braced herself to hear that Trent had moved a strange woman and two kids into the lavish home that Giselle had paid for. Karma was truly a bitch, but amazingly, Bailee took no pleasure in her mother's suffering.

"Trent hadn't been answering my calls. When three days went by without a word from him, I drove to his home. What a shock I had when I saw a 'For Sale' sign on the lawn. I gave him an obscene amount of money for that house, and he put it on the market like it was nothing."

"I don't understand why you'd be so generous with someone you should have regarded as nothing more than a boy toy?" It was difficult to speak of Trent as if they weren't connected, but she managed to emotionally disassociate in order to hear Giselle out.

"There's no explanation for how a woman responds when she's in love," Giselle said softly.

"Did you go to his office and confront him?" Bailee asked.

"Yes, and it was the most humiliating experience of my life."

"What happened?"

"I was barred from entering the premises by Trent's security detail."

"How is he able to afford a security detail?"

Giselle wailed in agony. "I paid for it."

"Oh, my God, Mom."

"I don't understand how he could treat me so cruelly, especially in my condition."

"Are you sick?" Bailee asked, her voice high-pitched and fearful.

"No, I'm not sick. I'm pregnant."

"Pregnant?" Bailee said, incredulous.

"I felt bad for him. He told me that you refused to have a child with him, and that it made him feel less than a man, so I—"

"But you're over fifty," Bailee reminded her, cutting her off. "How is pregnancy even possible? Wait, did you freeze your eggs a long time ago? No, you wouldn't have done that because you never wanted more kids. Mom, I'm so confused. How did you get pregnant?" Bailee demanded.

"I used an egg donor."

Bailee sighed. "Why? If you and Trent…" Bailee paused, finding it difficult to refer to her mother and her husband in the same sentence. "If you two agreed to lead separate lives, why would you go to that kind of trouble and expense to get pregnant?"

"It was stupid of me, but I hoped a child would bring us closer."

"How many months are you?"

"Three, but I'm seriously considering an abortion. I refuse to be stuck raising this child without a father," Giselle proclaimed, sniffling. "This fetus that's growing inside me doesn't have a drop of my blood. I doubt if I'd be able to love the child without Trent in my life," Giselle admitted mournfully.

"Surely, you wouldn't abort a baby that you went to such extreme measures to conceive."

"I can't imagine going through labor as a single parent. It's vile and low-class. I refuse to put myself through that kind of pain all alone. I need Trent," Giselle cried. "I need him by my side when I give birth to his only child."

Uncomfortably, Bailee shifted from one foot to the other. She wondered if she should tell Giselle about Trent's secret or if she was better off not knowing. A dull ache began throbbing at her temples, making it apparent that her mother's self-inflicted problems were affecting her. She'd left Philadelphia to live in peace and serenity, but if she allowed her narcissistic mother to draw her into her nightmarish world, all the hard work she'd put into building her confidence and self-esteem would go down the drain.

"Mom, I wish I could be there for you, but the wound from your betrayal is still open. On an emotional level, I can't afford to get involved in the mess that you and Trent created."

"I already apologized; what more can I do? Why're you trying to punish me for something I had no control over?" Giselle whined.

"This is not payback, Mom. It's called survival. I have to do what's best for me, and helping you deal with your current problems would be emotionally unhealthy for me. It would be disastrous. I'm going to hang up now. You can call me if there's an emergency, but otherwise, you'll have to work out your problems on your own."

Bailee heard Giselle take a breath, gearing up to say something else, but she disconnected the call. Overwhelmed with sorrow, she leaned against the wall, and took a few moments to pull herself together.

She opened the door, and there was Hayden, standing by the elevator looking down at his phone.

He gazed up in surprise. "Hey, pretty, I thought you went back to your hotel."

"I was on my way, but I had to take a call."

"Wanna grab dinner?"

"Yes, I'm starving," she said, giving him a warm smile.

"We can't go anywhere fancy. I'm too sweaty from rehearsal."

"I don't care if we eat at a taco truck. Anyway, you look sexy and masculine when you're covered in sweat," she said, leaning in and kissing him on his damp cheek.

The elevator dinged and the doors slid open, revealing an empty car. The moment they stepped inside, Hayden enfolded Bailee inside his perspiration-soaked arms and kissed her deeply.

All the unpleasant, chaotic emotions that Giselle had dumped on her began to instantly evaporate and she felt engulfed in serenity.

Chapter 32

Dressed in fashionable business attire, Jayla and Derek made a striking couple, and they looked extremely dignified as they swept into the auction.

No one at the auction would have guessed that they'd fallen asleep last night to the sweet melody of triple orgasms echoing in harmony throughout their bedroom.

Their fellow bidders would have been hard-pressed to imagine that the morning after a lewd ménage à trois, the elegant pair awoke to the overpowering scent of illicit sex hanging in the air. It was a pungent smell that permeated their bedsheets and clung to their skin.

No one would have been able to picture a scene where Jayla's thighs were clamped around another man's head while Derek crouched behind the same man, rhythmically slow-stroking into his tight anal passage.

A person would have to possess a truly warped and unstable mind to conjure an image of Derek working his hips and building momentum until he progressed from gentle gliding motions to deep driving plunges, inciting the third-party lover to deliver intense tongue-thrusts into the moist depths of the woman Derek intended to marry.

When it was time to bid on the house on Dearborn Street, Jayla's palms began to sweat and her pulse throbbed rapidly. The fear that a wealthy developer would outbid her and Derek prompted her to begin petitioning the Lord and pleading for His assistance.

Jayla bid on the property and amazingly no one tried to outbid her. Upon hearing the words, *going, going, gone*, she leapt to her feet and hollered. Derek joined her in the rowdy celebration, bellowing, "Yeah," as he pumped his fist into the air.

Neither Derek nor Jayla had any interest in prolonging the dignified and stately charade. They were ecstatic about their financial future and didn't care who knew it.

When Lorraine discovered that Jayla had used her money to invest in a raggedy, ghetto property, she flew into such a blind rage, her blood pressure went sky-high, and Jayla feared she would have to be hospitalized.

The only thing that calmed Lorraine down was the solemn promise that Jayla and Derek would stop living in sin and get married at Lorraine's church with her beloved pastor officiating.

Jayla had feared Lorraine would make her use part of the loan to pay for the wedding expenses, but to her surprise, her mother sprang for all the costs.

During the nuptials, Lorraine shed tears of joy and shouted "hallelujah" several times as she watched Deacon Webster escort her daughter down the aisle.

Bailee flew in from Miami to serve as Jayla's maid of honor, and of course, James, the pastor's son, stood beside Derek as his best man.

No time for a traditional honeymoon, the newlyweds and James spent a lust-filled night in the honeymoon suite at the Loews Hotel.

Returning home after the honeymoon, Derek and Jayla were unable to find a vacant spot in the parking lot of their building, and they were forced to park in front of the green house across the street.

Derek opened the passenger's door and bent at the waist, preparing to lift Jayla into his arms.

"What the hell do you think you're doing?" Jayla asked, laughing.

"I'm carrying you across the threshold."

"You're not supposed to pick me up until we get outside the door of the condo. You're so silly, boy," she said as she eased out of the car.

Outside trimming his rose bushes, Mr. Murphy glared at the happy couple as if they'd committed a crime by parking in front of his house.

Derek popped the trunk and he and Jayla moved to the rear of the car, laughing heartily. At the tinkling sound of their laughter, Mr. Murphy's frown deepened.

"What's old dude's problem? Why is he giving us the screw face?" Derek asked. "I never did anything to grandpop. Maybe his face is all twisted up because he needs a laxative," Derek said, causing Jayla to laugh even harder.

"The reason Mr. Murphy was looking at us all sideways is because he was offended that we parked in front of his house without giving him an explanation," Jayla clarified. "He swears he's the mayor of Mount Airy."

Derek grunted. "That petty muthafucka better get a life."

"Plus, he can't stand me," she further explained.

"What's his beef with you?"

"He's got a stick up his ass. A while back, he got in my face and told me that I was a loose woman with no morals."

Derek reared back in his chair. "He disrespected you and got in your face?"

"Yeah. He talked to me real greasy. I used to attend his stupid community meetings because I thought we were cool, but I haven't spoken to him since that day he showed his true colors."

"I'll fuck that old bastard up if he even thinks about coming out his mouth to my fuckin' wife!"

"Let it go. He's a miserable old man, upset because he can't get his fuck on without taking a cocktail of pills."

Derek made a chuckling sound, but Jayla could tell by the way his brows were knitted together that he was still pissed.

Later that night, after making love, instead of going to sleep, Derek sat on the side of the bed, studying the screen of his phone.

Jayla cracked an eye open. "What are you doing? I know you're not attempting to call up a nigga or a bitch and start cheating on me already," she said, half-joking and half-serious.

"Nah, why would I have to do that when we have an understanding?"

"That's what I'm saying, so, what are you doing?"

"I'm looking for something on eBay—a tool I need to work on the house. It cost a fortune at Home Depot, but I can get it much cheaper online."

"Oh, okay." Jayla patted him on the arm.

"Get some rest, babe. I'll be zonked out right next to you as soon as I make this purchase."

She giggled. "Check you out—the man who used to be intimidated by technology is wheeling and dealing on eBay."

"And don't forget that I can hold my own in restaurants. No more anxiety about ordering food—thanks to my baby for being patient with me and helping me out."

"Of course."

"I don't know what I'd do without you, Jayla."

"Hopefully, you'll never have to find out."

He flashed a smile, gave her a kiss, and then returned his gaze to the screen.

Three days later, when Derek's package arrived, Jayla handed it to him, noting that it was an extremely lightweight tool, but she didn't ask any questions.

"I'm gonna put this in the trunk, so I don't forget it when I work on the house tomorrow."

"Cool," she responded.

Derek left the condo, and she felt the intense loneliness that engulfed her whenever they were separated. Her love for Derek grew stronger every day, and she hated being apart from him, even for a few moments.

She found herself meandering toward the window, so that she could watch him strut across the parking lot. The way he held his broad shoulders erect when he walked was so damn sexy, it was no wonder that both men and women lost their minds over him.

As she secretly watched Derek with admiring eyes, it was a jolting surprise when she saw him exit the parking lot and strut across the street, still carrying the package.

Mouth agape, she wondered what he was up to when she observed him knocking on Mr. Murphy's door.

Smiling broadly, Mr. Murphy opened the door and welcomed Derek inside.

Fuming over Derek's deceit, Jayla stormed away from the window and began to pace back and forth.

What the hell is he up to? I know he's not sneaking around, getting his dick sucked by that disrespectful-ass, old man.

An hour later, Derek put his key in the lock and came inside, whistling.

This sneaky motherfucker is actually whistling after he did his dirt. Jayla's heart sank. She'd put her love and trust into Derek and had accepted a new lifestyle. A bitch couldn't win. Muthafuckas always had to feel like they were getting over on somebody.

"It took you long enough to put the package in the trunk," she said, baiting him.

"Yeah, I had to make a stop," he said casually as he pulled the fridge open and peered inside.

"Oh, so it's like that? You go across the street and get your dick sucked and now you're hungry after busting a nut." She fired off the words with her fist balled, ready to fight Derek.

"Huh? What're you talking about?" he asked, frowning in confusion.

Jayla stalked toward him. "I was looking out the window, and I saw you sneaking inside Mr. Murphy's house. I thought you had better taste, but I guess you're just a sleazy ho wanting the new thrill of getting your dick gummed by a senior citizen."

Derek burst out laughing. He laughed so hard, he stomped his feet and doubled over. He couldn't stop laughing, and when he finally got himself together, he said, "Babe, ain't nobody gumming my dick." Then he started laughing all over again.

"Ain't nothing funny, Derek," Jayla said in a hurtful tone of voice.

"Your accusation is hilarious. But, I can explain."

"Please do," she said through gritted teeth.

"I didn't want to violate my probation by whipping that old man's ass. So I approached him in a friendly way and told him I wanted to get involved in the community meetings. When he invited me inside, I sat and talked with him and his wife. And while we were kicking it, I slyly unleashed the present I bought for them."

"The package you got on eBay?"

"Well, I couldn't find what I wanted on eBay, so I had to resort to Craigslist."

"What was in the package?"

"Bedbugs."

Jayla's mouth fell open.

"It's the best way to legally hurt a muthafucka. We had a bedbug infestation in prison, so I know firsthand the havoc they can wreak."

"Oh, my God. You are vicious."

"Only when it comes to defending your honor."

"But…but, how did you find bedbugs online? What kind of maniac sells some shit like that?"

Derek shrugged. "You can buy anything online…from bombs to bedbugs. It's crazy out there, babe. Anyway, Mr. Murphy is gonna be too busy battling bedbugs to have time to frown his face up at you."

All Jayla could do was shake her head.

Chivalry was not dead and her husband had proven that a verbal attack on her was like an attack on him, and he wouldn't rest until he got revenge.

And he didn't mind fighting dirty, either.

Her mouth began to water as she thought about his gallantry and valor. Wanting to reward him, she sauntered toward him and said in a stern voice, "Zip those pants down, young man. I got something for you."

And Derek didn't hesitate to obey the command.

Chapter 33

Ten miles outside of Miami and quietly nestled in a beautiful community that resembled a tropical paradise was a Mediterranean-style home with a manicured lawn and lush, lavender gardens.

It was a home of distinction with exquisite Old World craftsmanship, and possessing all the features that appealed to Bailee. It was the perfect place to begin her new life, but the house was totally out of her price range.

She contacted Jayla and instructed her to handle the sale of her Philadelphia condo, although the money from the condo wouldn't help very much with the high cost of the Florida home. Even emptying her savings wouldn't help. She needed access to her inheritance. However, that wouldn't be possible for three years.

The next best thing was to ask for a loan from the woman who held the purse strings, Giselle.

Throughout the course of the day, Bailee would pick up her phone to call Giselle, and then argue with herself as her finger hovered over the screen.

My mother stole my husband, and the least she can do to try and repair the damage she's done is to lend me the money for the house. But I don't want to talk to her, anytime soon. It's unhealthy to listen to her ramble on and on about her dysfunctional relationship with my husband.

The internal dialogue that ran through Bailee's mind always culminated in her putting the phone down before placing the call to Giselle.

Before going to bed, she convinced herself that asking Giselle for a loan didn't require her to engage in any conversations that made her uncomfortable, nor was she obliged to be friendly toward a woman she couldn't trust.

Motivated by righteous indignation, she called Giselle and without a word of greeting, she blurted, "I need a loan—a substantial amount of money, but you know I'm good for it. I'll pay you back in full as soon as I get the money from my trust fund."

"I'm not in a position to give you a loan, Bailee."

"What do you mean? Daddy left you a fortune."

"Listen, Bailee, I don't have the strength for this conversation. This pregnancy is sucking the life out of me, and my doctor has me on bedrest. Trent is putting me through enough crap, and I don't need any additional stress."

"I'm not trying to stress you out. You know I wouldn't ask for anything if it wasn't important to me."

Giselle sighed audibly. "How much do you need?"

"Four-hundred thousand," Bailee said without emotion.

"I don't have access to that kind of money."

"Of course you do."

"I don't. When I changed lawyers, I made Trent the estate attorney, and—"

Bailee felt her ears began to burn. "You did what? How could you give my soon-to-be, ex-husband legal control over my father's money?"

"Correction...it's my money that your dear father bequeathed to me," Giselle said with an edge to her voice. "But, it was stupid of me—I admit it, okay? I've already sent Trent a letter, terminating his services, but the money's going to be tied up for at least a few months. I won't be in the mood for a big legal battle until after I give birth."

"Oh, so you've decided to keep your child?"

Giselle sucked her teeth. "I can't go through with an abortion… I don't believe in them. But it's unlikely that I'll keep a child that's no relation to me. I plan to put it up for adoption."

A look of disgust formed on Bailee's face. Her selfish mother had concocted the idea of fertilizing donor eggs with Trent's sperm, and now she planned on giving the child to strangers.

"Instead of getting another lawyer, why don't you go back to Tillery & Danton, the firm Daddy selected. They're highly respected and experienced, and I'm sure they'd be able to cut through a lot of the red tape."

Giselle scoffed. "I was happy to end my relationship with that firm. The last thing I want to do is give them control, again."

"I never realized you were dissatisfied with their services."

"I don't tell you all the ins and outs of handling your father's estate. It's personal. I need you to be patient and to wait a few months for the loan. Can you do that?"

"Well, I wanted to make an offer on the house and—"

"Bailee," Giselle uttered impatiently. "It's not as if you're home-less or down to your last dollar." She gave another audible sigh. "My head is killing me. Can we talk about this at another time?"

"Sure," Bailee agreed half-heartedly.

Unable to sleep, Bailee sat up in bed, troubled by the fact that Trent had his grubby fingers in her family's money. Bailee decided to call Tillery & Danton in the morning to find out if they were aware of any legal loopholes that would give her access to a portion of her inheritance.

When she awakened in the morning, she felt even more troubled than she had last night, and as soon as business hours began, she called the law firm that had handled her father's estate for many years.

She spoke to Mr. Danton, but he didn't want to discuss the matter over the phone. He suggested that Bailee come into the office for a meeting.

Although she'd visited her hometown only a week ago when she attended Jayla's wedding, after speaking with Mr. Danton, she immediately booked a flight to Philadelphia.

Tillery & Danton were very old men, and Bailee was surprised they were capable of still running their firm. Tillery wore round spectacles, walked with a cane, and for some ungodly reason, his sparse hair was dyed a shocking shade of dark brown while his wild-haired eyebrows were snow-white.

Danton was bald on top and his face and head were covered with age spots. Although both men gave the impression of being physically feeble, at the onset of the meeting, it was abundantly clear that they were mentally sharp.

"Thank you for seeing me," Bailee said as she joined the two men at the conference table.

"We're glad you got in touch with us," said Danton. "In light of the fact that Ms. Giselle Cormier Wellington has terminated our services, it's somewhat unethical for us to meet with you in this manner..."

"However, we have a moral obligation to your father that supersedes ethics," said Tillery, picking up where his partner left off. He leaned forward, and looking over his spectacles, he held Bailee's gaze. "It is our concern that Ms. Wellington is mishandling your inheritance with her reckless spending."

Troubled, Bailee leaned forward. Her worried eyes flicked from Tillery to Danton. "I was aware that my mother has been irresponsible with her own money, but I had no idea she'd managed to get her hands on the trust fund my father set up for me."

"Ms. Wellington doesn't have any money of her own," Tillery informed, crinkling his bushy, white eyebrows. "Ms. Wellington signed a prenuptial agreement that would have entitled her to your father's fortune after ten years of marriage. However, with his death occurring after only nine years of marriage, she was only entitled to a lump sum of five-hundred thousand, along with the house. Aside from various charities, the bulk of Andrew Wellington's fortune was left to you, his only child.

"As your parent and guardian, Ms. Wellington was provided with a rather generous monthly income to oversee the estate. We fear, however, that her wanton looting of your assets will leave you penniless if she's not held accountable for her actions."

Bailee shook her head, trying to clear it. Tillery's bombshell disclosure had come so far out of left field, it took a few moments for her to take it all in. With comprehension came a dry mouth and a thudding heart. "Are you saying that my father's entire estate belongs to me and not my mother?" Bailee asked in a choked voice.

"We assumed you were aware that you are the sole beneficiary of your father's fortune," said Danton.

Bailee shook her head slowly, unbelievingly. "I only knew about the million-dollar trust fund that I inherit at age thirty-five."

Danton snorted. "Multimillion-dollar trust fund is far more accurate."

Bailee gawked at the attorneys. "Are you telling me that my father left me millions of dollars and my mother never mentioned it? This makes no sense. Why didn't you guys tell me?"

"It wasn't our place to disclose the arrangement until your thirty-fifth birthday, but Ms. Wellington certainly had a moral obligation to make you aware," said Danton.

"Bailee, we've heard a great deal of talk of an unnatural and revolting relationship between your husband and your mother," said Tillery, grimacing as if there were a nasty taste in his mouth. "We're sorry that this unpleasantness is happening to you, and we implore you to put a stop to their flagrant thievery."

Danton cleared his throat and then spoke gently. "We've been in the business of estate planning for a long time and we have many contacts. It's been brought to our attention by a credible source that after Ms. Wellington allowed Mr. Trent Evans to siphon funds from the estate and deposit said funds into a bank account that he controlled, Mr. Evans then had the audacity to request an additional sixty-thousand dollars in legal fees, which Ms. Wellington paid."

"Oh, my God," Bailee murmured.

"It gets worse," Danton said in an apologetic tone. "With Ms. Wellington's full knowledge and permission, Mr. Evans has used funds from the Wellington estate to buy a house, a luxury sedan, an all-terrain vehicle, for credit card expenses, and to pay rent for the office space of his new private practice."

Bailee dropped her head into her hands. It was insane that all the luxurious gifts Giselle had showered upon Trent had not been paid for with her own money. It was yet another betrayal by the two people whom she should have been able to trust more than anyone else in the world.

It was hypocritical for Giselle to have enjoyed an affluent lifestyle while teaching Bailee to be frugal and responsible.

At some point during her marriage to Trent, he and her mother had ruthlessly conspired to betray and steal from her. The plan, however, had backfired against Giselle, and she'd turned to Bailee, of all people, for sympathy.

It was finally clear to Bailee why Giselle had become so detached and unloving toward her after the death of her father.

She had always assumed that Giselle disapproved of her weight and was disappointed and ashamed of her for not living up to her standards of beauty. Now Bailee realized that the reason for Giselle's coldness was the simple fact that she was greedy and heartless and extremely bitter over the fact that her husband left his fortune to Bailee instead of her.

Danton held a stack of papers in his hands, and as he thumbed through them, the rustling sound brought Bailee back to the present moment.

"It would be viewed as conflict of interest if we were to represent you after being terminated by Ms. Wellington, but we would like to recommend a very competent attorney, Richard Pennetta, whom we've already spoken to. Pennetta is prepared to bring a number of serious charges against both Ms. Wellington and Mr. Evans— charges that include fraud and embezzlement."

Bailee swallowed hard. Did she actually want to see her own mother imprisoned? Did Trent deserve to be disbarred and jailed? And most importantly, was *she* spiteful enough to set the wheels of justice in motion?

Hell, yes! Those two deceitful snakes need to pay for what they did to me!

Thanks to Jayla and her refined sleuthing skills, Bailee perused Trent's baby mom's social media pages. Her name was Lanay Strickland.

Bailee had only briefly seen the woman in the video Jayla had sent; the camera was more focused on Trent and the kids than her.

Bailee studied Lanay's photos. She was average height and weight, but though she possessed a pleasant enough face, there was nothing remarkable about her. No perceptible characteristics that would influence a man to deceive his wife and her mother and break the law to keep her satisfied.

Perhaps the secret to Lanay's amazingness lay hidden between her legs, Bailee surmised wryly.

Surprisingly, there were no images of Trent on her Instagram page. Lanay only posted pictures of herself and the two children. Getting another look at the children's uncanny resemblance to Trent, struck Bailee like a harsh kick to the gut. Stifling a gasp, her hand covered her mouth as she stared at their young faces.

Switching to Lanay's Facebook page, Bailee perused the various posts, but was particularly interested in the most recent: *Date night tonight at Fujiyama's, my favorite Japanese restaurant.*

Ironically, Fujiyama's had been a favorite of Bailee's and Trent's also. She wondered if he'd also dined there with Giselle.

Lanay had no idea there was a warrant for her baby daddy's arrest. If the police didn't catch Trent at home in his spacious, new digs or at his office, Bailee would be sure to tell them to check out Fujiyama's.

After logging off Facebook, she felt an overwhelming sense of sorrow. The life she'd known had been a sham from the age of nine until now. It was no wonder she'd turned to food after her father's death. Her mother's simmering resentment toward her had left Bailee with a void that she tried to fill with food.

She'd grown up with the false belief that she'd inherited Giselle's incapacity to love a child and had therefore decided it would be callous to bring one into the world.

But she'd been wrong. She was nothing like her mother.

She was already making plans to include Giselle and Trent's offspring into her life. Even if the child wasn't related to her by blood, it was an innocent victim, like she was.

If Giselle somehow escaped prison, which Bailee doubted, she'd step in and volunteer to adopt her stepbrother or sister before Giselle tossed the child to the wolves simply because she considered the baby to be a terrible inconvenience.

Despite the fact that the baby would be a constant reminder of the most heinous act of betrayal Bailee had ever known, she was still ready and willing to shower the child with love.

There was no doubt in her mind that Hayden, being the good man that he was, would easily open his heart to her adopted child.

Epilogue

The trial had been brief, yet sensational, and the courtroom was packed every day. It was big news for a Philadelphia socialite and her son-in-law to conspire to steal millions from *her* daughter and *his* wife.

Although Bailee had not told Giselle about Trent's secret family, Giselle found out from her lawyer before the trial began. During the proceedings, unable to conceal her rage, Giselle had leaned forward in an intimidating manner, grimacing obscenely and mumbling indecipherably when Lanay Strickland took the stand on Trent's behalf. Giselle hissed at the woman so viciously, the judge threatened to throw her out of the courtroom if she didn't control herself.

Giselle had withered down to skin and bones. She was eight months' pregnant, but her baby bump was barely discernible. A shadow of her former self, the hurt and animosity over Trent's deceitfulness had transformed her into someone unrecognizable. Her hair, once lustrous and coiffed, had turned dull and brittle, and appeared unkempt.

Her complexion was no longer radiant, and there were odd, purplish discolorations spotting her skin. The signs of aging that she'd skillfully kept at bay with the help of expensive dermatologists had found their way to the corners of her eyes, around her mouth, and were visible in the sag beneath her chin.

There was nothing remotely beautiful about Giselle anymore. Bitterness had taken a toll. The seething resentment that consumed her was clearly visible on her face.

Seeing Giselle looking gaunt and miserable in the courtroom every day was difficult, and despite what she'd done, Bailee often felt unexpected surges of pity for her.

She also found herself becoming increasingly concerned about the well-being of the baby she was carrying. She suspected that her mother was intentionally trying to starve the poor child. Giselle had said that she didn't believe in abortion, but she clearly had no problem with fetal abuse.

Unfortunately, there was no clear evidence (such as drug use) that could be used against her. Improper nutrition wasn't considered a crime. And even if her wrongdoing had been deemed to be a criminal offense, there was nothing more the judicial system could do to her after she'd been convicted and sentenced to serve three years behind bars.

Throughout the pregnancy, Bailee had wondered if the fetus felt unloved in the womb. Did the unborn child realize that its surrogate mother wanted it to suffer as a way to spite its father—a father who was equally unconcerned about its well-being?

Both Giselle and Trent proved to be contemptible people. Out of pure meanness, neither would agree to allow Bailee to raise the baby. The biological mother was unknown, and therefore, was unable to come forward and claim her offspring.

Bailee sat in the courtroom, day after day, within arm's reach of Trent's secret paramour. Seeing his wife and his mistress in such close proximity didn't seem to faze him, as he showed no signs of remorse or any amount of discomfort.

In the rare instances when Trent looked Bailee's way, she saw nothing but defiance in his eyes.

Something was wrong with him, she decided. A sensitivity chip was definitely missing.

At the conclusion of the trial, she derived immense pleasure when he was given a six-year sentence and was shamefully disbarred from the distinguished profession he was so proud to be a part of.

During the first month of her sentence, Giselle gave birth to a baby girl. She named her Sofia, and then handed her over to the state.

Sofia was sickly and woefully underweight. After spending a few weeks in the hospital, she was placed in foster care.

Worrying about Sofia's welfare, Bailee found it difficult to sleep at night, and she wondered if a guilty conscience prevented Trent and Giselle from getting any rest.

After weeks of legal maneuvering, Bailee's attorneys were successful in getting her a supervised visit with Sofia. When she held the tiny, warm bundle in her arms, the baby's eyelids fluttered open, and in that moment, there was an instant connection between them.

Sofia needed Bailee and Bailee needed her.

She didn't understand her strong maternal feeling toward Sofia, but accepted that some emotions simply couldn't be explained. Bailee fell completely in love with the tiny infant and made up her mind to fight for her, at all costs.

Through her attorneys, she appealed to Trent and Giselle in a language they both understood. She offered to clandestinely pay them to give up the rights of Sofia and allow her to adopt her.

They both readily agreed.

"I'm so happy you and Hayden and the baby decided to spend Thanksgiving with us," Jayla said as she put a tray of macaroni and cheese into the oven.

"I love Florida, but it doesn't feel right celebrating the holiday in eighty-degree weather, so thank you for inviting us."

"Of course," Jayla said and then turned on the blender. The loud whirring sound frightened Sofia, who was investigating the lower kitchen cabinets and trying to pull open drawers. She gave a little yelp and quickly toddled over to Bailee. Bailee picked her up and comforted her with a kiss on the cheek.

"Aw, I'm sorry, Sofia," Jayla cooed, "but I have to finish making my homemade eggnog."

"Wait. Let me take her to Hayden before you turn the blender back on." Rocking Sofia in her arms, she carried her into the living room where Hayden and Derek were watching the Thanksgiving Day football game.

When Bailee returned to the kitchen, Jayla gazed at her and smiled.

"What's the big smile for?" Bailee asked, looking around self-consciously.

"I can't believe you're a mother."

"I know, right?"

"And you're good at it," Jayla added.

"Thank you. Being a mom is much easier than I thought it would be. But that's probably because she's such a sweet little girl. But, enough about me," Bailee said, waving her hand. "I can't believe you bought this posh brownstone. Living downtown is so cool. I'm so proud of the way you took charge of your life, Jayla. You're happily married…have your own successful real estate business, and you're—"

Jayla cut Bailee off. "Thanks, but I can't take all the credit. None of this would be possible if Derek and I didn't believe in each other."

"So, when are you two going to start a family?"

"Girl, please. No time soon. I like spending time with my god-daughter, but I'm not ready for diaper duty quite yet. But, I can't let my mom find out, so don't say a word about this."

"I won't say anything. But I'm curious as to why you and Derek don't want children."

"We do want kids, but not right now. We're having so much fun enjoying our life together, we don't want to be responsible for molding and shaping a young life." Jayla made a face. "Does that sound selfish?"

"No, not at all. Parenthood shouldn't be taken lightly. After I adopted Sofia, I lost all interest in the business arrangement I'd made with Hayden. Luckily, he had the energy to pick up my slack. It's amazing that someone as business-oriented as I was would find it fulfilling to become a full-time mom. But I've never been happier or more at peace than I am now."

Jayla put on a colorful oven mitt and checked the turkey in the oven. "I'm sure that it wasn't hard to find peace when your coins are right. After your lawyer finagled a way for you to get your inheritance early, you don't have any reason to get back out there in the competitive, dog-eat-dog business world."

"That's true, but I also feel that my time is best served by making sure that my daughter is raised right rather than leaving it up to nannies. When she's older, it's possible that I'll return to work."

Jayla cast a glance at Sofia. "Does it bother you that she looks so much like Trent?"

"Actually, I don't see it."

"You're kidding, right? You know damn well that Trent spit that child out," Jayla said in a hushed tone.

Bailee shrugged. "I view Sofia as being her own unique personality with no connection to her biological father. If anything, she reminds me of Hayden with her mannerisms and her temperament.

I believe children take on the personality traits and even the physical features of the people that they're around."

Jayla nodded, but she didn't necessarily agree. To keep the peace, she changed the subject. "So...now that you're a divorcee, are you and Hayden thinking about tying the knot?"

"No."

Jayla lifted a brow.

"We like our relationship exactly the way it is. He has his place, and we have ours, but he's still the father figure in her life."

"I can't knock your arrangement. I learned the hard way that trying to follow society's guidelines for what's acceptable and what's not will have you out here fraudin,' chile."

Bailee wrinkled her nose. "Frauding? I don't believe that's a word."

"Here you go, Ms. Perfect Grammar. Girl, it's a Philly thing. Don't get new because you've been in Miami for a while. You know we Philadelphians speak our own language."

"That's true."

"Anyway, as I was saying... I was fraudin' like I was in a committed relationship with that bum, Sadeeq. What I love about being married to Derek is that we keep it real. Derek is attracted to men and I like freaky sex. Being honest works well for us."

Bailee frowned. "What exactly are you saying? Does Derek sleep around?"

"We enjoy threesomes. And let me tell you, honey, our sex life is never boring."

"It doesn't bother you that your husband goes both ways?"

"Nope. I'm not trying to be a smart-ass, Bailee...but you were married to a man for ten years and didn't know what the hell he was out there doing. There are no skeletons in the closet and no secrets between Derek and me."

Bailee laughed. "You have a point, girl." Her expression turned serious as she craned her neck in the direction of the living room. "I hope he's not attracted to—"

"He ain't thinking about Hayden like that. That's your man and a new friend to him. Being bisexual doesn't mean that he goes around hitting on every attractive man he comes into contact with."

"I apologize for making that assumption."

The old Bailee rarely apologized or admitted she was wrong, and it was clear that Bailee had experienced a great deal of growth. Making her aware that there were no hard feelings, Jayla placed a glass of eggnog in front of her. "Taste it."

Bailee took a small sip. "Mmm. I don't think I've ever had home-made eggnog before. It's really good, but isn't it supposed to have liquor in it?"

"It's my mom's recipe, and with her being all churchified and everything, she doesn't touch alcoholic beverages. But after she leaves, we'll pour in the whiskey," Jayla said with a wink. "Oh! Speaking of my mom, who do you think I got my former sneaky ways from?"

"Ms. Lorraine?" Bailee asked uncertainly.

"Uh-huh." Jayla smiled mischievously. "Her and Pastor have been smashing for years. She wants people to think of her as a pious, Christian woman, and she works real hard at being deceptive."

"Wow. I'm so shocked, I don't know what to say."

"There's nothing to say. My point is…you and I have come a long way, Bailee. We've taken off our masks and we're both proudly standing in our truth. It feels good to be able to be raw and vulnerable."

Bailee chuckled. "I don't think we have any other choice than to finally be our authentic selves, now that we don't have all that extra weight to hide behind."

"I'll drink to that," Jayla said, turning the glass of eggnog up to her lips again.

As if on cue, Derek entered the kitchen and Hayden was directly behind him with Sofia high up in the air, riding on his shoulders.

"We came to check on the grub and see what we can do to speed things up," Derek said.

"Can you cook, Hayden?" Jayla asked.

"Oh, yeah, I can burn," he said, laughing.

Bailee shook her head adamantly. "Oh, no! He can burn up pots and pans and set off the smoke detector."

"I thought you loved my crispy bacon," Hayden teased. "Sofia likes my cooking; don't you, baby girl?" he said playfully as she bounced up and down on his shoulder.

Smiling, Jayla observed Bailee, Hayden, and Sofia interacting, and it pleased her to see her friend in such a good place. That she and Bailee were in a good place at the same time was a small miracle.

"My mom and Pastor should be here in about fifteen minutes, and then dinner will be served promptly," Jayla said. "In the meantime, try some of my eggnog and let's make a toast."

Derek took over the pouring duties and when all four glasses were filled, he launched into a series of corny-joke-type toasts that had Hayden cracking up.

"Thank you, Derek," Jayla interrupted, teasingly rolling her eyes. "Okay, my turn, and I'll keep it simple." She raised her glass and said, "Here's to enduring friendship; beautiful, new family members...and eternal black love that can survive anything."